Forbidden Ice

Ice Breaker Cold Case Romance
Book 13

Cynthia Eden

HOCUS POCUS
PUBLISHING INC

This book is a work of fiction. Any similarities to real people, places, or events are not intentional and are purely the result of coincidence. The characters, places, and events in this story are fictional.

Published by Hocus Pocus Publishing, Inc.

If you have any problems, comments, or questions about this publication, please contact info@hocuspocuspublishing.com.

Solve the case. Save the girl. Stop the killer.

Protect Wren. The minute that Jacob Jones receives the text from his brother, he springs into action. Wren Maye is the golden girl from his childhood, the star of his teenage fantasies, and the one woman who was always off limits to him…because she was his twin brother's girl. Over the years, he kept a careful distance from Wren because he knew she was the one person who could wreck his careful control.

She's in danger, and he's the only one who can save her.

Jacob arrives just in time to stop Wren's abduction. Now he's going to be her shadow because Wren is the target of a killer bent on vengeance. Jacob has always maintained a careful distance between himself and Wren—but there is no room for distance any longer. There is danger. There is desire. There is a vicious obsession that will not end. So now, he's just going to take what he wants. And, yes, he will damn well fight his brother for her. He will fight the world for her. She will be his. No one will hurt what belongs to him.

She thought he hated her. Now he's being her hero.

What is a woman supposed to do? One minute, the delectable Jacob Jones is keeping an icy distance between them, and in the next instant, he's saving her. Kissing her as if his life depends on the task, and swearing that he'll keep her safe from any and all threats. And in order to do that protection bit? He has to assume the role of his brother.

He'll be her lover. Or...at least Jacob mistakenly believes that was the role Ebenezer "Eb" Jones had in her life. Newsflash—she has never belonged to Eb. How could she? For years, she's been hooked on Jacob. The intense and brooding twin who knows far too much about darkness.

A killer will use her to get vengeance.

It is Wren's connection to both Jacob and Eb that makes her the killer's perfect target. He wants to kill her in order to punish the brothers. A life for a life. The twins will pay for their crimes. And they will pay by losing a woman who is so very important to them both. A friend to one. A lover to another. An ice-cold grave for them both to visit as they mourn for what they lost.

Vengeance is best served ice-cold. And desire? It's best when it burns red-hot.

Author's Note: A cold case from the past is about to shatter Jacob's world. If he can't team up with the Ice Breakers and solve this case, he may lose the woman who has been his life-long obsession. The woman who owns his heart. Get ready for another Ice Breaker Cold Case Romance...danger, steam, a hero who will not fight his desire any longer. Be careful when you wake the beast. Because he will fight like hell for the woman he wants.

For my readers—thank you.
Let's go solve another cold case together.

Chapter One

PROTECT WREN.

He had one mission. Only one. A goal that burned through every single cell of Jacob "Jake" Jones's body even as two words played through his head on an endless loop. *Protect Wren.*

The order had come from his twin brother. The lucky sonofabitch who'd been involved with Wren Maye while Jake had to keep his distance from her. While he had to put a tight smile on his face and maintain a veneer of icy politeness when all he really wanted in the whole world was—

Wren.

Protect Wren.

He parked the Jeep in the bar's busy lot. It had been twenty-four hours since he'd gotten the text from his brother. Two words. No other details. Not like his twin was ever big on details anyway. And after that text, his brother Eb had gone completely dark. Not particularly surprising considering the guy was a CIA spook. Eb spent most days in the dark.

And so the hell do I.

Though Jake was sure as hell currently not affiliated with the CIA. He'd never been big on rule following. He'd tried that bit once upon a time and hated it. He'd gotten out of the government's web as quickly as he could.

And Jake's penchant for breaking rules had just gotten worse over the years. Lately, he was far too much in the mood to take what he wanted and damn the consequences.

Protect Wren.

He exited the vehicle. Glanced around to take in the scene. Nearing midnight, and of course, the busy bar in Hilton Head, South Carolina, was bursting at the seams. Nestled right along the beach, the place was packed with locals and tourists, and music drifted in the night as the tunes poured through the open doors of the bar.

An assortment of vehicles filled the lot. Trucks, two convertibles, at least three more Jeeps, and even one long, sleek limo. His stare lingered for just a moment on the limo. Then, squaring his shoulders, he stalked toward the bar. The place belonged to Wren's uncle. A dive on the beach that had attracted crowds for years. He walked right past the surfboards set up outside and the tall pole of directional signs that told visitors just how far they were from locations like New Orleans, Key West, and New York. He cut his head toward the bouncer in a rough nod, and then he was inside, his gaze slicing over the dancers and drinkers and—

Why the fuck does she have a bridal veil on her head?

Every muscle in his body locked down when he caught sight of Wren swaying on the tiny dance floor with a freaking white bridal veil perched on her head. For a moment, he could not move at all. His world crashed. Nah, more like his world exploded right in his face. *She's getting married? Since when?*

Laughter poured from her lush lips. Too far away for him to hear clearly, but he could imagine the sound perfectly. A soft, light peal that pulsed with happiness. He knew the sound of her laughter, he could pick her voice out instantly, knew the scent she always wore, and knew—

Her head turned. Mid-laugh, she froze as she stared at him. Then her eyes widened. The white veil slid over one shoulder as she lifted her hand and waved to him.

Her smile was bright. Beaming. So welcoming.

His chest ached as he began to cut a path toward her. No smile curved his lips. Grim determination filled every cell of his body.

Protect Wren.

She wasn't dancing alone. A cluster of women were huddled around her. Women he recognized since he knew Wren's friends. Old high school friends—they'd all gone to the same school back in the day.

"Oh, look!" The woman to Wren's right did an excited little bounce. Her white dress fluttered around her legs. "Eb is here!" Now she was waving merrily at him. "Hi, Eb! God, Wren, he is so hot."

Wren's cheeks flamed.

He stopped right in front of her.

"It's not Eb," she said at once. "It's Jake." She shoved back the veil. "Hello, Jake."

His friends—the few he tended to possess and actually keep in his life—called him Jake, not Jacob. He'd been in the friend-zone with Wren for far, far too long. *Don't lust after your brother's girl.* That was a cardinal rule. Or it should have been. Only he'd never been able to fully make himself follow that rule. *Don't lust after your brother's girl—*

"How do you *do* that?" The woman in white shook her head before draining her champagne flute. "You're the only person I know who can ever instantly tell the twins apart." She slapped the empty flute down on a nearby table. "Guess you have intimate knowledge, huh?" Her eyebrows wiggled. She gave an exaggerated wink.

Wren's cheeks went even redder. "No, I don't." Crisp. She yanked the veil off her head. "Time for you to get this back, Makayla. Definitely should stay on the bride's head." She shoved the veil at Makayla and then stepped forward to —to hug Jake.

Her arms wrapped around him. The scent of vanilla and honey filled his nose. Her softness pressed against him. A light, casual hug. She'd given him hugs countless times over the years. He'd always responded with a quick, affectionate hug of his own. Friendly. Super fast. Like it didn't matter.

Not this time.

His arms locked around her. His face nestled against her neck. "Thought you were getting fucking married."

Her body jolted in surprise. She pulled back. Tried to, anyway.

He didn't let go, not yet. Not like he often had the chance to hold her. So why not enjoy the hell out of the moment?

Her eyes—dark brown but infused with the faintest hints of gold—widened as she stared up at him. Then her sexy little tongue swiped over her lips—lips she'd painted a slick, light pink. "Don't you think I would mention something like that to you? An engagement is a pretty big deal."

"When you and Eb get around to tying the knot," he growled back, "I sure as shit hope you'd tell me about the big event."

Her elegant jaw hardened. Her eyes narrowed. "That's never happening." Curt. She stepped back. A hard retreat.

His hands fell to his sides. "You're never telling me? Hurtful. And here I thought I'd at least get an invite to your wedding." Talk about seeing hell up close and personally.

"I meant Eb and I are not getting married. Ever." Her arms crossed over her chest. She wore a pale blue dress, sleeveless. One that stopped mid-thigh and fit her perfect curves all too well. "So don't keep expecting to get an invitation. It's just not going to happen."

Good to know. Best news I've heard all night. Damn if he didn't have to control a smile.

"We need to talk," he told her even as...shit, was that some joy spreading through him? Probably. Definitely. Felt like it.

One dark eyebrow quirked. "Is that what we need to do, Jake? *Talk?* Pity." Her delicate nostrils flared. "I'd rather hoped we were going to do something else."

What in the hell did that mean? Suspicion filled him as the women she'd been dancing with stumbled away. "Uh, Wren, are you *drunk?*"

"Hardly." Her head tilted. "Maybe?" She expelled a long breath. "Look, focus, would you?"

Uh, he was focusing. The star of his fantasies was not. She seemed to be weaving a bit in her high-heeled sandals. "You never get drunk." A major rule of hers. Especially after that prick in college had spiked her drink. Jake had been close—he'd caught her just as she passed out. He'd taken care of her and made sure the dick who'd slipped that crap in her drink lived to thoroughly regret the move. Though for a time, he'd thought about not letting the asshole live at all.

He tended to be a dark and disturbed bastard that way. One of his many flaws.

Wren glowered at him. "This is a bachelorette party! I can drink at my uncle's bar during a *bachelorette* party for a friend. Jeez. Fun police, stop."

He had to unclench his jaw. Right. Eb was the fun one. The one who could put on a mask and pretend to be the life of the party. Did anyone but him realize that Eb held a darkness inside that rivaled Jake's own? But, unlike Eb, Jake didn't bother to hide his darkness. What would be the point in that? He liked to parade it around for the world to see. That darkness helped to keep annoying asshats away. "Sorry that I'm not Eb."

"Oh, that is it!" She surged toward him. Grabbed his arms. "I don't want Eb." Her hands tightened around his upper arms. She yanked him toward her. Surprised, he leaned in close. "I want *you*," Wren declared passionately.

Then her mouth took his.

Right in the middle of that little dance floor.

With people milling all around them.

With her bachelorette party friends watching them.

Her mouth took his.

Had to be a mistake. Wren definitely must be drunk. As her lips parted beneath his, he did taste the champagne on her lips and on that sexy little tongue that darted into his mouth. But...

Fuck it.

His dream was in his arms. He was going to enjoy the moment. And he was going to give in to the desire that he'd always chained up inside of himself and finally, finally take what he wanted so very badly—finally take Wren.

She whipped back. "You're not kissing me." A low mutter. Hushed. Embarrassed. "I'm kissing you. You're not kissing me." Her eyes darted around the bar. "*Why* am I kissing you?" Two steps in retreat. Her hands had snatched away from him.

"Wren?" Jake reached for her.

But she spun around and broke through the crowd. Her heels clacked on the floor as she darted through the dancers and bustled toward her friends.

He stood there, watching her. Frozen for a beat of time. His hand still reached for her. Slowly, his fingers fisted and dropped.

* * *

"So, which brother is the better kisser?" Makayla asked her, blinking her big, blue eyes as the bridal veil rested on the top of her carefully styled hair once again. "Inquiring minds want to know."

There was a twitter of laughter from the group around her.

Wren's stomach twisted. Of course, they'd all just seen the show. Her kissing Jake. Jake not kissing her back. Her making an absolute fool of herself.

Story of her life.

She supposed she could grab a flute of champagne. Toss it back. Laugh and say that Eb was the better kisser. Of course, he was. Eb was charming and fun, and he never would have just left a lady hanging in the middle of a dance floor as she utterly embarrassed herself.

Or at least, Eb wouldn't have done that to her. He was one of Wren's closest friends. The man would have at least pity kissed her back.

A pity kiss was clearly not Jake's style. She should have known that, though.

"Well?" Makayla pressed.

"And since when did you get interested in kissing Jake?" Jennifer Kent—maid of honor, she reminded everyone of that title about every five minutes—sidled closer. "Is this some weird twin fetish thing?"

Yeah, she probably should grab a flute of champagne. Maybe two? Only she didn't grab anything. What she did decide to do? Be honest. Because why the hell not? "When did I get interested?" Wren repeated the question. Mulled it over in her mind. "Pretty much always been interested." There. Done. Truth revealed. Deep, dark secret unearthed.

Shocked gasps came from the group.

Wren's eyes rolled. "Oh, come on. You all know he's hot." Her tone dared them to deny the truth.

"Eb and Jake are both gorgeous, but Jake…uh, he's *scary*," Jennifer corrected. "Ice cold and crazy intense."

Makayla nodded. She also fiddled with her veil.

"Fine, he's scary hot," Wren said, annoyed.

Again, Makayla nodded.

As for who was the better kisser—not a question Wren could answer. Mostly because Jake hadn't kissed her back. Like that knife to the heart had felt good. But Wren pasted a smile on her face. "Makayla, I am so crazy happy for you!" Time to wrap up this scene and get the hell out of there. "I've had a wonderful time celebrating you." She actually had. Until the last five minutes. "I can't wait to see you walk down the aisle with Tom. You will be the most beautiful bride ever." Now, how to get out of there without running into Jake again…

Makayla blinked. She craned her head to peer around Wren. "I think Scary Hot is coming this way."

No, no, no. She wasn't looking back. She was making a fast getaway. Throwing out polite chit-chat and then running. "I will be there for the wedding next month. Count me in. It's been a great night." A night that should have ended an hour ago, but the celebration had lingered.

Time to end that lingering before she had to deal with Jake again.

She threw her arms around Makayla Lane—her friend was soon to become Makayla Hadden—and Wren whispered, "Congratulations. I hope you're happy every single day of your life." Then Wren hurried to sidestep and—

"You're not leaving." From Jennifer.

Uh, yes, she was. Trying to, anyway.

"I'm the maid of honor," Jennifer said.

There were a few groans.

"And we should do shots until dawn, we should go hit another bar, we should—"

"I'm going to bed," Makayla cut through Jennifer's big plans. "This bride-to-be is partied out." She yawned. Swayed a little. "Besides, the limo has been waiting outside too long as it is. Let's hit the road, ladies." Another tug on her veil.

They were hitting the road. Wren was bunking at her uncle's beach house. It was a short walk away. No need for her to pile into the limo.

There were quick exchanges of hugs and promises to see everyone soon, and a flurry of perfume lingered in the air as the ladies departed. Wren swore she could feel eyes on her, but she didn't look over her shoulder. She wasn't quite up to dealing with the menace that was Jake just then. So, instead of facing him again, when her friends made their way to the front of the bar, she slipped off and skirted her way to the rear exit. Freedom was at hand. And, maybe by tomorrow, she'd be able to face Jake once more. Perhaps they could laugh off the embarrassing kiss.

Talk about reality not living up to the hype.

She shoved open the bar's back door. The slightly warm, night air teased her skin as she stepped outside. Silence. Not total. The roar of the waves hit the shore not too far away. But the music was muted. That pounding beat no longer seemed to shake her whole body.

You dreamed of kissing a man for too many years. You built it up in your head. And then...disappointment.

He hadn't even kissed her back. She'd licked his lips. Darted her tongue inside. Tasted him—

And he'd been a statue.

The man might as well have flashed a neon sign at her. *Not interested.*

A truth she'd long suspected.

Wren kicked off her sandals and held them with her right hand as she began the trek toward her uncle's place. Her purse banged against her hip. Uncle Milo was out of town. Correction, out of the country, as he so often was. Off on another of his adventure trips. She planned to crash at his beach house. A place that was a second home to her. Just as Uncle Milo was her second father. When she'd been a teen, he'd taken her in.

He'd loved her.

If it hadn't been for him and the twins...those brothers who had swept into her life when she needed them...

Nope. Do not.

She hated thinking about the past. Particularly hated driving down the dark and treacherous road called *what if...*

Her pace quickened as she headed for the beach house. Sand flew up in the wake of her steps and she—

"*Wren.*"

She was being followed. Right. Sure. Check. The deep voice had floated from the night. Coming from close behind her. She didn't look back. "Look, it was a mistake." Her own voice was cool. Pitched high to carry over the crash of the waves. "I promise not to kiss you again. Your virtue is safe." Did that sound flippant enough?

Silence.

Goosebumps rose on her arms. Why the goosebumps? The last thing she felt was cold. "Good night, Jake."

More silence.

Dammit. She glanced over her shoulder—

Not Jake.

A man was running toward her. Surging fast over the sand. The stars and moon illuminated the beach, and she could see that he was big. Muscled. A hoodie covered his head, and, oh, God, was that a knife in his hand?

She stumbled back. Dropped her shoes. Screamed.

Her scream was Jake's name.

She screamed for Jake right before she started running for her life. Only she didn't get very far. The man was too fast. He'd gotten too close while the sand cushioned his steps and the waves drowned out any other sounds to warn of his approach. His body slammed into hers. She tumbled right onto the sand. He grabbed her, twisting one hand in her hair while the other brought a knife to her throat.

"He can't fucking save you," he snarled. "You're coming with me."

The knife pressed against her skin.

A roar shook the night. A roar that was *her* name.

"Don't count on it," she told the man with the knife as her breath shuddered out. Relief had her feeling dizzy. Fine. Maybe it was relief. Maybe it was too much champagne. Maybe it was fear. Or all of the above. But she still told the jerk holding her, "That's Jake, and he is going to *kick your ass.*"

Another roar broke the night. A closer roar. An even angrier roar.

Jake might not want to kiss her. But she knew with utter certainty that he would never, ever let anyone hurt her.

Chapter Two

SOME PRICK HAD WREN ON THE GROUND. HIS HAND was tangled in her beautiful hair. He had a *knife* at her throat.

"*Wren!*" Jake roared as he closed in. Oh, but that jerk was about to get the ass-kicking of his life. No one—*no one* hurt Wren in this world. His heart thudded hard in his chest.

The man had a hoodie over his head. He hauled Wren upright as she sputtered out sand from her mouth. Her sandals were on the beach. Her body trembling.

The knife was still at her throat.

"Walk away, hero," the man ordered.

Jake stopped. He did not walk away. "You're confused."

Wren's eyes widened.

"You think you get to touch her. To hurt her." Jake shook his head. "You don't. I'll make sure you thoroughly understand the lesson before you leave tonight. And when you leave, you'll be going to jail. With a broken hand." Calm. Utterly truthful. Jake never liked to make a promise that he didn't intend to keep.

"You think you're gonna take me out?" A laugh.

"Yes." Another promise.

"Take us *both* out?" the man added.

Hell. A second attacker. Jake had been so focused on this prick and Wren that he hadn't sensed more danger. Could this night get worse?

Wren's head jerked a bit to the right, and Jake realized she was looking behind him. The knife was at her throat, and she should have been statue-still with terror. Instead, she suddenly flew forward with a scream and leapt right at Jake.

Her body hurtled into his. He caught her, his arms wrapping around her, and they both tumbled onto the sand.

"Gun!" Wren gasped as she held him. "Gun, gun, gun!"

He rolled her, putting Wren beneath him even as the bastard in the hoodie raced away. For a moment, Jake couldn't move. His body crushed down against Wren.

Stop the threat. Save Wren.

He heaved up.

"There was someone behind you with a gun!" Wren tried to heave him right back down. "It was aimed at you! I thought he was going to shoot!"

Both attackers had gotten away. Or, correction, they were trying to get away. He couldn't let that happen. He had promises to keep. He broke free of Wren's grip. "Get back inside the bar. Call the cops!"

"What? *Jake!*"

He took off after the fleeing attackers. Actually, he could only see one attacker. The bastard in the hoodie. He'd never seen the guy with the gun. The jerk must have seriously hauled ass because he was already out of sight. Jake picked up speed as he rushed after the SOB who'd put his hands on Wren. He'd promised the man broken fingers and a trip to jail, and that was exactly what the prick was going to get.

Except...

The guy wasn't running blindly. He wasn't heading back to the bar or a nearby beach house. He was rushing toward the little dock that waited in the distance. A boat was bobbing, someone already on the vessel.

What the fuck?

Jake had his own gun out. He didn't even remember when he'd grabbed it. Carrying the gun was second nature to him.

The boat's motor buzzed. The prick in the hoodie double-timed his escape toward the vessel. It had already been untied.

Shit. Jake knew a getaway scene when he saw one.

The asshole leapt onto the boat. It hurtled away even as Jake considered the jump that it would take to land him on that vessel. *Too damn far*.

The boat zipped into the night.

He stopped at the edge of the narrow dock. His gun up. Aimed. The prick in the hoodie was looking back at him. The man shoved the hoodie back. Too far away for Jake to see his face clearly. His face or the boat's driver. Two sonsofbitches on his new hit list.

His eyes narrowed as he prepared for the shot. He was going to—

"Jake!"

What the hell? Hadn't he told the woman to get to the bar? Jaw locking, he whirled to see Wren creeping toward the dock.

"I thought you might need backup," she said, voice breaking a little bit. "I-I was worried about you."

Worried about him?

The boat was gone. For the moment. But he would be finding those two bastards. He would keep his promises. This was a delay. Not an escape.

Protect Wren.

Yeah, okay, fine, so Eb had not been bullshitting or being melodramatic when he sent out that order. Someone wanted to hurt their Wren.

My Wren.

Not happening. He stalked toward her.

Her hands twisted in front of her. Her eyes were on the boat. "Guessing the bad guys got away?"

Only for the moment. He would find them. Make them pay. Make them bleed. Break the hand that had touched her.

She rocked forward. "I, um, I did call the cops. Then I chased after you. Or maybe I chased after you and called the cops at the same time, and I—"

He was right in front of her. Touching close. His hand curled under her chin. Tipped back her head.

"Jake?" Uncertainty. Fear.

His mouth took hers. Her lips were parted because she'd just breathed his name. His tongue thrust into her mouth, and he took. He tasted. He fucking claimed the way he'd always wanted to claim her but never had.

Instead of taking what he'd wanted—so many times— he'd held back. Stayed in the shadows.

Tried to be a *good* brother.

Screw that.

Wren had been attacked. A knife had been at her throat. And when she'd been terrified, she'd screamed for *him.* He could have lost her. If he hadn't been on that damn beach, his Wren could have been taken.

Taken before he'd ever had her. Hell, the fuck, no.

No more holding back. Forget being a good brother. Instead, he was going to have what he wanted.

A moan built in Wren's throat. Her body trembled against his.

She kissed him back. *Kissed. Him. Back.* Even after her attack, after having to feel completely terrified, she kissed him back.

He kissed her as if he had no intention of ever letting her go. Spoiler alert, *I will not let go. You will belong to me, Wren. Only me.*

But he couldn't very well fuck her on the dock with the bad guys zooming away on their boat. His head lifted. "I will keep you safe."

Her hands had balled up the front of his shirt. "What is happening right now?"

He was taking what he wanted. Protecting her. "Your time with Eb is over."

"*What?*"

He needed to get her off the dock. To a safe location.

His fingers slid down her throat. Touched something wet. Warm. "Wren?"

"What do you mean my time with Eb is over? Eb is my friend. I love him!"

The fuck you love him.

But he didn't say those words because his fingers were wet and warm from touching her. "Wren. You're bleeding?"

"Uh..." She stumbled back. "I think the knife cut me when I ran for you."

When she'd barreled forward to save him from a potential gunshot blast. Only the second attacker had never fired.

Her hand rose to her throat.

He winced. Oh, shit. Oh, no. The thing about Wren...

She touched her throat. Squinted at her fingers as she stared at them. Wren had never, ever been able to handle the sight of—

He caught her as she fainted. He scooped her into his arms. Not the first time Wren had passed out at the sight of blood. And not the first time he'd caught her so she wouldn't fall.

His forehead pressed against hers. "Don't worry, baby. I've got you." He had no intention of letting go.

* * *

THE BLOOD WAS EVERYWHERE. Her fingers. Her arms. Her face. She could feel the stickiness on her skin, and it absolutely horrified her. She wanted it gone, gone, *gone*, but she had to just sit there. He'd told her to sit there. To not move. To not make a sound.

She had to sit in the blood and not move.

But it was so sticky. It was hardening on her skin. She could feel it. Smell it. Taste it. How long had she been there, covered in blood? How long *would* she be there?

A scream bubbled in her throat, and Wren knew it was going to break free. When the scream erupted, she would be dead.

As dead as the two people near her—

The scream broke free even as her eyes flew open.

"Easy, Wren." A light flashed in her eyes. "You're good."

I'll never be good. A terrible truth that she kept deep inside. But...

Her gaze whipped around.

She was in an ambulance. On a hard gurney. A familiar face leaned over her. A handsome face. Boyishly charming.

Hayden Washington. His dark eyes held worry, but his

expression was reassuring. Probably because Hayden was in his EMT mode. "You're fine," Hayden told her. "Just a little cut. Doesn't even need stitches. I was worried when Jake brought you over and you were dead to the world, but he said you'd just had a bad fright."

A bad fright. Check. She'd certainly had that. "Some jerk tried to—" Wren stopped. Frowned. Sat up. As she sat up, her fingers automatically went to her throat. Instead of touching skin, she felt the edge of a bandage.

"All taken care of," Hayden assured her with a broad grin. Another old high school friend. Hayden had gone from being the star of the basketball team to being the hero who rode to the rescue as an EMT. "Though I can certainly take you to the hospital for observation...?"

"No." No hospital. That would be another trip straight to nightmare land for her. Not that any of her friends knew about her nightmares. Not even Jake and Eb. She swallowed. "I'm good but thank you."

"The sheriff is outside, talking with Jake. Wants to know about the guy who attacked you."

But it hadn't just been an attack. She replayed the scene in her head. The man's words haunted her. *He can't fucking save you. You're coming with me.*

"Good thing Jake was there, huh?" Hayden continued as he bent over his med bag.

A very good thing. And not something that she was willing to chalk up to coincidence.

"You know the sheriff is freaked. Can't have people getting the idea this isn't a safe tourist spot."

Right. Safe. That was the big word. The area was supposed to be safe. Her life was supposed to be safe. The past was dead and buried. *The attack can't be about my past. It can't be.* Her hand dropped. "Thanks for patching me up, Hayden."

He looked back at her. Worry lingered in the darkness of his stare. "You sure you don't want transport to the hospital?"

What she was wanted was Jake.

"I'm fine." *Liar, liar.* But she had been far from fine for most of her life, and no one knew the truth. Well, Uncle Milo knew. Only he would happily carry her secrets to the grave.

She scooted off the gurney and eased out of the ambulance. Her first goal would be to find Jake.

"What in the hell are you doing?"

Found him.

She turned to the right. Surprise, surprise, Jake was already closing in and glowering at her. The sheriff followed right on his heels.

"Get back in the ambulance," Jake ordered.

Someone was still as bossy as ever.

"You need to go to the hospital."

Had he missed her glamorous bandage? There was plenty of lighting around them—and a crowd, too. He'd carried her back to the bar's parking lot. Onlookers gawked. The parking lot lights—plus the swirling lightbars on top of the sheriff's department cruisers—illuminated the scene. She motioned to her neck. "All better."

"The hell you are."

"The hell I am." A nod. She squared her shoulders and stiffened her spine. "I'm not getting back in the ambulance." Not on the agenda. "I'm going home."

"Uh, hi, Wren." The sheriff waved to her. But the worried lines on her face seemed even deeper than normal. "Heard you were nearly mugged tonight."

She shook her head. "I don't think so." The guy hadn't gone for her purse. In fact, Wren spun around and swiped the bag from the back of the ambulance. She slid the thin strap on her shoulder before facing the sheriff again.

The sheriff—a family friend named Honey Jackson— frowned. "You weren't mugged? But Jake here was just saying that you were attacked on the way home."

"Attacked. Yes. But the man who put the knife to my throat didn't want to mug me."

Honey ambled closer. Her voice dropped. "Sexual assault?" The words carried just to Wren. And to a still fiercely glowering Jake.

"No." But she couldn't know that for sure, could she? She didn't know what the man had intended for *after*. After he'd gotten her away from the beach. "I-I don't know." Uncertainty. The hard flicker of fear.

Jake reached for her hand.

She pulled in a breath. "The attacker—the man said I was coming with him."

"Oh, hell, no." Honey cocked her head. The small, gold earrings in her lobes danced. "He takes you to a secondary scene, and your odds of survival in that situation plummet. We would have been lucky to ever locate your body."

Once upon a time, Honey Jackson had worked at the Bureau. Every now and then, she'd scare locals with her stories of tracking down serial killers. She'd retired and become sheriff in the area about ten years ago. Said it was because she liked the beach. And because there didn't tend to be serial killers in the picturesque town.

There usually wasn't much danger at all in the area.

Until now.

"Jake saved me," Wren said.

"So I hear." From Honey. She squinted at Wren's neck.

"The attacker sliced you with a knife?" Her brown eyes had narrowed.

"I lunged away from him." Had Jake already told the sheriff all of this information? "There was a second person there with him, aiming a gun. I was afraid Jake would get shot." The lunge had been an instinct. She'd just had to get to Jake. Knife or no knife.

Honey glanced toward Jake. Her lips—painted a bold red—pressed together for just a moment, before she questioned, "Bet that pissed you off, didn't it, Jake? When she got cut saving your hide."

"It didn't thrill me."

Honey grunted. "Understatement, I'm sure."

He edged closer to Wren. "I want her out of here. If she needs to come to the station tomorrow, I'll bring her in. She can answer all of your questions then. Right now, there are too many people here. Too many unknowns."

What was that supposed to mean? Her gaze cut around the crowd. Was he suggesting that her attacker could be in the crowd? Correction, her *attackers* could be there?

"Good thing you were on the beach tonight." Honey's hands went to her hips. Her badge gleamed. "Just what brought you to town, Jake? Not like you come around real often these days. Did you miss home?"

"I came for Wren."

Automatically, her stare jumped to him. She found his stare locked and loaded on her.

"I came for Wren," he repeated, a little rougher this time.

She shook her head. No way were those words the truth.

"Decided it was time to stop waiting in the shadows and finally take what I always wanted."

This was not happening. Had she hit her head when she'd fainted? The sand should have been a safe place to fall. She didn't actually remember connecting with the sand, though.

"You two some kind of couple now?" Honey wanted to know.

"No," Wren denied.

"Hell, yes," Jake affirmed.

Wren's mouth could not hang open more.

"What does Eb think about this?" Honey asked. One hand rose to lightly pat her short, dark hair.

"I don't really give a shit what he thinks." Jake smiled. Wren caught the shark's grin in the flash of swirling lights from one of the cruisers. "Now I'm taking *my* Wren home. You've got my number if you need to reach me." He let go of Wren's hand, but only so he could wrap his arm around her shoulders and haul her against him. "Let's go, baby."

Baby? What alternate universe had she fallen into? Wait. If she was having auditory hallucinations, then maybe she should take Hayden up on the offer of a ride to the hospital.

Honey stepped into her path. "I need a description of the attackers."

An important point. Definitely. But... "I never saw the man's face—uh, the guy with the knife, that is. He was big. Maybe around six-foot-two? Three?" Hard to say for certain. He'd been close to Jake's towering size, though. "He had on a hoodie. The hood covered his head. It was big and billowing so I couldn't see much about his body. Certainly not his face. And when he held me, he was mostly behind my body."

A grunt. Honey always grunted when she wasn't pleased. "And the other bozo?"

"I saw even less of him. My eyes were locked on the gun." She'd been freaking out. Her only thought had been of getting to Jake.

"One guy had the knife at *your* throat when you lunged for Jake?" Now Honey whistled. "You're lucky he didn't cut you from ear to ear."

*Ear to ear. Blood pouring down. Covering everything. Covering me. Dripping, dripping, dripping...*Her body swayed.

"Wren?" A sharp bark from Jake.

She blinked. Sucked in several, quick breaths.

"You look like you are about to pass out on me again."

"It's the champagne." Total lie. "I think it's hitting me too hard." She'd lied for so long. "Take me home?" He'd said that before, that he'd take her home. Wren desperately wanted to get out of there.

Jake nodded. But instead of heading toward the beach and walking toward her uncle's house, he led her toward a waiting Jeep. He opened the passenger door. Moving on autopilot, she climbed inside. Whispers and stares followed her. When the door closed, she actually managed to pull in a deep breath.

He jumped in moments later and had them wheeling out of the lot. Her head tipped back against the seat. The drive to her uncle's house would take longer than a walk because of the way the streets snaked, but after her last trip on the beach, she could certainly appreciate the safety of the vehicle.

"Don't ever do that again." Low. Lethal. Very growly.

Her head turned toward him. "Do what, specifically? It was kind of a big night." Did he mean...*Don't kiss me in a crowded bar. Don't run out into the night. Or don't—*

"He could have killed you right in front of me. You're lucky his arm dropped when you lunged forward."

A tired smile pulled at her lips. "I was happy to save you from getting shot in the back. That's what friends do. They save friends."

He braked at the light. A hard brake that had her shoving forward against her seatbelt strap. "We aren't *friends*." A fierce denial.

Well, now that was hurtful. "I've had a really crappy night so far." Oh, the things on her list. Why not just cycle through them? "You didn't kiss me back. Some jerk came at me with a knife. I passed out on a beach. And now, after I save *you*, you have the nerve to say we're not friends. That's just rude. Total jerk move. Typical."

The light changed. Green.

He didn't move the Jeep.

His hand did reach up and curve under her chin. "We will *never* be friends."

Why did tears fill her eyes? Right. Because he was being a mean asshole. "Now I get why everyone likes Eb better."

His jaw hardened.

Someone honked behind them.

He let her go, and the Jeep surged forward. Then he turned to the right.

Unease stirred within her. "Uh, my uncle's place is to the left."

"I'm taking you home, Wren. As in *my* home. You know I own a place in town. Might not use it much, but it's mine and it's safe. You're staying there with me tonight."

Oh, no. "That is way unnecessary." And so very problematic. For so many reasons.

"It's completely necessary. You were targeted on the

beach, Wren. The men who were after you both got away. That means they can damn well strike again."

Hello, new fear. So glad he'd unlocked that terror for her. "Why would they want to do that?"

"I don't know why they targeted you in the first place. And until I know more, I'm not letting you out of my sight." His hands tightened around the steering wheel. "Better get used to having me close, Wren. Because there is no way you are going to get away from me."

Chapter Three

Some memories were burned into your mind. Those were supposed to be the big, impactful, emotional moments. Those high intensity times that shaped you. That truly left a mark on your psyche. Could be something terrible. Like watching your friends die in combat.

Been there, done that shit.

Or maybe, just maybe, a memory that burned into your head could be something good. It could be the first time you met someone who changed your whole freaking life. The day you rushed off a sidewalk because you were being a teenage dumbass, and you nearly got your ass plowed down by a speeding truck. Only instead of dying right then and there...

A small scrap of a girl grabbed you and yanked you back even though you had to outweigh her by at least forty, maybe fifty pounds. A girl who'd been all big, intense eyes and shaking hands as she patted you down when you both fell on the pavement, and she was trying to make sure that you weren't hurt.

The stupid ice cream you'd been holding fell and

melted on you both and she smiled at you and told you that she'd saved your life and that she was pretty sure that meant your life now belonged to her and—

"*Jake*. Hello, Jake? Are you listening to anything at all that I'm saying?" Wren spun toward him. A barefoot Wren. He was pretty sure that her heels had been left on the beach some place. When she'd fainted, he hadn't given a shit about finding them. He'd just rushed her to safety. He had taken her bag with them. Did that count for something?

Wren let out a dramatic sigh. "I do not need to stay in this house with you. You don't need to do guard duty." A sniff as she waved one hand toward him. "I am absolutely fine."

"Bullshit. You're terrified. Your knees are practically knocking together."

She glanced down at her knees.

So did he.

Jeez. That dress was short. Sexy. Tempting. *Look back up, Jake. Look up*. He wasn't. He was still staring at her legs. Maybe imagining how it would feel to have those legs wrapped around him.

"They are *not* knocking together." She snapped her fingers. "Yo, Jake."

Finally, he looked up. Got distracted again because... hell, it was Wren.

Her hair should have looked disheveled. Tousled. It didn't. It looked sexy and full and thick and like some kind of shampoo commercial as the heavy locks tumbled down her back. She'd gotten the hair from her Spanish mom. Or so she'd told him, once upon a time. He'd never met Wren's parents.

They'd been dead before she blew her way into his world.

Her father had been a college kid backpacking his way through Europe. He'd met Wren's mother in Madrid and fallen instantly.

Again, so Wren had told him.

Back in the days when he thought she shared all of her secrets with him.

Back in the days before she'd become his brother's girl.

"You're glaring at me." She crossed her arms over her chest. The move just made her lush breasts shove harder against the already straining top of her dress. "Considering how many times I've saved your hide over the years, you should be so much more grateful to me. You should *smile* at me. FYI, that one simple act—an occasional smile—will not kill you."

He still stood near the front door of his beach house. He'd locked it and set the alarm and now, he began closing in on his prey.

She blinked. Frowned. Took a little step back and bumped into the back of the couch.

He kept advancing.

Her arms dropped. "Are you trying to intimidate me right now?"

He stopped right in front of her. Wren stood at an elegant five-foot-nine, but he still had her by several inches, and her head tipped back as she stared up at him. "You were almost abducted tonight," he said. A near kidnapping should have her being *grateful* to stay with him. He'd saved that sweet ass.

She bit her lower lip. A delectable lip. The pink gloss had long since worn away, but she didn't need gloss to make her lips appear sexy. Full and pouting, they'd haunted his dreams plenty of times. How often had he wondered how she would taste?

I tasted her tonight.

"I can remember the events on the beach quite clearly, thank you very much." Crisp. Her nose was in the air. Cute nose. Gorgeous woman. "Well, I can remember most of them." A quick clarification. "When I passed out, things got cloudy. I don't remember hitting the sand."

"You didn't hit the sand. I caught you."

Her eyes widened. Darkness and light all at the same time because of the gold that lurked in the depths of her gaze. An amazing combination. "You caught me?"

"I always will." Gruff. And, dammit, he probably should back off. He'd crowded into her space, and all he wanted was to put his hands on her.

Everywhere.

A swipe of her tongue over the lip she'd just bitten. "So we saved each other tonight." A nod. "Okay, let's just call the night even. You saved me. I stopped you from getting shot. Done."

He stared at her. They were not even close to done.

"Thank you." Her voice came out softer. "I don't want to think about what could have happened if you hadn't been on the beach tonight. Good thing you rolled into town, huh?"

Not good. Not random. Jake didn't want to think about what could have happened if he hadn't arrived that night. He'd *almost* gone to her house in Charleston, but some last-minute intel had sent him to find her in Hilton Head. "I meant what I said, Wren. You're not getting out of my sight. You're staying here tonight. With me."

"Unnecessary. Like I told you on the car ride, I could stay at my uncle's place—"

"*This* place has top-of-the-line security." As if he'd have anything else installed in one of his houses. "I need to know you're safe."

Fear came and went in her eyes. "One night." Such a grudging concession. "I'll stay here for one night with you."

She'd stay with him until the danger had passed. He'd be a domineering bastard about that. Oh, wait, he was often a domineering bastard. "Like I said, you aren't getting out of my sight."

A nervous laugh sputtered from her. "I just agreed to stay, but no need to go overboard!" More nervous laughter. Weak. "You don't have to keep your eyes on me at every moment. I'm about to crash, Jake. You hardly need to share the same bed with me. No need for that big sacrifice."

There's need, and then there's want. I want to share the same bed with you. "Hardly a sacrifice." Quite the opposite.

"We're in the same house, that's certainly close enough, proximity-wise. I promise, I won't go running out in the middle of the wee hours. All I'm going to do is sleep."

All he would do was think about her. "We have a problem."

"The men on the beach?" Wren nodded. "Yes, but I think as terrifying as they were—and trust me, I was plenty terrified—it was just some random attack. That's what it had to be."

He didn't think there had been anything random about it. "Eb sent me to you." His hands had fisted at his sides. The better to not touch her.

A little furrow appeared between her brows. "Why did he do that?"

"Not exactly sure. The guy has gone dark on me." Not an unusual circumstance, considering the work that Eb did on a routine basis. Going dark was pretty normal for a CIA operative. "Got a two-word text from him, nothing more."

Though he'd sure be trying to learn more, ASAP. If not from Eb, then from other sources.

"What exactly did this text say?"

Simple. "Protect Wren."

She blinked.

He stared at her. Drank in her scent. Thought about her mouth. Tried to tell his eager dick to calm down and—

"That's it?" Wren pushed. "Just protect me?"

A nod.

"And you—what? Expect me to believe you got some mystery text from Eb—no explanation, no context—a note to protect *me*, and you dropped everything you were doing and rushed to my side?"

"Yes."

She waited.

What was she waiting for?

His head lowered toward her.

Her hands flew up and pressed to his chest. "I don't believe it."

Her touch burned through him. It had always been that way. Even that long ago, first day, when she'd saved his ass, he'd been aware of the electric current that charged between them. He hadn't known how to handle it—or her— so he'd just fallen back on his usual routine of being a dick. Everyone said he did that routine particularly well.

One of his special talents.

"You spend your time bouncing around the world and doing crazy, dangerous shit!" Wren accused.

His eyes narrowed. "You mean...*hostage rescues?*" Because high-risk, hostage rescues in hole-in-the-wall locations were his specialty. When normal channels didn't work, when the danger was too intense and odds of success were exceedingly low, then he stepped in. His fees were astronomical, and his success rate? Damn astronomical, too.

"I mean you jump straight into danger at every opportunity. You're paid wild amounts of money to pull people out of hell, over and over again. When you got that message from Eb, you were—where, exactly?"

"South America." No need for specifics. His clients usually asked for complete confidentiality. In his world, lethal repercussions were a way of life. The less said, the better. There was a reason why non-disclosure agreements existed.

"You flew from South America all the way here...to protect me?"

He shrugged. She made it sound like a big deal. It wasn't. "I'd fly around the world in an instant to protect you."

"You don't even like me," she charged. A quick, negative shake of her head sent Wren's hair tumbling over her shoulders. "You don't ever come around me. Haven't in ages. You barely speak to me when we do find ourselves forced together. You won't spend any time alone with me and you always act like—"

"I don't want you fucking my brother."

Her mouth dropped open. Then snapped closed. Then...

The hands on his chest shoved him back. "You have issues!" Wren lunged to the side. Darted around him. Whirled. Angrily pointed her index finger at him. "I am having a bad night!"

Noted. Duly noted. His night wasn't exactly stellar, either. Except for the kiss. Two kisses, actually. Those would be on his highlight reel. As for Wren almost being taken *and* being cut with a knife right in front of him...*Bad. Night.*

"I need sleep. I need to wake up and have this all be a terrible dream. I don't need you telling me who—who I can or can't—ugh! Who I can or can't *fuck!*"

His back teeth ground together. She had no idea how tormented he was. His problem. Not hers. "You want me to apologize for the kiss?"

"What?" The hand she'd been pointing at him fell back to her side. "No, no, I don't. Because then I'd have to apologize for *my* kiss, and I did it first and—*heat of the moment!* The kisses came from the heat of the moment!"

Had it been a particularly heated moment in the bar when she kissed him? She'd seemed pretty calm and focused when she pressed those sweet lips to his. He'd been stunned. Halfway convinced he had to be dreaming.

"We are not ourselves," Wren added determinedly. "That's what is happening here. We're out of control."

He always held on to his control near her. Always.

"This is an adrenaline-rush deal, isn't it?" A vigorous nod of her head. "I get it now."

Adrenaline *was* rushing. Desire pumped in his blood.

"In the morning, things will be back to normal. You'll barely speak to me. I'll tiptoe around you. There will be no kissing. There will be no talk of f-fucking," she stumbled over that particular word. "And, hopefully, the sheriff will have caught those jerks. I can go back to my life. You can go back to yours. End of story." Wren spun around. Marched forward. "Where is the guest room? We are *not* pulling some one-bed drama. No way, no day."

He would love to pull some one-bed drama for her. *With* her. All night. All day. Anytime. "Eb asked me to protect you. Sorry the brother you wanted couldn't be here for you. You'll have to make do with me."

She stopped in the middle of what looked like a very angry stomp down his hallway.

"I'll assume Eb's role in your life," he added because with him suddenly erupting into her world, they should probably have some sort of cover in place. "You already laid the foundation when you kissed me in front of your friends. You'll stay with me tonight. That will make it look like we're involved. Our supposed involvement will make protecting you easier." Because he didn't believe that the threat would be gone by tomorrow. As much as he liked and respected Honey Jackson, the evil surrounding Wren wasn't going to be something that could be handled easily. The two men had been lying in wait for her. *And* they'd had a getaway boat prepped.

I need to find out what—who—we are up against.

"Involved," she repeated. She didn't look back. "Us."

"Yeah. We'll be lovers. Friends with fuck benefits. Whatever you want to call it."

"You are so clueless." She whirled toward him. "That's what you think Eb's role is in my life? You think he's my lover? Or—or my *friend with fuck benefits?*" Her voice rose at least two notches.

"I already told you," the words grated as they rumbled from him, "you are not fucking him—"

"No, I'm not. Not now, and newsflash, I never have. Did you hear that? Let me repeat it. Nice and slowly for you. I. Have. Never. Fucked. Your. Brother. There. Happy?"

This time, he was the one with the mouth hanging wide open. He should probably scrape it off the floor. Instead, all he could do was stand there and gape. As for being happy...

She smiled at him. A cold smile. And she took a few, slow, deliberate steps toward him.

He didn't hear her steps. Not just because she was barefoot. But because his pounding heartbeat filled his ears like the maddening beat of a drum.

"Just in case there is still any lingering confusion, let me repeat—one more time for fun—I have never fucked your brother. Never. As in, not even once."

He shook his head.

"Not. Even. Once. When we were teens, we did date. Briefly. Nothing came of it. We are friends. I love him. He loves me. But there is no *benefit* clause in my relationship with Eb. And there is certainly no *benefits* between you and me." Her nostrils flared. "Thanks for saving my life tonight, Jake. Tomorrow, the danger will hopefully be over. You can get away from me. You go back to your life, and I'll get back to mine. Done."

With that, she turned away once more. Began an angry stalk to the hallway.

His jaw was still open.

"Not even once, Jake!" Wren yelled back at him. "And, I don't care which room you wanted, I'm taking this first one. The one on the left. No one-bed situation, you hear me?"

He thought his neighbors might hear her.

A moment later, a door slammed.

Not. Even. Once.

His breath expelled on a long rush. She'd asked if he was happy by that news. He hadn't gotten to answer her. The answer, of course, was...

Hell, yes. Deliriously happy.

* * *

Her back pressed against the door. Her breath shuddered out. In. Out.

Rage battled with her fear.

Seriously? Jake had tossed that BS to her about Eb? Like she hadn't been dealing with those rumors for years. Just because Eb had a tendency to charm most women into his bed with minimal effort didn't mean that she'd been one in a very long line. Not like he'd crooked his finger at her and she'd eagerly jumped the guy.

She and Eb were friends. They worked *better* as friends. If they'd been in a romantic relationship, it would never have worked because—

Because he wasn't the right twin.

Her eyes squeezed closed. She still had her purse. She'd grabbed it from a table during her last angry stalk toward the hallway. Now she dug around inside the bag and hauled out her phone. Her fingers trembled as she grasped it tightly.

Then, keeping the phone, she tossed the purse onto a chair. Marched into the bathroom. She locked the door behind her before yanking the shower on full blast. The roar of the water would work to drown out her call. Just on the off chance that Jake might be listening...

I have always needed to be extra careful around Jake and Eb. Because they weren't typical civilians.

Neither was she. In fact, there was very little about her life that had ever been typical.

She dialed her Uncle Milo. Steam began to drift around her in the air. Wren stared at her reflection in the mirror as the steam slowly fogged the surface.

"Wren?" Not sleepy. Completely alert. Even though it had to be super late where her Uncle Milo was currently located. He was supposed to be on the other side of the world, after all. "What's happening?" Uncle Milo demanded.

Oh, just some madness. A little near-death experience. "Have you heard from Honey?" A not-so-little secret was that Honey and Milo had been lovers for years.

"Not since yesterday." A pause. "Today? Hell, the time shift has me all messed up." He hummed. "Heard from her earlier. A lot earlier." A pause. "Why?"

He was too calm. That meant he hadn't been updated on the recent activities. "Two men were waiting for me when I left your bar tonight. One came at me on the beach with a knife."

"*Wren!*"

He wasn't calm any longer. She spoke quickly, needing to get this recap out of the way fast as she told him, "The other was waiting with a gun. Luckily, Jake was there. I got away." She didn't mention the bandage on her neck. What would be the point in that? Uncle Milo didn't need to worry about a scratch.

"You *aren't* hurt." Not a question.

"I'm fine." *Mildly hurt.* She didn't mention the fainting episode. That would just be embarrassing. She hadn't fainted like that—from the sight of blood—in ages. Wren had hoped that she'd kicked the habit. Unfortunately, it would seem she had not. "They escaped. Honey and her team are looking for them now."

"Sonofabitch."

Her stomach twisted. "Uncle Milo..." Wren had to ask the next question. And maybe *it* was what had really driven her fear so high and caused her to faint. Because she'd been utterly terrified on that beach. "Do you think he found me?"

"No, no, dammit...*no*. Impossible."

He sounded so adamant. She released a breath as her shoulders sagged.

"No one knows outside of our little circle, Wren."

Their circle. Ha. It was more like a triangle. Her, Uncle Milo, and Honey. They kept her past secret from everyone else in the area.

"Whatever happened tonight, it wasn't related to *him*."

Uncle Milo wouldn't lie to her. He'd always been her one constant. She was okay. The past was still gone.

Buried. *If only*.

"And...hell, I was gonna wait to tell you in person, but... he's dead, Wren."

Maybe the roar of the shower was too loud. She must have misunderstood him.

"Did you hear me?" Uncle Milo groused.

No, not accurately. There was no way she could have heard—

"Your father is dead, Wren. That's what this trip is about. I-I got intel that he'd been discovered. Didn't want to say anything to you until I was certain. That's why I had to come and see for myself. I'm not on the other side of the world, kid. I'm in Colorado. And your father is *gone*. He's dead, Wren."

Most people thought her father was *long* dead. That he'd died before her fourteenth birthday. Those people were wrong.

"He can't ever find you. He can't ever hurt you. You will never have to fear him again," Uncle Milo promised her.

The mirror's surface had fogged completely. All she could see of herself was a hazy outline. A ghost.

Wasn't that what she was?

"I don't know what happened tonight, but it's not him. He did not come after you. He did not send anyone after you. He's dining with the devil, burning hot, and rotting in hell is exactly where he deserves to be."

She had to swallow the lump in her throat.

"Wren, where are you? Are you safe?"

"I'm safe." So why didn't she feel that way? *He's gone. The monster is gone. He can't ever hurt me again.*

"Where are you?"

"I'm with Jake."

"What?"

"I'm staying with Jake tonight. He saved me on the beach, then insisted that I come to his place. He didn't want me to be alone."

An approving hum. Her uncle had always liked the twins. "Good. Good. He'll keep you safe."

He'll break my heart into a thousand pieces. Oh, wait. He'd already done that. Been there, done that, would do it again.

"I'll talk to Honey," he promised. "We'll figure out what's happening."

Her cheeks were wet. Probably from the steam. No way was she crying. She would not ever cry over *him*. The monster. The monster who made the world red with blood. "I'm sure it was something random tonight. Random attacks happen. They're terrifying and horrible, but they happen." Because it hadn't been him. She could finally stop looking over her shoulder. She could stop being afraid to live.

He was gone.

"Everything is all right," she said. Those were the words Milo had given to her so many times over the years.

A mantra. A promise.

But right then, those words were a lie.

Things were not all right.

"Fuck," he breathed.

Had he heard the lie in her voice? Wren cleared her throat and tried to sound more composed. "Jake is here. No one will get past him tonight. I'm okay." Then, "Good night."

"Wren!"

She stopped before ending the call.

"Blood doesn't matter. You understand me? It doesn't mean a damn thing."

"Good night," she said again. This time, she hung up. She lowered the phone. Put it on the counter near the sink. Then her hand swiped over the mirror, clearing a path in the fog. The path was right in the spot that reflected the white bandage on her neck. The same hand reached up and carefully pulled away the bandage. She could see the splotch of red on the underside of the bandage.

Milo was wrong.

Blood mattered a great deal.

For some people, blood was the only thing that did matter.

The monster is dead. Maybe she should celebrate.

Instead, she stripped off her dress. Let it fall to the floor. Same with her panties and bra. She stepped under the spray of the shower. The water hit her cheeks and washed away the tears. Tears, not steam.

She *was* crying for the monster.

How screwed up did that make her?

I was screwed up from the beginning. Because I am the monster's daughter.

Chapter Four

THE SHRILL CRY OF HIS PHONE STOPPED JAKE JUST when he was preparing to pound on the guest room door. He'd been trying to figure out a way to apologize. Shocker, apologies weren't his strong suit.

Not apologies.

Not tact.

Not charm.

Eb excelled at all of that crap.

Again, Jake's skill set focused in the realm of being a world-class dick. He normally loved to tell the rest of the world to fuck off. But this wasn't the rest of the world. This was Wren. He knew when an apology was necessary, and he—

His phone rang again.

He hauled it out of his pocket. Glared at the screen. But answered. Because it was— "Milo." A sigh. "Let me guess, Honey called you?" Like he didn't know those two were involved? Please. Biggest open secret ever. He'd once caught them making out in the back of the hardware store. "Wren is fine. Anyone who wants to hurt her will have to go through me."

"Damn straight they will," Milo's slightly scratchy voice returned. "Wren needs you."

"Yeah, I'm right here. Not going anywhere." Right there, in front of her closed bedroom door. Trying to wrap his head around the fact that she wasn't tied to his brother. That there was no reason why he could not *have* the woman he wanted most in the whole world.

"No, dumbass, she needs you *now*. You don't have eyes on her, do you?"

He blinked. "She's sleeping." He leaned closer to the door. Was that the blast of the shower? "Showering," he corrected.

"She's not all right."

The fuck she wasn't. "She's safe in my home. Nothing will happen to her." A vow. Then, a new thought, "Milo, are you having some kind of episode?"

"*Get to Wren*. Don't let her be alone."

"Uh, she's safe." She'd also made it pretty clear that she did not want him near her that night. No one-bed situation, check. His fantasies would wait.

"She's crying."

The snapped words iced right through him.

"Take care of that shit," Milo ordered. The guy hung up. No other explanation. No pleasantries. True story, Milo had a talent for being a world-class dick, too.

Jake frowned at his phone. Then he frowned at the door. Then...screw it. He clutched the phone with his left hand while his right grabbed for the doorknob. The knob twisted in his grasp, and he threw the door open. Jake rushed into the bedroom. "Do *not* cry—" he began.

Her tears would wreck him.

But Wren wasn't in the room crying. She wasn't in the bed. Wasn't there at all.

Then the bathroom door squeaked open. His head automatically whipped that way in time to see Wren step forward. Steam drifted around her. Her wet hair slid over her shoulders, and a fluffy, white towel wrapped around her body.

She stared at him. Quirked a brow. "Lost?"

He'd been lost for years. Speech currently eluded him as he took in the vision right the hell there. Wren. In a towel. Still wet.

"It's your house. You should really know by now which room is yours and which one...is being used by your only guest."

He damn well did know. "I...Milo told me to check on you."

"Unnecessary. I'm fine. You know Uncle Milo is a worrier."

Was he? Jake stalked closer to her. The fact that the woman of his dreams was wearing only a towel didn't exactly make it hard to get close.

Want to touch. Want to taste. Want to take.

And it would be so easy to tug at the towel edge she'd tucked between those beautiful breasts.

Except...

His gaze sharpened on her face. "Have you been crying?"

"I've been in the shower. Didn't dry off thoroughly because I heard someone breaking into *my* room."

"That wasn't a yes or a no answer, so, let me repeat. Have you been crying?"

Her lips pressed together.

His stare dipped down the graceful length of her throat. "You took off the bandage."

"I was showering. The cut isn't bleeding anymore so..."

It was red. Angry. But, no, not bleeding.

"I cleaned it. I needed to get all the sand off me. Thus, a quick shower. No big mystery here, Jake. You can go to your room."

Yeah, he should leave. Every minute there made the temptation he felt for her just grow stronger. He nodded. Turned away. Except... "You don't have to act tough in front of me. It's okay to be scared. Or to cry. It was really one hell of a night, Wren. A night like this would be hard on someone like you."

Silence.

Check. She did not want to talk. Not like he was good at getting people to open up.

That was why he just took the high-risk missions. Did the most dangerous retrievals. Why he got rid of problems that others couldn't handle.

Rinse, repeat. *Why my life is lived in the dark.* He didn't get close to others, and other people tended to not want to get close to him.

He marched for the still open door. The phone remained gripped in his left hand.

"Someone like me..." Her musing words had him pausing. "I guess that means the, ah, activities wouldn't be hard on you, huh? Just another night in the exciting life of Jacob Jones?"

Having her in danger hardly qualified as just another night for him.

"I do have to ask, though, just what do you know about *me?*" An edge very much like anger had entered her voice.

Oh, just about everything. "I'm pretty much a Wren

45

expert." Probably not something he should confess, but, too late. He'd just done it.

"I don't think so."

He pushed the phone into his pocket. Turned back toward her. Sucked in the side of his cheek.

"I don't think you know me very well at all," Wren told him.

So wrong. She was his obsession. He knew all the important details about Wren. All the unimportant ones, too. He knew—

"After all, you thought I was fucking your brother. Wrong, wrong, wrong."

Okay, that was a direct hit. He had been wrong on that score. Something Jake wished that he'd discovered long ago. "I caught you kissing him on our eighteenth birthday." Talk about the worst birthday ever. "Then the next morning, you were coming out of his room, wearing his shirt." Did his voice roughen?

It did. The memory still pissed him off. He'd thought that Eb fucked Wren that night. Again, *worst birthday ever*. He cleared his throat. "Some women like screwing around with twins. Eb and I have gotten...offers like that before."

"Probably because you're both hot as hell."

He blinked.

She shrugged. The towel strained.

Sweet torture.

"We kissed at the big eighteenth birthday party," Wren confirmed. "You two had invited half the town."

Probably more than half. Eb had always loved to party. And it hadn't just been an eighteenth birthday party. It had been an eighteenth birthday party, a high school graduation celebration, and an unsupervised weekend all at the same time—the trifecta. That trifecta had equaled bliss in Eb's mind. It had been a pain in the ass for Jake.

"I had my first glass of champagne," she recalled. "I spilled champagne all over my shirt—that happened when I opened the bottle in order to get that big, exciting first taste." She ticked things off quickly. "Because I was a mega lightweight when it came to all things alcohol, I fell asleep on the floor of Eb's room. Then, bright and early the next day, I snuck out of his room because I didn't want anyone to find us and get the wrong idea. But I guess you got the wrong idea no matter what, didn't you?"

He...

Fuck. He'd been too furious to ask questions. It had taken all of his control not to beat the hell out of his brother. *Hello, jealousy.*

She took a step toward him. "I'll say again, you don't know me."

"I do."

"Prove it." A dare.

Fine. He was up to the challenge. "You like your eggs scrambled. Your favorite color is black. You dance in the rain."

Her chin notched up a bit. "What else are you supposed to do in the rain? It's made for dancing. Everyone knows that."

No, everyone did not. That was Wren logic. He advanced on her. "Your favorite holiday is Halloween."

"Of course. I've always liked to pretend I was someone else."

There was something about her tone... "Wren?"

"While this late-night chat is interesting, it really doesn't prove much. Surface material, that's what you know about me. You don't know the real me. Deep down, beneath the skin. But I know you, Jake. I know you so very well."

Then she surprised the hell out of him because she closed the distance between them. She stopped right in front of him. So close that he could feel the heat from her body.

"Want *me* to prove it?" Wren asked.

He nodded.

"You don't do long relationships. Because you're not the happily-ever-after type, are you, Jake? Your sister Marley, she is. I was at the wedding, after all. Saw her and all her bliss not too long ago."

He knew that Wren had been there. She'd been a freaking bridesmaid, for shit's sake. Hard to miss her. And when she'd come down that aisle, stunningly gorgeous in the cascading blue dress with a bouquet of pink roses in her hand...

No. Do not go there.

"You fuck and you walk away. And you look for the next big adrenaline rush. You don't let people get close because *you* don't think you can get close to people. You think people won't like what they find lurking inside of you."

His feet had rooted to the spot.

"Eb flashes his smile, and he charms the world. Surface," she breathed. "That's why Eb and I get along so well. We were both always so good at putting on that fake surface to make people think we're normal."

What in the hell? She was normal.

Wren rose onto her toes. Curled her fingers around his shoulders.

He bent toward her.

Her mouth went to his ear. "I always liked you, though,

because you didn't give a damn about the surface. You are dark and dangerous. Intense. Brooding. With an edge that can cut like a knife. There will never be anything *safe* about you."

He felt the edge of her sexy little tongue lick against his ear. "Don't play with me, Wren." He was far past that point.

"Why not?" She eased back so that she stared up at him once more. Those dark, deep eyes were on him. Seeing into him. "Why can't I play? At least, a little bit. After all, you were ever-so-wrong about me. You can say you've been keeping your hands off me because of Eb..."

"I *was*. I don't fucking share with my brother." And if Jake ever crossed that line, if he took Wren...

I would fight my brother for her. I would wreck the world for her.

Something he had long understood in that deep, dark part of himself that she seemed to know all about.

"Such a convenient story. The real truth is that you've been keeping your hands off me because you thought I was the good girl."

She was good. With a smile that had always lit up the room. Kind words. Sweet deeds. The person who never hurt anyone's feelings. The one who'd always made room at the table when someone needed a seat. Hell, Wren usually gave up her seat for other people. He distinctly remembered one damn time in high school when he'd caught her standing by the edge of the cafeteria table because Makayla Lane had transferred in, and the other girl hadn't known anyone. The table had been filled to overflowing by their group, but Wren had still brought Makayla right in.

And stood to the side.

He'd barked for some of the asshole guys to make room

because Wren needed a place to eat. Dumbasses had jumped fast enough for him.

"I'm not what you believe me to be." Her hand went to the knot of the towel.

He forgot all about high school. Stupid cafeteria tables. He just thought about what she would look like beneath that towel.

"No matter how hard I try, I will never be good." Husky. Sensual. She unhooked that knot. Let the towel go. It fell to the floor at her feet. "So how about we be bad together?"

Chapter Five

She'd probably just made a huge mistake.

The cold air teased her nipples, making them tight, hard peaks. She was completely naked in front of Jake, with goosebumps rising on her skin. Absolutely vulnerable. Her body on full display. Her pride gone because she was offering herself on a silver platter to the man.

And he wasn't saying a word.

Not really the way she'd hoped this would go.

"Just this once." Wren licked her lips and hoped she didn't sound quite as desperate as she felt. "This one time, we can both let go and take what we want." She wanted him and the oblivion she knew that she'd find with Jake. Her control was too ragged. *She* was ragged. On the edge. She wanted to fall, and he was the only one who'd ever caught her when she fell.

She needed him.

Pain and grief and fear were going to destroy her if she didn't get the oblivion that she needed.

The monster is dead.

So what does that mean for me?

What lived and breathed in her? Hadn't she always been afraid to find out? Hadn't she always pretended to be good because she was afraid of someone seeing past her careful mask to the true evil that waited inside? But if anyone could understand darkness, if anyone could show her how to face the dark over and over again without letting it completely consume her, that person had to be Jake.

A Jake who wasn't moving.

Who hadn't taken his gaze off hers even though she had just dropped her towel. He hadn't looked down at her breasts. Her body. Just kept staring into her eyes.

He kissed me, and I thought he wanted me. But he's not moving.

Her own eyes were on his face. A face that she knew so well. The hard angles, the sharp cheekbones. That square, granite jaw. A coating of dark stubble covered his jaw. His dark hair was barely mussed, despite the time they'd spent on the windy beach. And his eyes—those piercing, topaz eyes pinned her in place.

"Most people can't tell the difference between you and your brother." She had to keep talking because the silence chipped away at her too much. "I've never had that problem."

He shook his head once. Slowly. No.

"Want to know why?"

His eyes did not leave hers. But he nodded.

"Because you wear your darkness like a second skin. I see it every time I look at you. I see the savagery that breathes in you. The intensity. And I've never been afraid of it. Quite the opposite." Maybe that *should* scare her. "I want you because, unlike Eb, you don't pretend that you want to be a normal, *good* guy. You like the darkness. You like the danger. You like—"

His hands clamped around her arms. A fierce grip, but one that did not hurt. Jake had never hurt her. Not physically.

The battered pieces of her heart could attest to the fact that he'd shattered her a time or two, though. Oh, those tricky emotions. All the times he'd seemed to ignore her. The times he'd barely spoken to her. The times she'd wanted him to stop. To *see* her. To want her as much as she wanted him.

"You *need* to put the towel back on." Growled. Ordered.

But she could see the cracks, then. Finally. In his gaze as topaz burned. The flare of brutal lust. Could see it in the extra clenching of his already hard jaw. Feel it in the hands that pulled her closer.

So she smiled at him with a confidence she was far from feeling. But hadn't she warned him that she'd been good at wearing a mask?

Maybe I am my father's daughter. Her heart stuttered at the thought.

"Wren?" A furrow cut between his brows. "What's wrong?"

Only everything. "If you want the towel back on me, put it on," she challenged.

"You don't know what you're doing."

Actually, she didn't. They'd get to those specifics later. Or maybe not. For the moment, she admitted the obvious, "I'm trying to seduce you. Offering you a no-strings, one-night stand. Isn't that the kind of sex you enjoy?" She would not hold her breath. She would not show him just how frantically her heart pounded.

"What kind of sex do you enjoy?" Jake threw back at her.

The kind of sex I get to have with you. "Why don't you

find out?" Another challenge. One that was even huskier than the first.

"Don't. Play." Gritted.

"I'm. Not." She'd never been more serious. "You kissed me on the beach. Remember that? *You*, kissing me. Not the other way around." She might have been the one to start things in the bar, but he'd been the one to reach for her on the beach.

No denial came from Jake.

"Do it again." *Please, do it again.* "We both know you want to kiss me." Or, technically, she hoped he did. "We both know—"

He kissed her. Her lashes closed as tears stung her eyes because Wren was so relieved to feel his mouth against her own. It wasn't a careful, stumbling kiss. It was a kiss full of passion and need and a desire that raged wild and hard.

Her lips parted eagerly. His tongue swept inside her mouth. Took and claimed and demanded, and she met him head-on. She needed this, needed him, more than she needed anything else in the world. Her hands pressed to his chest. To his shirt. She wanted his clothing gone. Needed them to be skin to skin.

A moan built in her throat as his hands slid down her arms. Those warm, strong hands moved to curl around her waist. Slightly callused fingertips skimmed over her bare skin. Then those fingertips...

His right hand traveled a bit more down her body. Eased in front. Dipped down, down—

She pulled back, her eyes flaring open, before he could touch her core.

"Changed your mind, Wren?" Now he was the one to taunt and dare.

Cute. No. She shook her head. Caught his hand and pressed it between her legs.

She saw the lust blaze ever brighter in his gaze. Saw his face become brutally savage.

"You were just being too slow," she told him, again, speaking with a confidence that was not real. *He doesn't know. He can't know.* Not yet. She needed him past the point of no return. "Thought I'd, uh, help you out." She rose onto her toes as she guided his hand. Pushed him to stroke her just where she wanted him.

A gasp shuddered out of her.

"You're wet." His words were guttural. So thick and heavy with lust.

She managed a nod.

"Hot. Wet." A muscle flexed along his jaw as his gaze devoured her. "*And tight.*" She wasn't guiding his fingers any longer. He'd taken over and two fingers had thrust into her. Stretched her. Owned her.

She was still on her toes. Her body so tense and eager. Every part of her ached with a ferocious hunger. His thumb raked over her clit, again and again, even as those wicked fingers of his thrust into her and with shock, Wren realized she was about to—

His fingers pulled away.

Dammit! She was about to be seriously disappointed because he had not *finished.* "Jake!"

"Yeah, fucking *Jake.*" He swept her into his arms. "How about we make you scream that name?"

What? Really? This was happening? They were doing this? "Excellent plan." She curled her arm around his neck even as she pressed a kiss to his throat. "Make me scream." Then she licked his neck. Sucked a little. Felt the growl that rumbled in his chest right before he dropped her on the bed.

A hard drop because she bounced and frowned at him, but in the next moment, he'd caught her bare legs. Dragged them to the edge. Spread them far apart.

His gaze was on her sex. Locked on the V he'd created with her widely spread legs. She'd never been more exposed in her life. Wren could feel heat stinging her cheeks. Maybe if they turned the lights off this would be easier? "Jake, the lights…"

"I'll see everything. No way I miss it when you come for me."

Then he was on her. Right between her legs. She'd kind of expected more foreplay. Maybe some kisses. And he, uh, *was* kissing her.

Just not on the mouth.

His tongue slid over her clit. A delicious lick that had her hips surging off the bed, but his hands clamped around her and held her in place as he feasted. Licked. Sucked. Took.

Her head tossed against the bed. She grabbed for the sheets and fisted them in her hands. Wren held on for dear life as Jake went down on her. *Jake is going down on me.* Hello, fantasy.

Only this was way better than a fantasy. His wicked tongue worked at an expert level. He stroked and tasted, and one strong hand freed her heaving hips so that his fingers could join his mouth. Those two fingers thrust back into her again even as he licked. Wren was completely helpless because all of her control had disintegrated and there was no stopping the pleasure that flooded through her body. Did she scream?

Yes.

"*Jake!*" The orgasm thundered through her. So much more powerful than anything she'd felt before. Her body shuddered and pulsed. Her hands clenched around the covers so tightly that she couldn't believe the bedding didn't rip. Her whole body arched as pleasure consumed Wren.

"Fucking beautiful."

Her eyes snapped open.

His eyes pinned her.

Her breath shuddered in and out. Her breasts rose and fell.

"Do you always come so fast?" A careful question. A deep and dark one and something feral seemed to blaze in his eyes.

Her head moved slowly against the bed even as she fought to bring her breathing back under control.

"No?" A hard smile curved his lips. "Guess I'm special."

Oh, Jake, you have no idea.

"I'm going to fuck you, Wren. There will be no going back."

Did it look as if she was trying to go *anywhere?* She was currently just trying to breathe like a normal person again. Her body felt utterly limp.

And why did he still have on all of those clothes? The clothes needed to go, immediately.

He stood by the bed.

She missed his hands on her.

In her.

He yanked off his shirt.

Hello, muscles for days. She sometimes thought that Jake must spend every spare moment in the gym. The man was built. Had been, for years. Abs for days. A powerful chest. Shoulders that could block out the sun.

A few faint, white lines cut across the tanned expanse of his chest. Scars from attacks, from danger, that she'd never been told about. He'd always kept his secrets.

Just as she'd kept hers.

He kicked away his shoes.

She sat up on the bed. Then moved to crouch on her knees. Her breath still came too fast.

He tossed his phone on the nightstand, and then his hand went to the waist of his jeans. "Change your mind?"

What? Change her mind? Ha. Forget that. She reached for him. Unhooked the jeans. Lowered the zipper and she barely heard the hiss over the sound of her pounding heart. She shoved down his black boxer shorts—she just wanted them out of her way—and, acting purely on instinct, she lowered her head, and her mouth closed over the broad head of his dick.

"*Fuck, Wren.*"

She was trying hard to get the man to fuck her, yes. That was the goal. But now she was licking and tasting, and this was way better than she'd imagined.

Except, in a blink, she found herself back on the bed. Correction, on her *back*, on the bed.

"Unless you want me coming in your mouth, *don't do that again.*"

Well, she didn't hate the idea.

But he'd finished stripping. He'd hauled a condom from his wallet. Of course, he'd be the prepared type. Just another thing to love about Jake.

No, stop. Do not go there. Don't you dare.

"Wren? What's wrong?"

She blinked. Smiled brightly. Too brightly? "Just wondering why you aren't already in me."

Maybe that hadn't been the right thing to say. Because before she could pull in another breath, he was on her. On the bed with her. On top of her. Her legs were spread wide beneath him, and his dick lodged at the entrance to her body. He kissed her, his tongue thrust deep, and then his cock slammed hard inside of her. Wren could not hold back her quick, startled cry of pain.

So much for hiding that secret any longer.

He froze. That powerful body stiffened over her. Against her. And his head shot up as if he'd just been electrocuted with a powerful shock. *"Wren."*

Probably not the moment to say...*surprise, surprise.* He definitely did not look like a man who was in the mood for a surprise. Even though he'd clearly just gotten one. He suddenly didn't even look like a man in the mood for sex. Before, he'd appeared ravenous, and now, he looked... horrified and...

A slow smile curved his lips. "You don't know what you've done, do you, sweetheart?"

Just because this was her first time, it didn't mean she didn't understand how things worked. Her hands grabbed for his broad shoulders. Her head tipped back against the pillow as she stared up at him, and, deliberately, she tightened her inner muscles around his cock.

"Fuck."

Yes, good. Maybe they could get back to the business of fucking and forget all about that quick flash of pain.

And, good, he was moving, pulling out. Driving in. Only...

His fingers were between them. Working her clit mercilessly. And his mouth was on her breast. Licking and sucking and she wasn't feeling any more pain because need and desire rose within her again. She heard herself pleading with him. Demanding. Urging him on and he thrust over and over. Her nails dug into his arms.

Then an orgasm hit her again. This time, it was even more powerful. He didn't stop thrusting. If anything, the drives of his hips became more powerful and that just made her feel *better*. Wilder. Control was gone.

For her.

And, as she stared up at the brutally handsome lines of Jake's face, she knew control was gone for him, too.

Her rigid Jake. Always holding back. Always so strong. Always with that control of his firmly in place.

His control had shattered.

His hips pistoned against her. He plunged deep over and over again. One hard hand grabbed her leg and hauled it up higher so he could slam deeper. She was completely open to him, her orgasm still pulsed inside of her, and he was not done. He was frantic and consuming. Owning and taking. There would never be a chance to go back from this. She would always remember this moment.

Always remember him.

His eyes glittered with ferocious intensity as he stared down at her.

Am I coming again? Desire built. So much need. No pain. Just pleasure that filled her and wiped out everything else in her world. No more pain or fear or sadness.

She bucked beneath him. Her nails raked down his arms.

He came inside of her.

She cried out his name.

* * *

She heard thunder. Wren figured she should crack open an eye and check for a storm. Except she didn't really feel like it.

The thunder continued. Only, maybe it slowed.

Seemed softer.

More controlled.

"Wren..."

Jake's low voice.

He pulled out of her body.

The thunder came back.

Oh, wait. That thunder is my heartbeat. No storm.

She really should crack open an eye. But she didn't. She settled more comfortably against the bed. Then she felt a hand on her hip. "Wren." More demanding.

Her eyes fluttered.

"Wren...what the fuck?" Anger burned in those deep words.

Now her eyes were fully open. She stared at him and decided to be one hundred percent honest. Why not? Surely, there was a first time for everything. "I've got to say, Jake. You were worth the wait. One hundred percent."

Shock flashed across his handsome face.

She yawned. There was a whole lot more talking they should do. She got that. Definitely needed to give the man an explanation. But... "No strings." That had been the deal. If he was worried that she'd go back on that promise, she could reassure him of that before sleep claimed her. "A one-night stand with no strings. Even with my, um, surprise, that arrangement still stands. No worries on that score." That should make him feel better. Her lashes began to sag closed.

"Oh, trust me, sweetheart, there are strings."

She shook her head. "One night..." That was all he ever did. She knew the rules.

"We'll fucking see about that."

Chapter Six

He'd fucked Wren.

He'd fucked Wren.

And now she was asleep, and he was standing by her bed and...

He'd fucked Wren.

Jake kept coming back to that point. Probably because it was an exceedingly important point. A point that was changing his whole world.

He'd ditched the condom. Seen the bit of blood on it. Which brought up another utterly astounding point.

I'd been the first to fuck Wren Maye.

How in the hell had that happened?

How in the hell had he gone from having the woman as his dark obsession for years to—to actually *having* her?

He frowned down at her. She should get under the covers. She'd be far more comfortable under the damn covers. He bent and scooped her up. She cuddled against him as if it were the most natural thing in the world.

"Jake." A soft whisper of his name.

And he almost didn't put her back down. His stupid

arms wanted to keep holding her because if he let her go, he might lose her. This whole night might vanish. Be just another dream. One that made him wake up aching for her, in a cold bed.

Get your shit together, man.

He held her with one arm. Yanked back the covers and tucked her in and forced himself to let go. *Let go.* She was naked and delectable and if he didn't put the covers over her, he'd be trying to fuck her again.

Yes, let's do that.

No, dammit, no.

He snatched the covers in place. Covered that hot body.

Her eyelashes—those long, dark lashes—fluttered and opened and her gaze zeroed in on him. Sleepy, but aware. "Are you covering me up?" Husky. So sensual.

"Yes." Hissed.

"Why?"

"Because you could get cold."

"Not if you're in bed with me." Whispered.

She had no idea that she was playing with fire. "If I'm in bed with you, I'll be fucking you again."

"Okay."

His eyes squeezed closed. "You are pushing me." He was way too close to the edge. She didn't get just how desperate for her he truly was. She'd bled. She'd *hurt*. He wasn't supposed to screw her like crazy all night long. He was supposed to show tact. Care. Be a freaking gentleman. Because he'd been her first.

How in the hell had he been her first?

Why? Why had she picked him? Why in the hell hadn't she picked someone nicer? Some actual gentleman? Someone who didn't have so much blood staining his hands?

His eyes flew open because he needed the answer to that one, burning question. "Why, Wren?"

But Wren's eyes had drifted shut. She'd turned onto her side—toward him—and snuggled against the bed. "Safer that way," she responded. Her words slurred together.

Safer? What did that even mean?

"You can stay." So soft. He almost thought he'd imagined her words, but then she added, "If you want. Still night. Still counts...as one-night...stand..." A soft exhale.

"This is not a one-night stand."

She didn't respond. Because she'd gone back to sleep. Like the woman didn't have a care in the world. Like she hadn't nearly been abducted that night. Like some prick hadn't cut her neck. Like Jake hadn't fucked her like a possessed madman who would never, ever get enough of her.

"It's not a one-night stand," he repeated. How could it be when he just wanted more and more and *more*?

After he'd ditched the condom, he'd hauled his boxers and jeans back into place. No shoes or a shirt. He stood by the bed and kept glowering at her.

His phone beeped and vibrated. He wanted to keep right on staring—dammit, glowering—at Wren, but his gaze reluctantly turned to the phone. His eyes narrowed on the screen, and when he realized the text was coming from his twin, he grabbed the device and nearly shattered it in his hand.

Is Wren secure? The question on the screen had come from Eb.

Secure? Not quite the description he'd give. But texting back...*She's just been thoroughly fucked* didn't seem like the right thing to do. So, instead of saying that, Jake sent: *Call me now. 911.*

911—that meant serious emergency status achieved.

And the phone was ringing even as he turned away from Wren and hurried for the door. His fingers swiped over the screen. He put the phone to his ear right before crossing the threshold.

"What is happening?" Eb demanded and there was real fear in his voice.

"You haven't fucked Wren." He pulled the door shut behind him.

It clicked closed.

"What?"

He stood just beyond that door and tried to figure out how to not sound insane. "You haven't fucked Wren." Okay, yeah, same words. Still probably sounded crazy. Too bad. He felt crazy.

"Uh, yeah, I'm aware." Fireworks seemed to explode in the background.

Jake tensed. It wasn't the Fourth of July, and he'd bet his soul those were not exploding fireworks. "Eb?"

"Really kind of busy at the moment," his twin returned, "so if this isn't life-or-death, how about we chat later?"

More fireworks. Shit.

"Is Wren safe?" Eb bit out.

"She's with me."

A quick exhale. "Good. Keep her close. You know I love that woman."

Jake's heart stopped.

"I'd be there myself if I could—"

Fireworks. Nah. Correction, *gunfire*.

"But that can't happen. Not yet. Working on it, though. In the meantime, you have to stay close to her, bro. I get that you don't like the woman."

"I like her just fine."

"Uh, right. Wren tells me all the time she thinks you hate her but...you can keep her safe. I know you can do that."

Wren thinks I hate her? So why did she just let me fuck her?

"Don't let her out of your sight," Eb said. The words were an order, but held the tone of a plea. As a rule, Eb never pleaded for anything.

"What is the threat to her? Where is the danger coming from?"

"The past. Mine. Yours."

Oh, that couldn't be good. Their past tended to be a shitshow. "You're gonna have to be way more specific."

"I would be if I could be and—*dammit!*" An explosion of gunfire. "Way too close. Look, I got word that payback was coming at me. At us. Didn't know exactly how or when. I was already on edge, and...then, fuck, I received an email with Wren's pic attached."

Uh, yeah, so where was the big drama—

"In the pic, there was a bull's-eye on her face."

"Trace the email." Simple enough.

"You think I didn't try?" Eb's breath heaved in and out. "The fucker is good. He knows his way around tech. He *wanted* me to know what he was doing. Wanted me to know he was targeting her. I'm trapped here, she's there, and he wanted me to know she was in danger."

"How do you know this isn't just about *you?*" Because maybe this wasn't *their* past. Maybe it was just Eb's.

"Because the email had a damn message that said, 'The sins of the brothers will burn the bitch.' Brothers, as in plural. As in you are the only damn brother I have in this world. There. Does that get nice and specific enough for you and—shit, *way too close!*" Gunfire cut through his words. "Hell is raining on me, and I've got to go. Just—look, Wren is the target and the tool of someone's twisted vengeance and just *keep her safe*. Don't let her out of your sight. Take her off the grid. Make her go dark. Kidnap her if you have to do it, but she has to get out of sight until I can figure out more and—*people are shooting at my team. I have to go!*"

Well, great. "Stay alive, asshole."

"Working on it. You just keep *her* alive."

The call ended.

Keep Wren alive? Done. End goal. He pulled in a breath. Exhaled slowly. Eb was CIA. When he talked about his team, he was talking about the spooks that would have his back. His brother had damn well better stay alive.

The sins of the brothers...

Hell, they had committed far too many sins in their lives. Which one was coming back to haunt them now?

Jake opened the door. The lights in the bedroom were still on. He should turn them off so that the illumination didn't disturb Wren. She needed to sleep. The fingers of his left hand rose and pulled down the light switch. The overhead light immediately turned off, but the bedside lamp still glowed.

He walked silently across the room. Stared down at Wren. His beautiful Wren. She rolled away from him in her sleep. And as she did, the light fell on her back. Her bare back. He saw the scar that skated across her right shoulder. And the mirrored scar on her left.

What. The. Hell?

He dropped the phone onto the nightstand. His hand lifted toward her right shoulder. Almost touched the scar. A scar that sure as shit looked like it might have come from the blade of a knife.

Who had hurt Wren?

When?

And was the sonofabitch still alive? Because if he was, Jake would gladly send him to hell.

But his fingers stilled before he made contact with her skin. This wasn't the time to demand explanations. He'd get his answers soon enough. Instead, his hand pulled back.

Mirrored scars. Deliberate cuts. No way is that shit accidental.

He turned off the lamp. Then he climbed his ass in bed with Wren. He wasn't supposed to let her out of his sight, after all. So it looked like they would, indeed, be having a one-bed situation. But he eased forward just a little because those scars bothered him so much.

Wren shouldn't know pain. Not ever.

I hurt her tonight. I didn't mean to do it. If I'd known that I was her first, I would have been so much more careful. Would have made sure she was so lost to pleasure that she would never feel pain.

His lips brushed over one scar.

An old scar. It had faded a pale white against her golden skin.

He eased back against his pillow, but his arm locked around Wren, and he pulled her close. He'd been her first lover. Jake still had trouble wrapping his head around that fact. How did he get to be the lucky bastard?

As for Wren...

She was going to be the first woman he slept with. Actually, *slept* with. Because she'd been right. He didn't stay with lovers. There were no permanent ties in his life. Not except for his family.

And Wren.

His eyes closed.

What in the hell am I going to do with Wren now? Other than, of course, keep her alive.

Keep. Her.

* * *

HER EYES OPENED. She stretched and rolled slowly as awareness trickled in and she faced—

Jake.

A Jake who was right beside her. As in, beside her in bed.

Her lips parted.

His eyes opened. "Morning, sunshine." No sleepiness. Complete awareness.

Jake was in her bed. She was naked, and Jake was in her bed.

Wren screamed.

Chapter Seven

He winced. "Sure, I get it. Some women wake up and want coffee. You wake up and scream. New, fun Wren-fact."

She bolted to the other side of the bed, and she yanked the sheet with her. Her fist clutched the sheet to her chest. Her eyes decided to fall to *his* chest. His bare chest. Such a muscled chest. Then, her gaze dipped lower.

Hello, abs. Abs that she remembered. Because...

It had been real. Not a steamy dream.

She'd had sex with Jacob Jones. Mind-blowing, body-thrilling sex. Then she'd fallen asleep. And he'd...stayed? Slept in the same bed with her?

He folded his arms behind his head. "Did you sleep well?" His voice was all pleasant and warm. Deep. A little rumbly.

She squeaked. Immediately snapped her mouth closed.

"You looked like an angel while you were asleep. Especially when you snuggled up against me. Though you did snore just a little bit at one point."

"I did *not*." Horrified.

His lips curled upward. "How would you know? Not like you've slept with anyone else who could say otherwise. After all, I'm the first."

Oh, crap. He'd just walked her right into that trap.

His gaze pinned her. "What a surprise that was." A brief pause. "Want to explain?"

"Not particularly." What she wanted to do was flee to the bathroom. But her side of the bed pressed against the wall, and in order to flee, she'd have to jump over him. Or maybe do a shimmy off the foot of the bed. She could do the shimmy. That would probably be the better option. She prepared to shimmy.

He sat up and caught her wrist in a deceptively lazy movement. "I think I need to insist on that explanation."

She was naked, and Jake was chatty. New, fun Jake-fact. He was chatty in the morning. "Do you always demand explanations from your one-night stands?"

"Oh, my sunshine, you are no one-night stand."

She wasn't? Wild hope began to bloom because maybe Jake was about to say—

"We're lovers."

Yes, yes, they were. They were—

"In deep. We fell hard."

She could not *breathe*. Was that joy exploding in her chest?

"That's exactly the story we're going to tell the world. Because I've got strict orders from Eb to stay close to you. To not let you out of my sight until the danger to you is gone. I talked to him while you slept last night. He says the past is coming back to bite us in the ass, and I'm not about to let you be collateral damage for something my brother and I have done."

And she was a deflated balloon. Her breath left her in a

whoosh, so she even sounded like a balloon deflating. How fantastic. She'd just gotten her first ever real lover, and he wanted to go straight to being pretend the day after they'd had sex. Both sad and typical. "The story we'll tell the world." A nod. "That's just...something." She wiggled her fingers. "Want to let go of me?"

He looked at her hand. Then back at her face. "No."

"Okay, let me rephrase...let go."

Jaw locking, he grudgingly did so. She shimmied her heart out and hopped off the foot of the bed. With her back to him, and the sheet covering all her important parts, she bounded toward the bathroom door.

"Who hurt you?"

She reached for the doorknob.

"Who sliced your shoulder blades with a knife? Who took a knife to *you*? You tell me his name, and I will put him in the ground for you."

Her hand froze. Correction, her entire body froze.

She heard the squeak of the mattress. The rustle of the bedding. Her left hand still grasped her sheet to her chest, and she slowly turned toward him, making sure to haul the sheet around, too.

He had on his jeans. The button was undone, though. Sexiness personified. The stubble of his cheeks was darker, deeper than it had been the night before. His eyes gleamed as he closed in on her with a predatory grace that should have scared her.

Instead, it made her ache.

Get a grip.

"Tell me his name," Jake said. He stopped in front of her. Put his hand up and pressed it to the doorframe near her as he leaned in. His left hand curled under her chin.

"Tell me his name, and I can have him dead by dusk for you."

She wet her lips.

His stare fell to her lips. Did she imagine it, or did that stare heat? She was about ninety percent sure the heat had been real. But then again, she was one hundred percent sure she'd just heard him offer to kill a man for her, and she had to be wrong about that.

Didn't she?

An auditory hallucination?

"Wren."

"It was an accident." Same old story. Same old lie. "I fell on a fence. I was climbing into a tree house when I was a kid. I slipped. Hit right along my shoulder blades."

My precious angel. Let's just see if there are wings hidden beneath your skin...

She bit her lower lip because she was afraid it might be trembling.

She didn't have wings beneath her skin. She wasn't an angel. The daughter of the devil could never be an angel.

But Jake didn't know that. Just as Jake didn't really know her. No one knew her.

His eyes narrowed. "Are you lying to me?"

Yes. She let go of her lower lip. "Why would I do that?"

"Because you don't want me to kill for you. But it's not a big deal. Promise."

"Murder is always a big deal."

"No one hurts you and walks away."

The man with the knife last night had walked away. Correction, he'd run. "You don't have to kill someone for me. Totally unnecessary." Especially if Uncle Milo had been correct. The monster who'd hurt her so long ago was dead.

"The offer will stand." His thumb swiped softly over her lower lip. "Don't bite. No sense ruining perfection."

He thought her lips were perfect? Since when?

"Why did you wait for me?" he asked.

"Excuse me?"

"I was your first. Me. Not Eb."

"Hate to point this out, but you have an obsession with your brother."

"No, I have an obsession with you."

She blinked.

Another slow swipe of his thumb over her lip. "Eb wasn't your first. Neither were any of those dumbasses I've seen you with over the years."

Her college dates. Then the perfectly behaved gentleman she'd met post-college. The ones who knew nothing about darkness or death. They smiled easily. Laughed. Joked.

She had nothing in common with them.

"Why me?" Jake wanted to know.

Wren had her own questions. The first... "Why does it matter? It was one night. I'm not asking for anything else." She was trying to play by his rules. The man should be thanking her.

He glared. "Why the hell aren't you asking for more? I know you enjoyed yourself." He leaned in even more. "You screamed for me."

Yes, she had. No reminder necessary. "Just because I hadn't done the actual deed before doesn't mean I didn't have experience. I'm not exactly a complete amateur. Let's move forward, shall we?"

"Why me?"

Because you're the one I always wanted. Because the

monster is gone. I don't have to worry about him coming back and ever taking me away. I could finally live. Take what I wanted. Take someone who might understand me. She didn't say any of that, though. Instead, Wren went with, "You're asking a lot of questions for a man who seemed to have himself one hell of a good time."

He stared at her and—smiled. A wide, satisfied, dimple-winking grin. It was a rare smile for him. Eb would flash his dimple all the time because he knew that dimple could get him anything he wanted.

But Jake...

Jake...

He didn't usually smile at her. His smiles were reserved for Eb. For his sister Marley.

He usually just stared at Wren... "As if you hate me," she whispered.

His brow furrowed. "What?"

A quick recovery was necessary because she'd just slipped up. "You seemed to have one hell of a good time last night, for a guy who claims to hate me."

"I've *never* claimed to hate you." Then, growling, "That's the second time someone mentioned that shit to me."

He was caging her in, and she needed to get away. "Well, you sure don't act like you're thrilled whenever we're together. But we exploded last night in that bed, and I have no regrets. Zero." Her shoulders straightened. "You were a great first lover, Jake. Thank you."

He blinked.

"You don't need to feel guilty or weird about being the first." She did not want guilt. "I have no regrets." *I hope you don't, either.*

"Guilt?" He backed up a step. His hands fell to his sides.

"Yes, guilt. I don't feel it."

"Trust me, sunshine, I don't feel guilty. Not even a little bit."

Sunshine? He'd called her that before. She wasn't anyone's sunshine.

"I am territorial as fucking hell. I want to take you again and again and have you scream my name because I loved hearing you and *feeling* you when you came around my dick."

Was it hot in there? It felt hot. She was hot.

"I don't feel weird. I don't feel guilty. But I do feel like I want to fuck you again."

But...fucking her again... "Doesn't that go against your one-night-stand rule?"

A muscle jerked along his jaw. "You think once was enough for me?"

How was she supposed to respond to that question?

"Was once enough for you?" Before she could answer, he tapped his chin. "Oh, wait. You didn't just come once for me, did you? Was it twice?"

Jerk. "It was three times, thank you very much." She lunged for the bathroom and slammed the door shut on him. Breath heaving, she flipped the lock into place.

There was a soft knock at the door. Glaring, she did not open the bathroom door.

"Wren?" He cleared his throat. "You're welcome."

Then she was pretty sure she heard whistling as he walked away.

* * *

"WE DIDN'T NEED to come here." Jake surveyed the driveway. The empty road. The quiet beach house as it waited on stilts. Milo's place. Sunlight spilled around the looming structure, and waves pounded into the nearby shore.

"We absolutely needed to come here." Wren put her hands on her hips. Hips that were covered by her short, blue dress. The same tempting dress she'd worn the previous night. "In case you missed it, I'm in full walk-of-shame glory over here."

Behind the lenses of his sunglasses, Jake's eyes narrowed on her. "There is no shame." Was that how she felt? Ashamed because of what they'd done? Because, if so, that shit needed to stop.

He didn't want her regretting their night together or the fact that he'd been her first.

First. Yeah, he still couldn't quite wrap his head around that bit of knowledge. Everything that he *thought* he knew about Wren had just blown up in his face.

Plus...

She's lying to me. The scars on her back hadn't been made by a fence. No way. There was more going on, and he would find out the truth.

"When you're still wearing the dress you had on the previous night at nearly ten a.m. the next day, and when you come home with *no* shoes on your feet, your hair in total disarray, and zero makeup on your face, people tend to assume you're doing the big walk of shame because you spent the night in a stranger's bed."

He marched beside the Jeep and stopped right in front of her. He could hear the muted roar of the waves, and the smell of the ocean teased his nose. "I'm no stranger." But she absolutely had been in his bed. Or, well, the guest room bed. With him. "From now on, I'm going to be very close to you."

"Because you think I'm in danger and you're my protector."

Damn straight, he was. "You were attacked last night, sunshine. That counts as danger."

A shiver worked its way over her body. "Don't call me that, please. I'm hardly your sunshine. I get that you're big into pretending that we have some passionate affair happening, but you don't need to use fake endearments with me."

So was this not the time to tell her that he did think of her as damn sunshine? Especially when she smiled at him? Probably not the moment. As for some passionate affair happening…"If we weren't passionate last night, then how would you describe things? Please, take your time. I'd love to hear your summary."

Her lips parted.

The breeze caught her hair and tossed it against her cheek.

And frantic honks from a car horn filled the air.

His body tensed right before he lunged in front of her. His hand went for the gun he'd tucked beneath the back waistband of his jeans when he exited the Jeep. He didn't think Wren had even noticed that he was armed. His head whipped toward the loud honks.

"Oh, no." Dismay filled Wren's voice. "I will never, ever live this down."

A white convertible honked more before screeching to a stop at the end of the driveway. A woman with billowing, blonde hair popped her head out of the driver's side. "Wren!"

"Jennifer," Wren whispered.

Yes, he knew the other woman's identity. Jennifer Kent. She'd been at the bar the previous night.

As for the woman hopping out of the passenger side...

She's not wearing a veil this time. But he still recognized Makayla Lane.

"You weren't at the farewell bridal brunch!" Jennifer called loudly. Then, she, too, hopped out of the convertible and hurried toward Jake and Wren. "You were supposed to arrive at eight a.m. sharp, and you weren't there."

Wren's fingers pressed to Jake's back.

Reluctantly, he stepped to the side just as Makayla barreled toward Wren. Jake made sure his gun remained concealed.

Makayla wrapped Wren in a tight hug. "I was worried about you."

He heard those words clearly.

"We tried to call, but you didn't answer." This chiding charge came from Jennifer as she closed in. "But luckily, Deputy Blake was at the beachside breakfast buffet. He told us what happened to you last night."

Makayla released Wren. "You were attacked?" Her eyes swept over Wren. Lingered on her throat and the faint wound that remained.

"Attacked and, um...you're still wearing that dress?" A bit sharper from Jennifer. Then Jennifer's gaze darted to Jake. Then to Wren. And back again to Jake. "Oh." A nod. "Did...*someone* spend the night with Mr. Scary Hot?"

What?

"Walk of shame," Wren sighed. "I told you, Jake." She squared her shoulders. Lifted her chin. "Yes, Jake and I spent the night together." Then she surprised the hell out of him by reaching for his hand. Her fingers threaded with his.

"He saved me on the beach. Then insisted that I stay with him for my own safety."

"Uh, huh." Jennifer's green eyes were very, very wide. "Safety." She fanned herself a little.

"And he just brought me home because, clearly, I need to change my clothes."

Both Makayla and Jennifer were staring at Jake in shock.

He almost said, "*Boo!*" just to see their reaction.

"What is Eb going to say?" Makayla whispered.

Jake narrowed his eyes on her even as his brother's words played through his head. *Keep her close. You know I love that woman.* Jake's hold tightened on Wren's hand. "He's going to say...thanks for taking care of her, bro. Appreciate it."

Jennifer coughed. "You have one...uh, weird relationship with your brother."

He locked his stare completely on her.

She backed up. Two steps. A third.

"Wren and my brother were not involved. Wren and I are." He rolled one shoulder in a shrug. "From here on out, it will very much be a Wren-and-me situation. She belongs to me, not my brother."

Wren sucked in a breath. "I-I need to get changed."

A brisk nod. He'd be going with her because that was part of the whole not-out-of-his-sight deal.

"You missed the brunch!" A whining tone had entered Jennifer's voice. "I'm the maid of honor. The least you could have done was call and tell me what was happening. We waited like, ten minutes for you before we began the breakfast toasts. Not that I drank because I was the designated driver. But, seriously, why not just pick up your phone?"

"I'm sorry." Wren let go of Jake's hand.

His fingers flexed.

The thin strap of her purse hung off her left shoulder. Wren fumbled and yanked her phone from the purse. She frowned at the screen. "It was off. I-I don't even remember turning it off." She hurriedly turned the device back on. "Last night was, um, a lot. I spoke with my Uncle Milo and things got—" Her gaze rose to collide with Jake. "Complicated." A slow release of her breath. Then her gaze was flying back to Makayla. "I'm very sorry I missed the brunch." She shoved the phone back into her bag. She reached for her friend. Hugged her again. "I am so happy for you, Makayla. I want you to only know joy." Another squeeze before she released the bride-to-be. "I won't disappoint you again."

But Makayla just laughed. A sweet sound. "Forget disappointing me. I'm pretty much just thrilled that you're still alive." She sent a wink at Wren even as she fluttered her fingers toward Jake. "And, apparently, living the dream."

"A scary, hot dream," Jennifer muttered.

Was that supposed to be praise or an insult?

"After Deputy Blake told us about what happened, I asked Jennifer to swing us by your uncle's place because I wanted to check on you." A nod from Makayla.

"I'm okay. Promise."

Someone was trying to kill Wren. That was not "okay" in his book.

But Makayla seemed to buy the story. Her big smile came and went again. "I'll call soon, and we'll talk more, okay?"

"That would be great." Wren looked down at her dress.

She hauled her keys from the bag. "I'm going to get changed. Bye, Makayla. Jen." She darted away.

He immediately moved to follow her.

Only to have Makayla step into his path.

"Oh, no," Makayla told him. She didn't sound quite so sweet any longer. "Maybe you missed the tears in her eyes, but I didn't."

"I didn't miss them, either." Jennifer took up a position at Makayla's side, effectively blocking his path. "She never cries, but I saw them, too." A glare slid over her face. "Just what did you do to Wren?" A long sigh. "Scary hot guys are always the *worst* trouble."

* * *

HER FEET POUNDED up the wooden steps that led to her uncle's elevated beach house. Her breath came too fast, and she had to blink away those frustrating tears. Jake wanted to be all-in on a pretend relationship, acting like they were finally a couple. A dream she'd had for far too long. One that had come true because of a nightmare.

He doesn't know about my past. Makayla doesn't know. Jen doesn't know. Because she'd kept it all so secret. If they knew, the women wouldn't want to be her friends. Jake wouldn't want to touch her.

No one would want her.

How could they?

She shoved the key into the lock. Threw open the door and rushed inside. The door clicked shut behind her. She'd taken a few steps in when—

No alarm is beeping.

Uncle Milo had a great security system. She'd set it when she left the previous day. It should have been beeping until she typed in the code to disengage the system. Only it wasn't beeping.

Before she could run back for the door, powerful arms grabbed her. And something sharp—sure felt like the tip of a knife—pressed into her side.

"How about we try this again?" A male voice. Angry. Rumbling. "My orders are to kill you. Right here and right now."

Chapter Eight

He needed the bride and the bridesmaid to get the hell out of his way. "Ladies, move."

They did not. Well, Makayla did not. Jennifer squeaked and sidestepped before catching herself.

"You aren't going to break her heart," Makayla told him.

He blinked. "Is that what you're worried about? Wren's heart?"

"She's our friend!" Jennifer declared. "As maid of honor, I—"

"Of course, I'm worried about her heart," Makayla fired back. "Not like yours is involved. Last night, I watched you. You were stunned when Wren kissed you. And you saw an opportunity. What was it? A chance to one-up your brother? Everyone always liked Eb better—something that had to piss you off—so you thought maybe you'd take something away from him?"

"Thanks for telling me I'm the popular one." He didn't see Wren. She'd made it into the house, and he didn't like that. He should have searched the place before she went inside. "And what is happening between me and Wren has zero to do with Eb."

"So you had sex with her because you're hopelessly in love with her?" A careful question from Makayla.

His eyes were on the beach house.

"I don't hear a yes," Jennifer pointed out. "Say it with me. '*Yes, I passionately love Wren.*'"

"Wren wanted me. I wanted her. And nothing else is your business." Politeness had never been his strong suit. *I should have checked the house first.* "Honestly, nothing is your business. I have Wren."

But...he didn't have Wren. She'd gone into the beach house. "Excuse me." He stalked around the women.

"Obsessive much," Jennifer groused behind him. "Jeez, let her change clothes. She'll be right back. Seriously. This is why smart women should avoid Scary Hot guys. Like, it should be a life lesson."

* * *

"Didn't know if you'd show up here or at your uncle's bar." His breath blew against her ear. "I came here, and my partner is staking out the bar. Guess it was my lucky day, huh?"

If she screamed, Jake wouldn't hear her. He was outside with her friends. The ocean pounded too loudly, too close. No way could he hear her.

"He's not going to save you this time," the man said, as if reading her thoughts. "I am going to slice you into pieces. He'll find you bloody and broken."

Bloody and broken.

Slice you into pieces.

Bloody and broken...

"No." She shook her head.

"You'll be begging soon." Sick enjoyment and anticipation filled his voice. "I am gonna love it when you beg."

She rammed her elbow back into his stomach. She grabbed for his wrist at the same moment and shoved the blade to the side, so it didn't slice over her skin.

Uncle Milo had drilled self-defense into her. Over and over.

She kicked back with her heel.

He cursed and fought, and so did she. With every ounce of her strength and will. Wren spun, and she shoved that knife right at him. The blade pierced his stomach, and he howled even as his blood flew out and soaked her fingers.

"Maybe *you'll* beg," she told him.

His eyes widened. Fear flashed for a moment. Too brief of a moment. Then rage overshadowed the fear. A killing rage.

She yanked the knife back.

"You—" he began.

She shoved the blade in him again. Harder. Deeper.

He screamed and surged away from her. He fell backward. Hit the floor. She rushed for the door. She hadn't locked it, and she threw it open. Wren darted onto the wooden deck. She could see Jake below, standing near the Jeep with Makayla and Jennifer. He still had on his sunglasses. Could he hear her? See her? Her hands waved frantically. "Jake!"

Arms locked around her stomach and hauled her back. "*Fucking bitch.*"

* * *

"WREN!"

"Yeah, that's exactly who we are talking about." The women had scurried into his path again. A decisive nod bobbed Jennifer's blonde hair. "We are talking about you and your obsession with Wren. You're freaking out right now, and the woman has barely been out of your sight for a few—"

He flew past the women. "*Wren!*"

She was out of his sight again. But she'd been on the wooden balcony a moment before. Waving desperately at him until someone had snatched her back.

He hauled out his gun.

"*OhmyGod!*" Jennifer's terrified scream. "He's lost his mind! He's going to kill her!"

The fuck he was. But he was going to kill whoever was attacking Wren.

He rushed up the stairs, taking them two, three at a time. He flew onto the wooden deck. Bounded toward the door. It was shut, but he didn't even stop. Just kicked it open. "*Wren!*"

She was on the floor. Fighting an attacker who straddled her. Blood covered her dress. Her arms. And there was a knife plunging down toward her. The bastard shoved his bloody knife toward Wren.

"Stop! Get the hell away from her! *Drop the knife!*"

Growling, the bastard ignored Jake. He never looked away from his prey. The blade thrust down at Wren. *My Wren.*

With zero hesitation, Jake fired. The bullet hit the bastard in the back. He jerked. Twisted, with the knife still in his hand. His head finally wrenched toward Jake.

Jake fired a second time. A hit in the chest.

The man collapsed near Wren. A bloody and silent Wren.

Jake rushed to her. "Baby?" He dropped to his knees beside her.

Wren leapt at him. Her arms wrapped around his neck. She trembled and her breath heaved, and he looked over her shoulder at the man on the floor.

Blood pooled all around the bastard.

"Where I go, you go," Wren gasped. "From now on. The most wonderful plan ever. The best. Where I go, you go."

Footsteps pounded up the stairs outside the beach house. He surged to his feet, dragging Wren with him. He took aim at the door with his gun.

Makayla flew over the threshold. She was followed immediately by Jennifer. Their eyes widened when they took in Jake's gun. Then the man on the floor. And, finally, Wren's blood-covered form.

Their screams pierced the air.

* * *

"WREN..." Honey Jackson slowly approached the back of the ambulance.

Wren perched on the gurney. "It's not my blood." The blade hadn't sliced her. It had been coming at her, plunging right toward her chest in the first of many promised stabs, but Jake had stopped the attacker.

She looked down at her hands. Bloody hands. Blood also covered her arms. Her dress.

Everywhere. She'd been told to sit. To wait.

Evidence, right? She was the evidence.

Sticky. Hardening. Blood. The coppery scent was all she could smell. All she could feel.

Don't move. Don't make a sound.

Her lips pressed together. She couldn't let the scream erupt.

"Wren."

Her gaze lifted.

Honey frowned at her. "Are you hurt?"

"It's not my blood." Hadn't she said that already?

"Maybe it's not, but you still have to tell me, are you hurt? Being hurt isn't just about blood."

Physically, she wasn't hurt. Maybe a few bruises, but those hardly mattered. "I stabbed him." A confession she'd given to the first responders on the scene. "Twice. He had the knife, but I got it away from him, and I stabbed him twice. He was bleeding like crazy, and that's where all the blood came from." Should there be more emotion in her voice? It sounded too flat. Maybe that was good. Or bad? Her gaze jerked to the left. "Jake?"

"Still right here, sunshine."

She flinched. "Don't call me that." *Not sunshine. I'm not an angel. No wings. I'm just like him...*

"He's dead," Honey said.

Wren sucked in a breath.

"The man who attacked you died on the scene. I'm thinking that was due to the bullet in the heart, but we'll let the ME rule on all that."

"A bullet to the heart does tend to be fatal," Jake murmured.

Honey glanced over at Jake. "Guessing you took the shots? The one to the back, then the one to the heart?"

"He was driving his knife at Wren. I told him to stop.

To get away from her. Instead, he drove that knife toward *her* chest."

Jake stood just beyond the open ambulance doors. He'd been there the entire time she'd been inside the emergency vehicle. Wherever she went, he was a few steps behind her.

"That what happened?" Honey asked as she turned her focus back on Wren. "Jake told him to stop, and the guy refused?"

"Y-yes. Jake saved me." Without him, she would have been the one loaded into the black body bag.

"I should have been with you the whole damn time," he suddenly snapped. "*My* mistake. It won't happen again." A pause. His shoulders rolled back. "Sheriff, did your team get the other bastard?"

Because Wren had told the first responders about the man who was supposed to be waiting at her Uncle Milo's bar. The dead man's partner.

Honey shook her head.

Fear twisted in Wren's stomach. *Still on the loose.*

"We will, though. We will find him," Honey promised.

The EMT hunched in the corner. Everyone just kind of lingered there, and the blood was dry, and it felt horrible, and Wren was pretty sure she was about to jump straight out of her blood-covered skin.

But at least I haven't fainted. That's something, isn't it? This time, instead of blood making her sick, she'd...

Been the one to use the knife.

Her stomach twisted. For a sickening moment, the familiar light-headedness returned. Pinpricks seemed to shoot across the skin of her face. "I want the blood off," Wren said. "I need the blood *off*."

"Surprised she hasn't fainted yet," Jake noted.

"Me, too," Honey admitted, voice more guarded.

Wren glowered at Jake. She also tried to breathe. *Don't faint. Don't faint.*

He winced. "Honestly, baby, you're doing great."

She was not. A scream threatened to break free from her at any moment. The past and present were colliding, and as far as fainting was concerned? Hell, maybe fainting would have been good. It would have stopped her from slipping into the memories that haunted her. It would have stopped her from breaking when and where others could see her. Where she might say or do the wrong thing and give everything away.

Tremors shook her body. The cold pinpricks turned to heat on her face.

"I think she's in shock." From the EMT. Not Hayden this time. A stranger. "Pupils are dilated. Rapid heart rate. Shallow breathing..."

"Get her to the hospital," Honey directed. Her lips tightened.

Wren shook her head. She hated hospitals. *Woke up in one once, tied down. Screaming. My whole life gone.*

"*Hospital,*" Honey snapped. "That wasn't an option, Wren. It was an order. I want you away from this scene before it turns into a circus. And—what in the hell are you doing, Jake?"

Jake had just climbed into the ambulance. "Going with her. The other bastard is on the loose, per your words. You think I'm letting her ride off without me?"

Wren didn't want to go anywhere without him. She had been one hundred percent serious about the whole "where I go, you go" business earlier. He could be her shadow. Her fake boyfriend. Her real lover. Anything. Everything. She just wanted him close.

"Before this ride goes rolling away, I need to talk with

Wren. Alone." Honey jerked a hand toward the EMT. "Get out of the ambulance."

"But—"

The keys on Honey's belt jingled. Light hit her badge and made it gleam even brighter. "*Out.*"

He got out.

Jake didn't.

"You, too, hero," she demanded with a wave of her still lifted hand. "Give us three minutes alone. I need to talk with Wren without eyes and ears on us."

Jake settled beside Wren. "Talk freely. I'm not going anywhere."

Honey leaned inside the ambulance. "Wren is safe. I will be right here with her. *Go.*"

He didn't.

Wren knew she should say something. Do something. But all she could feel was the blood and the past. "I stabbed him."

"You did what you had to do," Jake assured her. "You stabbed him, and you got away long enough to call for help. *Dammit, I should have been there.*"

"I stabbed him twice. I would have kept stabbing him, if it meant I survived, and he didn't." Her head turned toward Jake. A new emotion had joined her fear and rage. Sadness. "I didn't want to be like him."

Jake's brow furrowed. "The guy who attacked you? Trust me, you're nothing like him. You were fighting to survive."

He didn't understand. "I don't have angel wings. I'm meant for the dark, not the light. Didn't you see that? *Can't you see that?*" Of all people, he should have seen the truth the most clearly.

"Wren?" The furrow deepened.

"I didn't want to be like him," she said again, "but I am my father's—"

"*Wren.*" Honey bounded into the ambulance. The fastest Wren had seen her move in years. "You're in shock. You're saying things you shouldn't. I want you to look at me. *Look at me.*"

Reluctantly, her stare pulled from Jake to land on Honey. "I'm not in shock." At least, she didn't think she was. "I'm just not in denial anymore, either." You could learn a lot about yourself when you stabbed a man. Twice.

"Jake, *go.*" A sharp, barking demand from Honey. "Wren, *watch yourself.*"

"Why does Wren need to watch herself? What is happening?" Jake still didn't move. "Someone explain to me, now."

Honey shook her head. "Some things can't be taken back, Wren. I talked to your uncle this morning. He told me the news. I'm sorry, and I know it's hitting you hard on top of everything else that's happening—"

Why would Honey be sorry? She'd wanted Wren's father dead, too. For years, she'd hunted him. "I'm not sorry he's dead. You're not, either. Don't pretend otherwise to be polite."

Honey didn't have a comeback for that.

"I'm glad he's dead. But...him dying didn't change much about me, did it?" The blood was all over her hands. "What's inside can't be changed. He always told me that. I wanted him to be wrong, but, here I am."

"Here you are *surviving.*" Honey was adamant. "You fought to live today. You're a good person, Wren."

No, she pretended to be good. She'd mastered the art of deception. She could play the good-girl role in her sleep.

"Class president," Jake rasped. "You led every volunteer

effort in high school. Still do that same shit today. Most likely to succeed, that was you."

Most likely to kill. That should have been her. If they'd known the truth, it would have been.

Why did she feel so cold? Clammy?

"Someone wants me to die," Wren announced, and, yes, her voice broke a bit around the edges. "It has to be about the past."

Jake stiffened. "I told you—"

"My past, Jake, not yours or your brother's." *It has to be.* Her father died and this happened, all so close together? "It has to be about what he did. He's dead, and I'm targeted, and it *has to be* because someone wants payback."

"Fuck." From Jake. "Baby, this is about—"

"It's about me and it's about my dad."

Honey's eyes fell closed.

"My dad," Wren repeated. "A serial killer. A man who murdered seven different couples. A man who covered me in blood and made me into a monster." The big, twisted secret was out. There was no pulling the words back. No stopping them. "That's who you saved today, Jake." *That's the woman you fucked last night.* Shame swept through her, and she couldn't look at him again. She simply stared down at her fisted, bloody hands. "That's who the man in the house wanted to die. He wanted me to suffer, and it has to be because my father made so many people suffer. Someone learned the truth about me, and now I'm targeted for death."

Chapter Nine

"What in the hell is happening?"

Honey whirled toward Jake. They were in the hospital's hallway, right outside of the exam room that had been assigned to Wren.

She'd already been cleaned up—*the blood had better all be gone*. And a doc was currently examining her, thus the reason Jake was cooling his heels in the hallway with the sheriff. A sheriff who had apparently been keeping far too many secrets from him. Secrets about Wren.

"Wren was in shock when she spoke earlier." No emotion entered Honey's cool voice. "Clearly, she did not know what she was saying."

"Clearly, that's some bullshit," he tossed right back. They were alone in the corridor. Makayla and Jennifer had tried to push their way back to the exam area, but the two women had been detained in the waiting room. Right now, he wanted answers, and Jake was going to get them. If Honey wouldn't give him what he needed, then he'd be ripping his way through every contact he had at the FBI. "You're a former Fed. A damn FBI profiler." He knew she'd been one of the best at the job. "Did you work her dad's case?"

She didn't speak.

His patience was long gone. All the stuff he'd thought that he knew about Wren? *Wrong.* And the idea that Wren had been carrying this burden while he just stood there, unknowing, for so many years, made him ache. "You think I don't know that Milo is a former Fed, too? Seriously? Do you know how many government contracts I've worked? And don't go forgetting my brother is CIA."

"As if I could forget." A roll of her eyes. "You twins were always pains in my ass. Still are, by the way."

He was about to become an even bigger pain. "Milo *isn't* her uncle, is he?"

Her lips pursed.

"Her father is a serial killer."

She rocked onto the balls of her feet, then dipped back onto her heels. The woman was all of five-foot-nothing. The faintest threads of gray slid through the darkness of her black hair. Her sharp gaze assessed him, and he could practically see the wheels grinding in her head as she tried to figure out what BS to feed him. "Wren was confused," she began.

No, she had not been. "I've seen the scars on her shoulders."

She swallowed. "Have you now? I heard she fell when she was younger. Some kind of tree house accident." A shake of her head. "Painful, but those things happen."

"Bullshit." Honey was normally a much better liar. "Did he do that to her?"

"Wren is—"

"Do not tell me she's confused again. She's not. She's strong and she's determined, and she survived *two* attacks in two days. I don't think those attacks had a damn thing to do with her father." Eb had been too certain that this madness was tied to their own bloody pasts. But with this new reveal from Wren, he needed to know more in order to be sure. Maybe he and Honey should both put all of their cards on the table. "Eb sent me to her. He thinks one of our enemies is targeting her. The nightmare that's happening to Wren? These attacks? He thinks it's because of us. And that's what I thought, too, until this new bombshell made me start second guessing." What had his Wren endured? And how could he take all of her pain away?

Honey's dark lashes flickered. "That would track. Trouble coming from you two bozos. Trouble follows you both everywhere like a shadow." A brief pause as she seemed to consider things. Then she exhaled and admitted, "More likely that it *is* related to you two, especially since her father's remains were positively identified recently. After being hidden for years, an off-the-books team closed in on him. Only to discover that he was already dead. DNA verified his identity." Her gaze darted along the empty hallway before returning to Jake. "Her father is dead, and as far as the rest of the world is concerned, his only child—a daughter—died years ago, too. She died as a result of injuries she'd sustained courtesy of her dear old, freak of a dad."

It felt as if he'd just taken a bullet to the heart. "Who was he?"

"One of the most twisted bastards I've ever seen. Handsome as sin, charming as a snake, and sadistic enough to give you nightmares for the rest of your life."

That wasn't a name.

"He targeted couples. See, his wife left him when she realized he was, you know, fucking demented. As you do.

Only he tracked her down and killed her. First order of business."

Fucking fuck.

"Then he got this idea in his head that there were no perfect couples in the world. That when times got hard, even the most loving couple would turn on each other. Survival of the fittest at play. These people would do anything to escape, to survive, even betray the one they claimed to love most. *Hurt* the person they loved the most. Romantic love to him—it was a lie. The only thing that mattered was blood. As in, your own freaking DNA. A blood connection—a familial connection—was the most powerful thing in the world. And since the only person bound by blood to him was his daughter..."

"She was all that mattered." His hands were fisted.

"Yes. So he liked to give her an up close view of his attacks. He never wanted her to be confused or misled by someone the way he was. Love is a lie. Blood is truth. It was a lesson he worked hard to instill in her."

This couldn't be happening. Dammit. Dammit! *How* could this have happened to his beautiful Wren?

Honey's gaze darted toward the closed exam room door. "The first time I saw that girl, she was covered in blood. It had dried on her skin. Coated the poor thing. Her eyes were so dark. Huge. And she had her hand on the throat of a vic, like that was going to stop the blood from pouring out of the dead woman. All that blood had just drenched the girl. She was so still. Frozen like a statue in that pose, and I knew, I *knew* she'd been that way for a long time. Hell, if she hadn't blinked, I would have thought I was staring at a dead girl."

He lunged for the exam room door.

It opened before he could touch it. A doctor stood in the doorway. "She's good." His gaze was steady and reassuring behind the lenses of his glasses. "Very determined to leave, and asking for...Jake?" A nod. Then a wave at Jake. "I'm assuming that's you."

If Wren wanted him, then Wren was getting him. "I'll be taking her out of here." He'd take her wherever she wanted to go.

"Thought as much." An incline of his head toward Honey. "Sheriff Jackson." Then the doctor bustled away.

Honey grabbed Jake's arm before he could enter the exam room, and she hauled him close. Her voice dropped to a husky whisper as she said, "Outside of a few shrinks that she was forced to see when she was younger, Wren has *never* spoken about her past to anyone but me and Milo. Just so you understand how delicate this situation is, Milo told me that he informed her of her father's death last night. Last. Night. This shit is fresh, and it has to be hitting Wren hard."

He looked down at her hand. "When, exactly, last night?" His voice had gone wooden. Low, but wooden. "You got a specific time?"

"I don't know—sometime after you took her off the beach. She called him to check in, probably so he wouldn't hear the news from me and freak out about the attack."

Wren had checked in with the older man, then Milo had called Jake. Milo had said that Wren was crying. *Sonofabitch.*

Everything that had happened afterward...

It has to be hitting Wren hard. Honey's words slid through his mind once more.

"I don't know what the hell just put that look on your face, Jacob Jones, but don't you dare go treating that girl any different, you understand me?" If possible, her voice had dropped even more. A soft but lethal order. "She has fought to be good for as long as I've known her. She lived through hell, and she came out freaking valedictorian of her class. She put the past behind her. She did everything right and, from the sound of things, if *your* past hadn't come rearing its head, Wren would be safe and happy and living her best life about now."

Honey thought he would treat Wren differently because her father had been a monster? The sheriff had no clue. The only way he wanted to treat Wren was like the fucking goddess that she was to him.

"Always knew you'd be wrong for her." Honey's brows beetled. "Too intense. Too growly all the time. Wren needs someone who smiles and laughs and who can chase the shadows from her life."

Wren smiled. She laughed. She did that stuff plenty.

But...was any of it real?

"Eb should be here with her," Honey suddenly declared. "He's the one who's always been her best friend. Thought if she'd tell the truth to anyone, it would be him."

"I'm more than her friend." *I'm going to be her fucking future.* And he was done waiting. Waiting in the hall. Waiting on the outskirts of Wren's life.

He broke away from the sheriff and surged forward. Hurried into the exam room. Then drew up short when he saw Wren standing near the exam table in green scrubs.

She winced. "Don't judge the outfit. It was all that was available, okay? I am seriously in need of new clothing. But at least the blood is gone."

Her skin was clean. No more blood on her arms or hands.

Honey shut the door after she slipped into the room. "Wren, we all need to talk."

Wren slanted her gaze toward Jake. "Did she tell you all the dark and dirty details about my past?"

"Some of them." He had the feeling there was plenty more darkness to share. "She also said the man was dead."

"My father? Yes. Or at least, that's what I'm hearing."

"It's what you heard last night. Right before I came into your room to check on you." He needed to be very sure about this timeline.

"Yes."

Hell. The truth was like a knife blade to the heart. He'd been tasting heaven, and Wren had been trying to claw her way out of hell. "You said I didn't know you." And he'd rattled off crap about the way she liked her eggs and her favorite holiday. His eyes squeezed shut. "Of course, you like Halloween." How could she not? His eyes opened, and Jake pinned her with his stare even as her previous words played through his head. *"I always liked to pretend I was someone else."*

She stepped toward him. "I'd like to leave now, please."

He was in front of her in an instant. His hands rose and curled around her shoulders. Delicate shoulders that had been carrying a heavy burden that he'd known nothing about. "Eb had no clue?"

Her head turned to the side. Not looking at him any longer but focusing on Honey. "I would like to continue keeping my past as under wraps as possible. I understand that if this investigation leads to anything linked to my f-father, then the truth will have to emerge." Her lips pressed together.

His hands lightly squeezed her shoulders.

"That's why I spoke up to Jake," Wren continued determinedly. "If he's offering his protection to me, I thought it was only fair for him to be fully aware of what was happening. And just who it was that he was protecting."

"What in the hell is that supposed to mean?" Jake demanded. He knew exactly—

Her long lashes swept down to conceal her eyes. "Maybe you don't want to protect someone like me."

"*Wren.*" The horrified cry burst from Honey. "You are nothing at all like your—"

"We need time alone, Honey." Firm. Flat. Jake and Wren needed to clear the air, and he was one hundred percent gonna clear it. "Wren has to understand a few important facts before we walk out of here."

Those long lashes of hers swept up. The darkness of Wren's eyes almost swallowed him. "I understand plenty, I can assure you of that."

He wanted to kiss her. To sweep her into his arms and run the hell away with her. To protect her from any and every threat. All items on his agenda. But first...His head angled toward a watchful Honey. "Perhaps there is an update waiting on you? Maybe while Wren was getting checked out, one of your patrols got lucky and found our second suspect. You should go look into that."

"Are *you* feeling lucky?" Honey asked him as a twisted smile curved her lips.

He'd never been the lucky one. And he'd killed a man not too long before. Honey had already grilled him about that scene. There would be official statements to make. So many questions to answer, and, yes, when the story spread, people would be digging. The first place they'd dig?

Wren's life. Her past.

She wanted her secrets to remain hidden. But she had to understand that the truth might emerge. And if—or when

—it did, Jake would be right at her side. Or, screw that, he'd be in front of her. Shielding her from any and every threat.

"I'll just step outside for a bit," Honey conceded after a stare-off with Jake. "I'll let Wren's friends know she's good."

But as he looked back at Wren, he saw her flinch at that one word. *Good.*

Ah, sunshine, we are going to have a problem. Because she needed to stop thinking of herself as—

"That word really isn't part of me." A careful clarification from Wren. "I just pretended."

Honey had already swept out of the small hospital room. She hadn't heard Wren's words. Jake had.

Wren backed up one step. Two.

His hands dropped to his sides. "Eb doesn't know." This time, he didn't phrase the words as a question. Eb was hell on wheels when it came to keeping secrets. He had to be, as a CIA spook. But this...

Wren shook her head. "Uncle Milo said I should tell no one. My fa—the killer was in the wind. I was hidden. Given a new name. A complete new identity. I even looked different." Her lips pulled down. "The last time he saw me, I was a scrawny, blood-covered thirteen-year-old. I don't look anything like her any longer. I'm *not* her." Adamant.

"Wren..."

"I was placed in protective custody at thirteen. The first placement—it didn't go so well. I guess I had issues."

Probably a major understatement.

"Uncle Milo kept checking on me. And, he—when I needed another cover, he's the one who stepped in. At sixteen, I came here with him. But one of the rules was that Uncle Milo said I couldn't talk about the past. If I said the wrong thing to the wrong person, then the truth might get out. I'd have to be relocated again. Or maybe, even before I could be relocated, my fa—the killer would find me." She wrapped her arms protectively around her stomach. "I didn't want him to find me. So I followed the rules. I never told anyone. I did everything just like I was supposed to do."

"Perfectly," he rasped, thinking of her life.

She frowned.

"You played by the rules. Toed the line." He had to advance on her. But when he did, she instantly backed up. He stopped. "You didn't even take a lover." *Until me.*

"How could I? A lover wouldn't know me. Not the real me. I pretend enough. I didn't want to have to keep pretending about who I really was, ah...*then,* too."

"But then you let me take you." The words fell between them. "Want to tell me why?"

"No."

Just that. He waited. There was no more. "Wren..."

"He was dead. Milo wouldn't lie to me about something like that. He said they confirmed his identity with DNA. The monster was dead. Since he was dead, I-I thought the attack on the beach had to be random."

It had been far from random.

"I thought I was safe, and if I was finally safe, then I could have something of my own."

Now they were getting somewhere. "Why me?" He wanted to close that last bit of distance between them. To pull her into his arms.

Never let go.

But she wasn't speaking.

He pushed, "Was it because I was there, Wren? Convenient for you?"

Laughter spilled from her. "Jake, I hate to be the one to tell you this, but you are pretty much the most inconvenient guy I've ever met."

He loved her laughter. He loved—

Jake shut down the thought. "Why me?"

Her head had tilted forward. But at that stark question, she angled back her head and stared at him.

"It's just us here, Wren. What you say to me isn't leaving this room. I get that you carried secrets your whole life, and the weight of them had to nearly suffocate you."

Her lower lip trembled. She caught it. Bit it.

"You don't have to carry them alone any longer." *Let me carry them for you. I'll carry any weight for you.* If she would just let him.

"If the truth gets out, my business will be ruined. I worked hard building up my real estate firm."

A successful firm that she ran in Charleston. Yes, he knew she'd poured her heart and soul into the business.

"But no one will want to buy a house from a serial killer's daughter. No one will want to do business with me. No one will even want to be near me." One hand rose and gestured toward the door. "The 'friends' waiting outside? Makayla and Jennifer? Do you think they would have even talked to me back in high school if they knew what my father had done? He *tortured* those people. Then he made them torture each other. It was all a test, and they just failed over and over and over again. Because love—love won't last. He taught me that. People will swear that they'll stand by you. That they will help you, but when it comes right down to it...that's just not how it works."

"And how does it work? Really?" How in the hell had she silently battled these demons for so long?

"My fa—the killer believed that blood was stronger than anything else. Give someone a choice of saving a blood relation versus a friend or a lover...and the choice goes to blood. But even then, he said people would turn on family members if it meant saving their own lives. Survival at its core is about caring for no one but yourself."

Jake shook his head. "You don't believe that."

A tear slid down her cheek.

That lone teardrop gutted him.

Before she could reach up and brush aside the tear, he was there. His hand rose and caught the tear. Her hand slid against his. Her eyes widened.

"He didn't want you to believe in love because the bastard's own heart had been broken. Honey told me that your mother left him."

"She left him. He killed her." Pain twisted in Wren's voice. "He didn't have a heart."

But you do. Baby, you do. "What happened to your shoulders?"

She sucked in a breath. Shook her head. "I don't—"

"You fucked me because he was dead, and you didn't have to worry about protecting a lover anymore." The conclusion he'd reached. "You were free for the first time in your life, and you turned to me."

Her gaze searched his.

"That's one explanation. Or we could say that you fucked me because you were being torn apart by adrenaline and grief, and you needed a release, so you used me." His hand lingered against her cheek. "That's fine, too, baby. Use me. Use—"

"*No.*" Hard. Angry. "How about this explanation? I had sex with you because I wanted you. Because I've wanted you for a very long time. Because *you* carry darkness, and you are probably the only person out there who wouldn't turn away from me in horror if you learned all my dark and twisted secrets." Her fingers curled around his. "Case in point, you're not running away from me right now."

"Hell, no, baby. I'd never run away from you." They should get that clear. "I'd run *to* you, every single time."

"Jake—"

He kissed her. Not hard and demanding. Not consuming. Not with the raw passion that wanted to rip him apart anytime he thought of sex with Wren. But with care because he could do that, too. He wasn't a full-time bastard. Just a part-time one. So his lips pressed lightly to hers. Softly. A kiss of promise.

There were an awful lot of promises that he wanted to make her. But he would not lie. He couldn't.

His head lifted. "The truth about your father may come out to the rest of the world. I killed a man today, and death tends to attract attention. I don't know how deep and hard the Feds buried your past, but you have to be prepared in case the news about your father goes public. If that happens, I will stand with you."

"My real estate business..."

"Maybe you'll get new clients who are curious as hell about you. Maybe business will boom, sunshine. Let's think positive."

"I'm not sunshine. I'm death." She let go of his hand.

"Nah. That's me." His hand darted up to cup her chin. "Eb thinks the danger you face is because of us—because of him and me and someone who wants to get at us through you. That the past is biting back. Our past, not yours. And like I told you before, you will not be collateral damage."

"You don't know that this is about you and Eb! You can't know for certain."

Uh, he'd been sent there by Eb to—

His phone rang. A loud, pealing ringtone that he'd assigned just to one person because, dammit, it was a happy freaking sound, and he liked to know exactly when *she* was calling. Not that she normally called.

Not that Wren made a habit of calling him…

The phone rang again, and Jake hauled it out of his pocket. He glared at the screen.

"Are you answering that, *now?*" she asked, shocked.

"Yeah, I am. Because *you're* the one calling."

"No, I'm not, I'm right here and I—"

His fingers swiped over the screen, and he put the phone on speaker. "Who the hell is this?"

Laughter. Grating. Robotic.

"You have Wren's phone," he snapped. Had her phone been left at her uncle's place? At the crime scene?

"I saw your *face.*" The robotic voice blasted so loudly and hard that Wren flinched. "You thought she would die, and I saw your fear."

"Fantastic for you. Why don't you come find me right now? I can show you all kinds of things." He wanted to shatter the phone and destroy the caller. "All up close and personal-like." A grim promise.

"You saved her this time. You won't again. You and your brother will lose her. Do you hear me? You will *lose her.*"

"Never gonna happen," he snarled right back. "But you try and take her, and you *will* lose your life. Understand me?"

The caller hung up.

Jake forced his jaw to unclench. "I think it's safe to say," he gritted out, "the attacks on you are because of me and Eb."

Chapter Ten

SHE WAS SUPPOSED TO SPEND ANOTHER NIGHT WITH Jake.

Wren curled up on the couch. She'd gotten new clothes —currently she wore jeans and a black top. She'd needed clothes—and not just the borrowed scrubs—for her very long visit at the sheriff's station. A visit that had come immediately after she'd left the hospital. Luckily, Honey had gotten a deputy to bring Wren's travel bag over from Milo's place.

The crime scene.

The deputy had brought the bag to the sheriff's station. There had been tons of questions to answer about the attack. Forms to sign. So many statements to give.

Her phone had been located.

It had been tossed in one of the garbage cans outside of the hospital. Jake said the caller had done that act deliberately, to let them know just how close he had been the whole time.

Her friends had been terrified when they saw Wren.

Jennifer had been crying loudly, and Makayla hadn't been able to stop shaking.

She hadn't mentioned anything about her father to them.

So far, Jake was the only person—besides Honey and Uncle Milo—who knew her secret. Years ago, Uncle Milo had insisted that she talk with a few shrinks. But those psychiatrists had never learned the full story from her teenage self.

And Jake, well...

He'd just strode into the den. He had his phone to his ear. "Yeah, dammit, Eb, you heard what I said." Tension practically poured from him. "One dead attacker and another in the wind. I don't know if they are lackeys just following orders or if the one in the wind is the jerk pulling the strings." His intense gaze landed right on her. "The sonofabitch said we'd lose her. Hell, no, it's not happening. I don't need to be told that shit by you. I know it won't go down."

Fear curled tightly within her stomach.

He marched toward her. "I get that it's someone we've both pissed off. Only there is a long line of those assholes. This person dug into our lives. They found out that *she* is our weakness."

Wren shook her head. She wasn't a weakness for the twins. Just a blip on their radar.

"That means this creep is close. Came back to our home base kind of close. I'll be using my resources, and you use yours—and, hell, yes, we're gonna get Marley to call in the Ice Breakers. Why not? They excel at digging, and this is Wren's life we are talking about. But not just the Ice Breakers. I want Declan Flynn on the job. That guy can follow any breadcrumb that he finds online. Declan *and* his buddy Hunter. Hunter is shady as hell, one of the things I quite enjoy about the guy. He doesn't mind getting his hands dirty."

She curled her legs beneath her as she perched on the couch. Her gaze fell to her hands. All of the blood was gone. It had been long gone. So why did she keep checking her hands so much to make sure they were clean?

I stabbed a man today. Twice. I would have killed him. To get away, she would have taken his life and never hesitated. Hadn't her father told her that would be the case? That if the choice came down to survival or death, people would do whatever was necessary?

He hadn't just been some wild maniac. Once upon a time, he'd been a respected psychology professor. He'd worked in an ivory tower for years. Then he'd fallen in love with a student.

Her mother.

The story she'd told Jake and Eb about her father traveling in Madrid and falling for her mother? That had been part of the cover Uncle Milo created for her.

Wren's mother *had* been from Madrid. She'd come to the US in order to get her degree. She'd been a student who'd gotten swept away in a romance with a handsome, young professor. For a time, the relationship had been great. Wren had some happy memories. But then, her mother had fallen for someone else. She'd left and...

And all of the cracks in her father's perfect surface had begun to appear.

"The guy is ballsy. To be at the hospital? He must have swiped her phone from the scene at Milo's."

She didn't even remember dropping her phone. Maybe it had fallen during the struggle? Had the phone been with her when she'd run out onto the balcony and tried to get help?

"He was right there. No, there isn't a camera that can show us his face from the hospital. The SOB knew exactly where to go so there would be no footage."

She looked up. Only to get caught by his blazing eyes.

"Is there anything else you need to know?" Jake's jaw hardened. Wren realized he'd repeated a question his brother had asked. Jake paused, as if mulling over what his response would be.

She held her breath.

"Yes. You need to know that Wren and I are lovers."

She felt her eyes widening.

"That's the story we're telling everyone. That's why she's staying with me. Why I won't let her go anywhere without me being by her side. So when you get to town, be prepared for the news. Deal with it."

Her breath shuddered out.

"Start making that list of names," Jake ordered. "Every enemy we've got. People who could find out about Wren. The caller was very specific. Said we would lose her. And that's not ever going to happen." A pause. Then, "Good. Glad you escaped the hail of gunfire. Now get your ass on the next plane." He hung up and tossed the phone aside.

The moments ticked by. She should say something. So how about... "Just what kind of cases have you and Eb worked that would make someone mad enough to kill?"

He sat on the couch. Right beside her. The heat of his body stretched out and curled around her. "You think you're the only one carrying around secrets?"

"I figure everyone carries them." True. "Some are just a whole lot bigger than others."

His head tilted as he studied her.

Wren had always thought her secret was particularly big. *Hello, twisted serial killer father.* "I told you my secret. Don't you think you should tell me all of yours?"

"You told me *one* secret. Granted, it was a major one. Definitely caught me by surprise. But you've hardly revealed all." His hand reached out. Caught a lock of her hair. "I don't want you to be scared of me." He fiddled with the lock of hair, seemingly unaware of his movements.

Meanwhile, she was far too aware of everything he did. "Story of my life," she muttered.

He frowned.

"Uh, thinking people would be scared if they learned the truth about me," Wren hurried to add. "My...father..." She hated calling him that. "He murdered people in front of me like it was one of his behavioral experiments." Because that was all it had been. Worse, *she* had just been an experiment. She knew that. "Trust me, there isn't anything you could say that would make me scared of you." But how did Jake feel about her? Deep down?

He leaned in closer. "Don't be so sure."

"Jake, you killed to protect me today." If he hadn't come barreling inside, that knife would have plunged into her. "I would never be afraid of you."

"I *killed*." Grim. "And now you're pulling away from me."

Uh, no, she wasn't. She was right there. Maybe even leaning toward him because she couldn't help herself.

"In the hospital, you retreated from me. You're scared of me now. If you learn more about me and Eb, the truth will just terrify you even more."

Really? That was what he thought? She moved quickly, shoving toward him in a fast burst of energy. Wren caught his shirt in her hands. Fisted the material. She'd risen onto her knees as she twisted toward him. "Does this look like a retreat?"

Then she kissed him. Not with a whole lot of tact or seduction. More like too wildly. Definitely a bit clumsily. With all the emotions and fears that bubbled inside of her.

He growled and his hands rose to clamp around her shoulders. The heat of his body tempted her to get even closer. She opened her mouth because she wanted to—

He pushed her away. Gently. Firmly.

Her breath sawed in and out. In and out. His eyes glittered at her, and her stomach twisted once more. The bad, sad kind of twist. "Now who is retreating?" Maybe he didn't want her anymore. Now that he knew the truth about her past and just how twisted she really was, he didn't feel the same desire any longer.

At least we had one night together.

In the next breath, Jake hauled her back against him. His mouth locked onto hers. His tongue thrust into her mouth as he kissed her with a ferocious need. A stark possessiveness that drove straight to her core. This wasn't a seduction type of kiss. It also wasn't clumsy or a bit awkward like hers had been. This...this was claiming. Owning.

Consuming.

His head lifted. "Understand this, I will never retreat from you." Guttural.

Her breath did the sawing-in-and-out routine again as her heart raced.

But he pushed her back. Once more, *back*. His stare seemed to singe her as he said, "I *am* trying to not fuck you here and now. Because when we fuck, I tend to lose my mind. I have questions that need answering. First and foremost...why me?"

"Why you...what?"

"Why did you pick me to be your first lover? Was it because you were trying to escape the grief of knowing your father was dead? Did you turn to me out of desperation?"

Had he just called her *desperate*? Insult much? One thing at a time. She sucked in a breath. "First, I did *not* grieve for him." A hard, negative shake of her head. "I got the news, and I was *free*. For the first time, truly free. Uncle Milo would never have told me that my fa—the killer was dead if it wasn't true." He was gone. "I don't have to worry any longer that he will come back for me. That I will wake up and be part of his experiments again. After Uncle Milo told me the news, I could finally take what I wanted without fear. So...I took it." *I took you, Jake.*

A muscle jerked along his jaw. "You wanted me."

"I pretty much have for years. Only every time I tried to get close to you, you'd step away from me."

"Because I thought you were fucking my brother."

Her teeth snapped together. "Can we get past that? I never did. Never will."

"Damn straight, you won't."

"I love Eb and—"

"Yeah, got it. He loves you, too. Bastard says it all the time." And he was off the couch. Towering over her. "So you can get why a guy might wrongly assume you two were an item?"

"Sorry. Guess I just don't go for the fun and outgoing twin. My heart belongs to the broody bastard who kills for me." Mocking words. Mocking just so that he wouldn't see how very true the statement was.

My heart has always belonged to you, Jake.

Even when he'd shattered it by walking away so many times.

But Jake's face changed as he stared down at her. It hardened, even more than normal. His jaw tightened. His eyes narrowed. Brightened. His nostrils flared.

The silence stretched to an uncomfortable level.

Slowly, she rose from the couch. Time to recover some ground and guard her heart better. "That is the story you want us to spread, right? That we're lovers now? That you're the one I've always wanted?" Before he could respond, she shook her head. "Let's just focus on the problem in front of us. The jerk who tried to kill me and his partner who got away. If this is about the past, something they blamed you and your brother for, then why come after me? I don't mean to seem cold, but if they are pissed at you, why not just kill you? Why not come after you and Eb directly?"

"Because we're tough bastards to kill."

"I could be tough to kill," she muttered.

"And because, sometimes, it's not just about death. It's about pain."

Unease slithered through her. Her father had been all about pain.

"It's about torturing your enemy. Taking what he wants most in this world and ripping it away from him."

She licked her lips. "I'm not what you want most."

He didn't speak.

"I-I...I'm just some random woman in your life. In Eb's life."

"Bullshit. You said you loved him. He loves you. Like I said, Eb spouts that shit all the time." A little line appeared between his eyebrows. "Maybe the wrong person heard him say it."

"He *loves* your sister." Fear burst inside of her even as she made that fierce declaration. "Marley! If someone wants to hurt you and Eb, the number one way to do that would be to go after Marley." The beloved sister, *not me*. Wren lunged forward because she had to get a phone and call Marley and *why* hadn't they already done that very thing from the first moment?

He caught her before she could make it toward his phone. His, because hers was in the sheriff's possession. His arms locked around her stomach, and Jake hauled her back against him. "I notified Marley about the mess the minute I got on the plane out of South America. I made sure that billionaire psycho husband of hers had a full brigade of protection around her. Getting to Marley would be harder than getting into Fort Knox. The minute she wed Declan Flynn, she became off-limits to basically everyone in the world."

His hold burned through her.

"Marley is safe," he said. "My priority is you."

She tugged against his hold. He just tightened his grip. Wren felt her heart thudding far too hard. Could he feel the frantic beat, too? "You can...you can let go."

"What if I don't want to?"

"Then you shouldn't have stopped kissing me on the couch." She turned in his arms. Was so very, very close to him. Her head tipped back.

"Maybe I stopped because I don't want you making a mistake you'll regret. Maybe I don't want to be your mistake."

"I don't think of you as a mistake." Soft. Right then, she thought of him as the man who'd saved her life.

"The first time we fucked, you'd been attacked on the beach. You'd just found out your father was dead. Your emotions had to be out of control and the adrenaline you must have been feeling probably seemed to be ripping you apart."

"Are you explaining how I felt...*to me*?" She glowered. "Thanks. Thanks so much for that. I was super confused."

"I'm trying to—fuck it. I'm trying to *help*." He cleared his throat. "I understand adrenaline. You think I'm not riding an insane wave of it right now? You were on the floor of Milo's beach house. The prick was above you with a knife. If I'd been slower, if I hadn't kicked open that door and rushed inside right then, you'd be dead."

She swallowed. "Your emotions are out of control because you had to kill for me." They were both too on edge. Check.

"I'd kill for you over and over, no hesitation. You will not be hurt. You will not be threatened. And I will not let my past destroy you in any way." He dropped his hold. Stepped back. "Just as I won't destroy you."

"Didn't realize you were in danger of doing that." She missed his touch.

"Adrenaline," he bit off like the word was a curse. "Adrenaline, fear, fury, and a lifetime of longing lead to control that *will* shatter. I stopped kissing you because I am trying to not take everything I want from you. I barely held onto my control with you last night."

That had been controlled? What would uncontrolled sex be like with him?

"I'm far from a gentleman. Always have been. But I'm also trying not to be a monster with you, though, so there's that. No knight in shining armor. Just not the dragon, either."

"You aren't a monster." Definite. She tucked a lock of hair behind her ear. "I've seen monsters." Up close.

"My past is the reason you're in danger."

"Just what terrible crime is it that you committed? Because I don't exactly see you as the cold-blooded killer type."

"Everyone always thinks I'm cold."

True enough. They did say that about him. *Ice in his veins.* "In school, people just thought you were...less emotional than Eb."

He laughed. A sharp bark of laughter.

She'd always enjoyed his laughs. Though he hadn't laughed much with her. His laughs had been reserved for Eb and Marley.

"Sunshine..."

Her shoulders tensed.

His stare sharpened. "Wren," he murmured. "Everyone thought—still thinks—that Eb is fun and charming, and I am a cold-blooded bastard. Those individuals are not wrong."

"I happen to think they are. I find you quite charming. And fun."

"Really?" His arms crossed over his chest. "When do you find me to be fun?"

"When you're making me come three times in the middle of hot, sweaty sex."

He surged forward. Reached out for her.

But stopped before actually making contact. Jake fisted his hands.

She smiled at him. A sweet smile. Dare she call it... sunshiny?

A muscle flexed along his wonderfully square jaw. "The first time I killed, I was twenty-two years old."

Her smile instantly wiped away.

"Not quite so fun and charming, am I?"

Goosebumps rose on her arms. "You killed to protect me today."

"I'd kill to protect you any day of the week."

And I would do the same for you. The knowledge was just there. Strong and clear in her mind and in her heart. She'd never, ever thought she'd be the type to kill. Mostly because she'd never wanted to be like her father. But today, when her life had been on the line, the brutal instinct to survive had kicked in and she'd fought back with all her being.

And, if Jake was in danger, if someone had been lunging at him with a knife, Wren knew she would have done anything necessary to save him. No hesitation.

"Wren?"

She blinked. Schooled her expression and wondered what she might have already given away. "My Uncle Milo respects you. You and your brother. No way would he do that if you two were bad guys. I'm guessing you worked for the government. I mean, I know Eb still does work for the Agency." The Agency—also known as the CIA.

"That CIA business of his is supposed to be confidential."

Yes. But it wasn't. "Eb shares things with me. I also figure things out because Uncle Milo has been telling me confidential stuff for years. Goes along with the whole me already being in witness protection bit and being basically adopted by the federal agent who was working to bring down my biological father." A roll of one shoulder as she ignored her goosebumps. "There are lots of shades of gray in my world with Uncle Milo. But if he had thought you were bad news, he never would have let me be around you or your brother. Instead, he invites you to every family dinner we have."

"The man does a mean crawfish boil."

Yes, Uncle Milo did. He'd been born and raised in New

Orleans, and the man was a crawfish king. "Are you CIA, too? Like Eb?" Only better at keeping that info secret?

"I'm freelance. Hostage rescue, you know that."

"But *were* you CIA?"

His arms were back at his sides. His fingers loose. "Let's just say that it was very convenient for a certain government agency to have two operatives who shared the exact same face. Made things easy. And...complicated. For enemies, that is. We could literally be in two places at once. We could be, and we were."

So, yes, she took that to mean he'd been CIA. Or—or something else way off the books.

"We eliminated threats. We'd both done time in the military, and when we came out, we had jobs waiting for us. Our specialized skill set was needed. We both got the missions done because we understood what was on the line."

Only Eb had kept working for the government. Jake hadn't. "Why did you get out?"

"Because I'm not big on rules."

She snorted at that understatement.

His face never softened. "Because...the work was dark, and it was just making my own darkness worse." A long exhale. "So instead of hunting down predators and the MVPs on the Most Wanted List, I shifted to hostage rescue. Sometimes it's good when you get to bring people home alive, and you aren't just burying bodies."

"Jacob Jones...are you saying you wanted to help someone? Because if so, that sounds like hero material to me."

"No. You shouldn't ever call me that. The pay is better in my current gig. The adrenaline high is just as strong. And I make the rules. All things that appeal to the arrogant asshole that I am. I don't do the shit to be a hero. I do it for the cold, hard cash."

"I think you're protesting a bit too much." She wanted to touch him. Okay, fine, she always wanted to do that. "You saved my life today. For zero payment. I think I know a hero when I see one." Just so they were both very, very clear. "Jake, you're a hero to me."

"Fuck."

She smiled at him. "You don't take a compliment well."

"You don't need to give me compliments."

"No, I don't suppose you need them, do you? I'm sure women toss their bodies at your feet all the time as they tell you how dead sexy you are."

A blink. "Wren?"

"No? They don't do that?" She deliberately crept closer to him. Not dropping at his feet, but definitely blocking his path. "Then let me assure you, you're dead sexy."

"*Wren...*" A warning note had entered his voice.

She just wasn't particularly in the mood for the warning. He was right. Her emotions were raw. Adrenaline had savaged her. And she needed Jake. "I don't feel like I have to be careful with you. You know all the ugly and twisted parts of me, and you are still here."

"There is *nothing* ugly or twisted about you. You're fucking perfect."

She laughed. "No. I'm fake. I pretend and I lie and I act like I'm this really good person, but deep inside..." Her hand rose and pressed to his chest. "I feel the darkness and I worry that one day it will take me over, the same way it did my f-father. You call me sunshine, but I'm not. I'm the exact opposite."

"You flinch every time I call you that."

"Because I'm not bright. I'm not happy. I'm not some

light." The smile that had been on her lips faded away. "I know what I am and what I'll always be. And you are the only one I can tell that truth to."

"You can tell me anything."

Could she? Could she reveal another big, bad secret to him? Could she stare right up at him and confess...

Jacob Jones, I love you.

Chapter Eleven

Don't pounce. Don't pounce. Keep your hands *off her*.

Wren's soft hand patted his chest. "I think I've shared enough for tonight. Let's stop while I'm ahead. Not like I want you running away in abject terror."

Her words were probably supposed to sound mocking, but he'd caught the quaver in her voice. "Told you already, I run to you. Not away." Her touch scorched him. "Actually, I don't run from anything." Not his style. Never had been, never would be.

"No, big, bad you wouldn't run." Her fingers flexed against his chest. "So which enemy do you think has come demanding his pound of flesh?"

"Don't know yet. But I'll be finding out."

"Guessing the dead man at the beach house didn't look familiar to you?"

"Never seen him before in my life." Her scent flooded his nostrils. So sweet. "My money says he was a hired thug. But we might be able to trace him back to the person pulling the strings."

"You don't think the guy who was with him on the beach—you don't think that could be the person pulling the strings?"

"Maybe." He wouldn't rule out that option yet. "We'll find out. Honey turned over the dead perp's phone to some of her FBI buddies. They'll try and retrieve every bit of useful intel on there." Intel that had better lead to some results. "To be clear, until the danger has passed, you're stuck with me."

She started to speak, then seemed to catch herself. Her lush lips pressed together before she told him, "I have to get back to Charleston. I can't stay here forever."

"It's Saturday. You can stay until Monday." But, hell, Monday might not be an option for her. "Honey may need us staying longer." Probably better to go ahead and prepare Wren for the change in her travel plans.

Her dark gaze was very serious. "Because you killed a man to save my life."

"Usually, the authorities don't like it when you scramble out of town after killing someone. Self-defense or not. Tends to look bad."

"I would hate for you to look bad."

Fuck looking bad. "Whenever you do go back, you'll have a boyfriend in tow. A real possessive prick." He'd be in tow, either in Hilton Head or in Charleston. Wren wasn't getting away from him.

"You're...going to stay at my home with me? When I go to Charleston?"

Why was she having trouble with this? "I let you out of my sight for two minutes at the beach house, and you rushed out screaming. I lost ten years of my life getting to you. Not gonna do that shit again, thanks. I will absolutely be staying with you. Here or in Charleston. Have you forgotten already? Where you go, I go. Thought you wanted things that way." He sure wanted that deal.

She rose onto her toes. "I have a confession for you."

He should stop staring at her mouth.

"If you come home to Charleston with me, it will absolutely be a one-bed situation."

His dick saluted her. Hell. Who was he kidding? His eager dick always saluted her.

"I don't have a guest room," she informed him sweetly. "So you'll have to share the bed with me."

"I can...sleep on a couch. Or the floor."

"That's cold, Jake. Ice cold." She backed away.

His hand flew out and curled around her wrist. He'd been trying to do this all *nicely*. Screw nice. Time to be blunt. "You think I can keep fucking you and let you go? Baby, I will *own* you if I have you again. Then I won't give you up just because the danger is over."

He'd said too much. He knew it. But the words weren't coming back.

Her eyes were wide and stark and right on him.

Let her go. Back away. Act normal. Not like a possessive prick who wants to horde his treasure and never, ever let the rest of the world get near her.

"Go to bed," he ordered gruffly as he freed her. "I'll secure things here. I need to make some more phone calls. Check in with some contacts." Get the Ice Breakers moving. Get Declan Flynn's arrogant ass on the line so he could use the man's assets. It was an all-hands-on-deck situation.

She didn't move. "Do I get to own you, Jake?"

Every muscle in his body tightened. When she'd said his name, there had been longing in her voice. A sweet, savage hunger. He kept warning the woman. He'd told her how very close to the edge he was.

For fuck's sake, he was *trying*. Attempting to do the right thing and not absolutely devour her. Maybe he should be even more blunt.

She batted those dark lashes at him and said, "Hardly seems fair that you're staking possession but I don't have the same right."

The same right? His hands reached for her. Again. And as soon as he touched her, yes, major mistake. Need spiked through him. "You've owned me since you were sixteen years old."

"Wh-what?" A little stutter. A tremble.

"You made the mistake of saving my life. That means I *owe* you my life, don't I? Isn't that what you told me back then? So I think you've owned me ever since that moment. When you pulled me away from the truck careening toward me, when we fell onto the pavement and my ice cream went all over us both. You've been in my mind since that moment. In every single fantasy that I've had. Even when I fuck other women—"

"Don't want to hear about that," she snapped.

"It's you. You're the one I want. So, yeah, you own me. Lucky you."

Her chest rose and fell quickly. "You saved my life today. I guess that means you own—"

He kissed her. Could not hold back any longer. What did a man have to do in order to save a woman...from himself? He'd warned her that he wanted her too badly. Warned her that his control was shredding. Tearing apart more and more, minute by minute. She should have heeded his warning and gotten the hell away from him.

Instead, she moaned. Instead, her lips parted beneath his. Instead, she pressed her breasts against him and she held on and she let him taste her need and her desire and the wild want that equaled his own.

His hands slid down her body. Curled around the sweet ass that he adored. He lifted her up against him, and she wrapped her legs around his hips like it was the most normal thing in the world. Like he wasn't about to fuck her until she couldn't walk.

When she'd been a virgin the night before...

She's mine now. I won't give her up.

He intended to keep her. Somehow, someway.

With her legs around his hips, with her arms around his neck, he began to walk. He knew how to get to his bedroom. No problem. He'd have her on the big, king-size bed. And he'd be in her as deep as he could go.

He'd make her scream again.

I tried to warn her. She chose this. She chose me.

Need grew to a dangerous degree. A white-hot lust that consumed and burned and destroyed all other thought.

He lowered her onto the bed. Stripped her clothes away. Had her naked and spread before him and what else was he to do but feast? He'd already gone too long without her taste.

He spread her legs wide. Put his mouth right on her core. Licked and sucked and tasted what belonged to him. His tongue swept inside of her.

Mine.

He pulled back. Licked her clit. Heard her sharp cry of pleasure.

Mine.

His fingers dipped into her as he licked and kissed. Sucked. Teased. Tormented.

He worked her again and again and her whole body

jolted when she came. A sharp and hard release that had her crying out his name.

Perfect.

He rose to the side of the bed. Yanked open his jeans and reached for a condom that he kept in the nightstand drawer.

She slid off the bed. Hit the floor right beside him, with her knees touching down. And her mouth locked around the head of his dick.

The world stopped. He wasn't even breathing.

Wren Maye's mouth was on his dick. Not a fantasy. Insane reality. She'd gone down on him the night before. It had been heaven. Hell. He'd wanted to explode down her throat.

I want it again.

She sucked him. Her tongue swirled over the head of his dick, and then she opened her mouth wider and took him in deeper.

He forgot the condom. His hands sank into the thickness of her hair as he guided her and fucked that sweet, wicked mouth. A mouth that Wren was using so temptingly on him. She'd taken him into her hot, tight sex, and now she was letting him fuck her mouth again.

Taking and taking, and he was going to explode right there. In her mouth, down her throat. He was going to—

"*Wren.*" He pulled back. His hands dropped to her shoulders as he carefully pushed her back.

Her lips were swollen. Red. Wet.

"I like the way you taste," she told him.

He pretty much threw her on the bed. Grabbed the condom. Shoved it on and then shoved his dick into her. Deep and hard and *mine*.

Over and over, he pounded into her. When it still

wasn't deep enough, he just grabbed her legs and heaved them over his shoulders. His hips thrust wildly. Again and again and again.

She screamed his name when she came, but it wasn't enough. Not nearly enough.

He drove into her. Faster. Harder. The bed groaned and squeaked, and his hands were too rough as he held her hips. His thrusts too fierce. But there was no pulling back.

There was no control.

There was only Wren.

His Wren.

He came inside of her.

Mine.

* * *

"My God, sweetheart, are you all right?"

Makayla Lane forced a weak smile when her fiancé rushed into her den. His pale green eyes were wide and worried. He pulled her into a fierce hug and held her tightly.

"I heard the story on the news," he told her. "Then my phone was lighting up with calls—someone tried to kill Wren? And you were right *there?*"

"It's all right, Tom." Thomas Addison Hadden, the Third. Banker. Just like Thomas Addison Hadden the Second. And the First. Only her Tom had also been the homecoming king and the high school track star, back in the day.

Back then, he'd been way, way out of her reach.

They'd reconnected in the last year, when she went into the bank looking for a loan.

And she'd wound up with a fiancé.

"It's *not* all right." He pulled back. Stared down at her with his perfect, handsome face, and his steady but worried gaze. "A man is dead, Makayla. Some crazy guy with a knife attempted to kill your friend. And I heard Honey Jackson thinks this nut job tried to attack Wren the previous night, too? Weren't you all at your bachelorette party then?" Alarm sharpened his voice.

"It was after the party." A chill skated over her skin. "Most of the ladies had left. We'd piled into the limo. Wren wasn't with us because she was walking to her uncle's beach house." She hugged him again. "I'm glad you're here." She hadn't exactly been looking forward to spending the night alone. Not after everything that had happened. "There was so much blood," she admitted.

"Wren's blood?" Tom sounded horrified.

Makayla shook her head. "I thought it was hers when I saw her after the attack." Wren, covered in so much blood. The blood had dripped down her friend's arms. "But it wasn't hers. It was her attacker's. Jake shot him. He saved her life."

"Jacob Jones."

They'd all known each other for so long. But she nodded anyway. "He—he and Wren are a thing now." How had she not realized that? "He flipped out when she was attacked. You should have seen him." She stared up at the face of the man she was going to marry. "He killed to protect her." She knew that should probably scare her. No, no, Jake *had* been scary. Scary and intense and... "He carried her out of there." Wren had been limp in his arms. Had she fainted? Maybe. Everyone knew Wren hated the sight of blood. At a high school party, a guy from out of town had gotten cut once on a broken beer bottle. The blood had been dripping from the side of his neck. The cut hadn't been that deep. Hardly life threatening. But Wren had taken one look and hit the ground. Correction. She'd almost hit. Jake had grabbed her before she could connect with the hard earth.

Makayla pulled away from Tom. "There was blood all over Wren." She looked down at her hands. "I thought it was her blood. I thought she was dead. But she'd been fighting her attacker. She'd broken free, and then Jake rushed to her—he *saved her*." She'd never forget all of the blood that had been on Wren. "I've never seen that much blood in my entire life."

"And I hope you never do again." He caught her hands. Squeezed. He was a strong man, but his hands were soft. No calluses. No old scars. And he always touched her with such care. "I hope you are never around anything like that again. Dammit, I can't believe I was gambling in Vegas, and my fiancée was dealing with some psycho murder scene. That is *not* what I thought you'd be doing during your bachelorette time with the ladies." He sent her a weak smile. "You were supposed to have a spa day."

"We did do that." On Thursday.

"And then maybe go to a strip show."

They'd done that, too. Friday evening. Jennifer had known just where to visit.

"And then maybe you were all going to drink a little too much and wind up dancing on the beach..." A long sigh from Tom. "But no one was going to *die*. That was not on the agenda."

"The bridesmaids didn't die. Wren is okay. Like I said, Jake saved her." But he'd been so scary as he did it. A shiver slid over her. "We went to the hospital—Jennifer and I did—to make sure she was okay. Jake barely let anyone near her. The man is in serious overdrive protection mode with her."

"Huh. I wonder how Eb feels about that."

Yeah, she wondered, too. She also wondered…"Would you do it for me?"

Tom frowned at her. "Do what?"

"He didn't even hesitate. You should have seen how fast he ran to her. I-I didn't even realize what was happening. He shoved me out of the way—"

"What the hell? He'd better not have hurt you!" Anger heated his words.

She shook her head. "He didn't. He just—he had to get to her. It was like nothing could stand in his way, and he *killed* for her." That wasn't supposed to happen in real life. She bit her lower lip. "Would you do that for me?" Why was she even asking? Not like she wanted him to do it.

"Would I stop a depraved madman from attacking you? Sweetheart, let's hope that event never, ever happens." He shuddered.

Only that wasn't an answer. That wasn't an overwhelming, *of course, I'd kill for you in an instant.* But then, Tom wasn't like Jake. Tom was culture. Tom was class. Tom was the million and one things she'd always wanted and never had in her life growing up.

She forced a smile for him even as she pulled her hands from his careful grip. "I do hope that never happens." If it did, would she fight like Wren?

She never would have thought that Wren would be such a fighter. Wren had always held herself back. Been so very cautious all the time.

"Darling." His fingers slid under her chin. "I would kill for you in an instant."

A warm glow filled her chest. Not that she wanted him killing. But…still, it was kinda nice to know.

"You are going to be my wife. I would never allow anyone to jeopardize you. You mean the world to me."

He cared. No, he loved her.

His mouth pressed lightly to hers. "I am so glad you're safe." Another light kiss. Not deep and wild. But...

Good.

Steady. Reassuring.

Her eyes had closed.

"I missed you," he murmured against her mouth.

"I missed you, too," she replied dutifully. *But, no, I did miss him. I'm not just saying the words. I'm going to marry him. Going to promise to love him forever.*

She eased back. Her lashes lifted.

And she caught him staring at her...

With doubt in his eyes.

Worry surged. "Tom?"

But he just smiled. He caught her left hand. Lifted it toward his mouth. Her engagement ring—the "mega-rock" as Jen called it—gleamed right before he pressed a kiss to her knuckles. "I want to hear everything that happened. Every detail. You must have been terrified."

"Not half as scared as Wren. But Wren is okay, really." Had Wren and Tom dated briefly back in high school? And why was she suddenly remembering that random bit of gossip now? Wren had pretty much just been connected at the hip with Eb back then but...

Why does it matter?

"Wren is staying with Jake. There was a second attacker. He wasn't caught." The words tumbled out from Makayla.

He backed up a bit. "Did you see him?"

"No, no, I didn't. I don't think he was at the beach house. I heard that he was—um, he was on the beach, the first night. When I was already gone in the limo. The men tried to get Wren then, but Jake stopped them. He saved her twice."

"How very fortunate that Wren has a lover who just won't let her out of his sight."

The words were wrong. They felt wrong. They sounded wrong.

Tom smiled. "Never would have picked those two as a pair."

"Most people wouldn't pick us as a pair, either." She hadn't grown up with the rich kids of Hilton Head. Her mom had been a waitress. Her dad? She'd never known him. She'd always wished that she had. She used to dream that he'd rush back into her life.

He never had. At this late stage in the game, she knew he never would.

"My darling..." Tom smiled his perfect smile. Perfect white teeth. Perfectly even. A perfect product of expensive orthodontics. "You are beautiful and charming and smart and graceful and...a hundred other things I do not deserve. I am the luckiest man in the world to have you as my bride-to-be."

He could also be so *perfect* with his words. She smiled at him. "You are lucky."

He nodded. "I know." Another kiss on her knuckles. "Though it does sound as if Wren is lucky, too. We don't always get to cheat death."

No, people didn't. Sometimes, death would take you in an instant and leave nothing but heartache in your place.

"I hope the other man is caught soon," Tom added. "Would be terrible if he struck again."

"I bet Jake can handle him."

His face darkened. Just for a moment.

"Do you think it was hard?" The question nagged at her. "Killing someone, I mean. Do you think it was hard to do?" It had to be. To feel that heavy knowledge weighting down your soul. To know that you've taken a life. That wouldn't be an easy burden to carry, even if the kill was done in self-defense.

"I don't think it was hard at all for Jake Jones. Something tells me this isn't the first time he's pulled a trigger."

Her chill was back. The goosebumps even bigger than before. "How would you know that?"

"Let's just call it a guess."

Who guessed about death that way?

"I know what he does for a living." A slight pause from Tom. "I...know people who've used his services in order to get back loved ones who've gone missing in very dangerous places. It's not an easy job. It's not pretty. It's violent and intense and it requires someone who isn't afraid to make a life-or-death call."

She couldn't decide if he admired Jake or if he...

Hated him. Feared him?

After what she'd witnessed that day, Makayla had to admit that a part of her feared Jake, too. She threw herself against Tom. Curled her arms around his neck. Wren could keep her "scary hot" guy. Makayla would stay with her safe fiancé.

After all, sometimes, a little safety was the most important thing you could have in your world.

"Wren should be careful with him," Tom continued, voice thoughtful. "Jake isn't a man who will ever give up something he wants easily."

"He wants Wren." She was sure of this.

"All the more reason for her to be very, very careful..."

Chapter Twelve

His fingers trailed lightly over the scar on Wren's right shoulder. "Are you going to tell me what happened?"

She stiffened.

"If you don't want to talk, that's fine," he hurried to add. "Go to sleep. Crash. Hell, all you probably want to do is shut your eyes and forget this day." He hadn't intended to fuck her again.

Okay, fine, he *had* intended to fuck her. Fucking her endlessly would always be on his to-do agenda. Not like he could lie to himself about that. Wren breathed, and he wanted her. Done deal. But he'd seriously planned to be the gentleman—or at least, try to act like one for her—that night. She'd been attacked. She'd been questioned and interrogated. Exhaustion had to claim her. He'd truly, truly intended to keep his hands off her.

But she'd wanted him.

He would never be strong enough to turn her away.

"You killed to keep me alive today," her soft voice replied. "I'm pretty sure that entitles you to a few of my

137

secrets." A little sigh. "But be warned, you probably won't like what you hear."

She was naked. Still in his bed. He wanted her to stay there the rest of the night.

No, not just the rest of the night. *Always.*

But not the time for that confession. Not yet. He was trying not to absolutely terrify the woman. Or at least, not terrify her more than she already was.

As for not liking what he was about to hear... "I'll never like anything that involves you getting hurt." This time, it was his mouth that brushed across one shoulder blade.

"Jake?"

Another kiss. "Talk, don't talk." He shouldn't have asked the question in the first place. If she wanted him to know her secrets, she'd tell him. If she didn't, hell, he'd take her exactly as she was. "Your past is yours and you don't have to parade it out for anyone to see. Sure as hell not for me." He eased back toward his pillow but moved his hand to curl around her stomach. "You'll be safe tonight, I swear it."

"Because you're sticking close to me?"

Damn straight, he was. Skin-to-skin close.

A soft sigh rustled from her. "He wanted to see if there were wings beneath my skin."

Jake couldn't have heard her correctly. "What?"

"There are scars on each shoulder because he figured if I had wings, they would grow from my shoulders. So he cut the right shoulder first, looking for a wing. Then he cut the left because he said he had to be sure one wasn't there."

Shock and rage surged through his body. "*Wren.*"

"That's not the name I was born with." A quiet confession.

He didn't even know her real name? *Doesn't matter. I know her.*

"But it's the name I chose," she explained as she turned on the bed. Darkness covered the room, so he couldn't see her eyes, not clearly. He wished that he could. "Want to know why?" Wren asked.

He wanted to know everything about her. *And particularly why the fuck your father thought there were angel wings beneath your skin.* But he locked down his emotions, and, against the pillow, his head moved in a nod. When she'd rolled, he'd pulled his hand away from her.

"Wrens are small birds, but they sing such a beautiful song. My mom..." Pain seemed to stop her voice. A tense moment passed. "My mom could identify any bird based on the way it sang. We'd walk through the woods when I was younger, and she could always call out the birds before she saw them. Just by hearing them. She *loved* birds. And the wren? It was one of her favorites." She tugged the covers to her chest. "The wren is a symbol for all kinds of things... determination. Happiness. Change." A low exhale. "And trickery. At least, in Irish myths, it was. When Uncle Milo found out that I liked the name Wren, he said it was a good choice for me, and then he told me this old Irish tale."

Milo O'Shaw would know plenty about Irish tales.

"He said that, once upon a time—I mean isn't that how all stories start?—well, once upon a time, there was this contest. All the birds got together because they wanted to see who would be king. The winner was going to be the bird who could fly the highest." She swallowed. He heard the soft click. "I don't have wings," she suddenly said. "I couldn't fly. I could never fly away."

Baby, you are ripping out my heart.

He had to touch her again. His fingers skimmed over

her cheek. And when he touched the wetness of a teardrop, pain knifed through him. "Wren…"

"So the birds…" Brisk. "The birds were having their big contest. The king would be the one who could soar the highest in the sky. And, of course, the big, bad eagle took off. He was so confident because he knew how powerful he was. He knew he was stronger than all the others, and the eagle soared so very high, and he thought that he'd won. He'd thought no one would ever beat him."

Jake brushed away her teardrop.

"But what the eagle didn't realize was that the little wren had hidden on his back during the flight. And even as that eagle was claiming his victory, the wren crept from the hiding spot and flew above the eagle. The wren won. The wren tricked the eagle and won."

"You faked your death. You got a new identity. You got away from the bastard. You won." Hell, yes, the name fit her. His beautiful and strong Wren.

"Uncle Milo and I knew we were tricking the powerful hunter, and yes, Wren seemed fitting. But I didn't know that I would win against him. I was always terrified. Always sure he'd come back and kill me."

Over my dead body.

"That's why, at first, things were so hard for me. I trusted no one. I was afraid every moment. I wasn't with Uncle Milo in the beginning. The Feds tried to put me with what they said was a 'normal' family, only I'm not normal so that didn't work out so well for me. When I'd wake up screaming or when I didn't want to—to *attach*, as one long ago psychiatrist called it, they got scared of me."

"They were worried about you—"

"No, they were worried I was too much like my f-father. I heard them. I know what they believed. They said I didn't love. That I couldn't connect. That I was too cold and closed off and that I made them nervous. The mother said she couldn't sleep at night because she was afraid of what I might do to her real children."

His back teeth ground together. "You wouldn't hurt *anyone*."

"You might want to tell that to the man I stabbed today. Twice."

"You mean the man I killed?" He *needed* to see her better. Damn the darkness. "You fought back because you're a survivor. Not because you're a monster." What should she have done? Let the bastard kill her? Uh, hell, no.

"My...f-father, he, um, thought I wasn't like him. Said that maybe I had wings beneath the skin. Maybe I was an angel sent to lift up the devil. But he cut me, and there were no wings there, and he left me bleeding and I couldn't make a sound because I was so afraid that if I did, he would come back and finish killing me." Her words came too quickly.

His rage built too strongly.

"He had two victims. Always two, that was how he worked. His MO. That last time, the, um, the male was...he was dead, but his wife was still alive. She'd been trying to escape, you see. She'd left her partner. Left him right before he died. My fa—the killer always said that people leave each other. They turn on each other in the darkest moments." A shuddering breath. "She'd gotten away and was running, but the killer caught her and dragged her back, and I found them, just as he sliced her throat." No horror. No terror. Just flat.

When fear and horror must have nearly ripped her apart so long ago.

"I screamed and I broke and I...attacked him. I'd tried to stop him before. This wasn't the first time. But he was always so much stronger. Told me that I was wrong, he was right, and that they deserved everything that happened. Because they were weak."

Jake wanted to pull her against him. To stop the words he'd asked to hear, because each one was like a knife stabbing into him. Wren had been through hell, and he'd never known. All of these years, he had never known. He'd put a careful distance between them, believed she was involved with his brother, but the truth was, Wren had been facing hell all by herself.

Never again.

"I jumped on his back. He was so much bigger, but he didn't expect me to fight so hard. I jumped on his back, and I held him as tightly as I could, and he let her go while he grabbed for me. I screamed for her to run, and she did. He whirled. Threw me down and..." A ragged exhale. "He said I was the first one who'd allowed someone else to escape while I stayed behind. That I'd sacrificed. That I had to have an angel inside me. He was...so excited. Almost proud. Then he flipped me over and sliced into my shoulders. I didn't cry out. I'd...learned he liked that."

He wanted to kill the bastard. Slowly. Painfully.

"But there were no wings beneath my skin. Just so much blood. Blood all over me. And then he let me go. He left only to...he ran out and he came back with *her. He caught her again.* She was so still in his arms. She hadn't gotten very far. She was alive, but he'd cut her more. Sliced so deeply into her neck this time. He put her in front of me, and I covered her throat with my hands as I tried to help her and he just—*he left us like that.*"

Emotion broke through those last words. So much pain.

"Wren..." *My beautiful Wren.*

"I didn't make a sound. I didn't cry out," she said once

more. "I-I'd learned he liked that. Did I tell you that already? I'm sorry. I-I don't mean to repeat things."

She could repeat anything she wanted. "You never need to apologize to me." Sure as shit not for repeating something about a memory that must have savaged her.

"I was still in that spot, still trying to stop her from bleeding so much, when Honey and Uncle Milo burst in. Only, he wasn't my uncle back then. He was just one of the Feds who swarmed with guns drawn. My father was gone, and I was a broken bird who didn't know how to sing anymore. I was Wren."

"You *aren't* broken."

"I didn't speak for three weeks. Trust me, I was plenty broken."

Screw it. He hauled her against his chest. Held her as tightly as he could and—

"I don't want your pity." She shoved against him. Harder than he expected, and, stunned, he let her go.

She scrambled to the other side of the bed. Wren had hauled the sheet with her. Clasping it to her chest, she threw out a hand and turned on the lamp.

He blinked against the sudden flood of light. "Wren?"

"Don't look at me with pity." Anger hummed in her voice. "I made it through that nightmare. I survived. I was the only one he attacked who actually survived. Don't pity me. Pity the victims that I didn't save. Pity them and their families. *Don't pity me.* I don't want that from you. Not you, understand? I need you to want me. To still see me as a woman you desire and not just some freak's daughter—"

He surged toward her. Caught her chin. Kissed her. He took her breath and gave her his. He claimed her mouth. Thrust his tongue past the sweetness of her lips. *Claiming.* Jake made sure she understood...*Mine.* "I will always want you. I've wanted you since we were sixteen years old, sweetheart. That shit isn't going to stop just because I find out how amazingly strong you are."

Her head shook. "I'm *not*."

"Yeah, you are." Another kiss. Because he needed it. And maybe so did she. "You survived hell. And I *hate* that you had to endure that nightmare. So do I feel fucking sorry for what you experienced? Yes. Do I want to find your father, hunt him down, and make him pay for every moment of pain that he gave you? For every second of terror? For every breath you took that held fear? Damn straight, I do." One more kiss. "Here's the thing, I would want to kill *anyone* who hurt you."

"Jake..."

Another kiss because this was his Wren. "Nothing would ever make me stop wanting you. That's just not possible. You need to understand that now."

She let go of the sheet. Grabbed his shoulders. "Since... we were sixteen?"

"Um. This gorgeous girl saved my ass from a brutal hit by a truck. We fell on the pavement together. My ice cream went all over her, and all I wanted to do was kiss her." Which he did. Right then.

Then he lifted his head because there were a few other things to say. Things she needed to hear.

"You didn't kiss me back then," she reminded him, confused. "You yelled at me that day."

Yep. "Because a sixteen-year-old boy can be a damn idiot. The prettiest girl in the world had just saved my life, and I was embarrassed as hell." More than that. His whole world had been realigning in that moment. "I've never been the smooth talker, Wren. My brother always knows what to say. I just know how to make other people scared or uncomfortable the longer they are near me. That would be my superpower of being a prick, and it was in full effect that day."

"Jake..."

"I've wanted you for years. That wanting has only gotten stronger as we grew older, and I learned so much more about you."

Her long lashes flickered. "Bet you never imagined you'd learn all this, huh? Surprise, surprise."

No, not in a million years would he have imagined this. "I told you that I killed for the first time when I was twenty-two."

Her head moved in a slow nod.

"Did you stop wanting me when you learned what I'd done?" Jake asked.

"I, um, just had sex with you so...clearly no."

"Then know that—clearly—I will *never* stop wanting you. Just not going to happen." He needed to reveal his past to her. It wasn't fair that she'd cut herself open for him, but he hadn't told her more about his life. "I killed for the government. They sent me after high value targets. Bastards who were twisted and depraved and who had plans to hurt an awful lot of people." Specifics couldn't be shared, not even with Wren. Some secrets had to be taken to his grave. "I got in close. Eb and I handled the missions. We did whatever was necessary. Sanctioned by the government, sure, but death is death, and we were very good at delivering death." A pause. "Knowing I can kill so easily, does that change how you feel about me?"

"No."

"Why not?" He really wanted to know. "You should be scared of me." Something *he'd* feared for a long time.

But she smiled at him. That sweet, heartbreaking, Wren

smile. "I told you, I have my own darkness. I more than have it. I'm just good at disguising it from most people." The smile wiped away. "I didn't want to be relocated again when I moved here at sixteen. I wanted to stay with Uncle Milo. I wanted to stay in this life with these two annoying boys who became my friends. This one boy in particular—the growly one—he was always watching out for me. Catching me when I fell."

He tucked a lock of hair behind her ear. "I will always catch you."

"You know all my secrets, and you're still touching me." So husky.

His forehead rested against hers. "You know what I've done, and you're still fucking me."

"You're the only person I want to fuck."

He lifted his forehead from hers, just a little. "Is this where you say you were saving yourself for me?" He tried a smile, wanting to lighten the load she carried even though he was far from being a joking kind of man. "Because, sweetheart—"

"Yes." No joke. No load lightening. Just that. "Yes," she said again. "I was waiting for you, Jake. No one else would do. The minute I knew I was free of the past, I went straight to you. I wanted you, and you were the best first lover that I could have ever—"

Her words stopped because he was kissing her. Feverish and wild. But her words played in his head on an endless loop. *I was waiting for you, Jake.*

How was a man supposed to stay sane when his woman said that to him? Not that he'd ever been the sanest when it came to Wren. But this...

This...

His hands curled under her delicate jaw. Her taste maddened him.

He was going to fuck her again. And again. And again.

And never let go.

But...she was pulling back. Her breath sawed in and out. "You...still want me, Jake?"

"How can you even ask?" His dick was so big and thick that she had to see it bobbing toward her. Had to feel it.

"I was there when they died. I was there for his crimes. He said I'd be just like him and when I stabbed that man today..." Now she didn't just pull from him. Wren rose and left the bed. She wrapped the sheet around her body as she paced across the room and toward the window. "It didn't feel wrong. I shoved the blade in him a second time without hesitating. My father— he would have been proud of me. *Proud.* Because he always told me that I was more like him than anyone else in the world."

He wanted her back in his bed. In his arms.

"I lied to you." Her hair trailed over her shoulders. "I lied to everyone. And I've done it for years. Those women who think they are my friends? They would run if they knew the truth. They wouldn't want me being close to them. My clients at my business would be horrified. And you..." Still near the window, she angled her body toward him.

He was still in bed. But when she broke off, he tossed aside the covers, and, naked, he stalked to her.

Her shoulders stiffened. Her chin notched up.

He stopped right in front of her. Close enough to touch. As he always wanted to do. Touch. Take. Claim. "Do I look horrified?"

"Of all the people in my life, I always thought you would be the most likely to understand me. Everyone else pretends the world is this bright and happy place, but you've always known darkness is there."

But he wished it could be a bright and happy place for her. "Do I look like I'm running?" Hadn't he already covered that he would only run to her? "And does it look like I don't want to get close to you?"

Her lashes fluttered. "Jake..."

"I will never run away. I will never be horrified. Not by anything about you. And I will always be between you and any danger." Didn't she get what gutted him? "It's *my* fault you are in jeopardy now. It's my twisted past that is hurting you. It's me. If anyone should be running, dammit, baby, it is you. You should be running as you try to get far away from me."

But she shook her head. "I will never run away from you."

"Maybe you should." If she knew all the things he wanted to do with her. The way he wanted to keep her, forever.

"I will never be horrified," she said, giving his own words back to him.

Are you sure? "I killed a man today." Right in front of her.

She put a hand over his heart. "Thank you for saving my life."

Always. He would do anything to save her.

"But you don't need to stand between me and danger." Wren wet her lips. "I'd rather if the choice ever comes up, how about you save yourself?"

Screw that. His hands curled around her hips. Clutched the soft sheet and wished it was her skin. "How about I just eliminate every threat? That work for you?"

"I don't want you hurt. I-I saw couples. I saw the ones

my father took, their bodies when he was done, and I..." She stopped.

He now understood so much about her. "You don't believe in love, do you, sweetheart?" He was deliberately not calling her sunshine because she didn't like that nickname. Even if that was exactly what she was to him. Fucking sunshine. Always would be. Sunshine in the darkness.

"They said they loved each other. He made them turn on one another—they abandoned the ones they swore to love the most. They hurt each other. You can't count on love."

Were those her words? Or her father's? Jake wanted to swear that he would never leave her. Because he wouldn't.

Because he loved her.

But she wasn't ready for the stark truth that he'd hidden for so long. And if he told her now, she might run away. So he'd tread carefully. Slowly. A bulldozer wasn't going to work in this situation.

"You can count on me," he finally said as the silence stretched between them. "My past is trying to hurt you. I won't let it. I will do anything necessary to protect you."

"By pretending to be involved with me?"

His hold tightened on her waist, and he lifted her up. Her eyes widened, and she grabbed onto his shoulders.

"Sweetheart..." Jake smiled at her.

She inhaled.

"We *are* involved. No pretending necessary. Danger brought us closer. Brought down every wall that had been between us. There is no lying. Just truth. You're mine, and I'll protect you. No one will use you as some pawn against me or my brother." He turned and carried her back to the bed.

"Jake..."

He lowered her onto the mattress.

"This will be the second night," she whispered. "Not gonna qualify as a one-night stand any longer."

"You were never going to be just one night for me." He turned off the light. Climbed in bed beside her.

Her warm, soft body pressed against him. "Then what am I?"

End game, sunshine. End game.

He kissed her.

* * *

MAKAYLA SLID OUT OF BED. Her fiancé rolled onto his side, but his eyes didn't open. His breathing remained deep and even, and she carefully tiptoed out of the bedroom.

The big bachelorette weekend had not gone as planned. There had been blood and death and now...

She crept down the hallway. Turned to the right. To the room where she'd been storing her wedding dress. Her hand trembled as she turned on the light. The flood of illumination filled the room, and the glow fell right on the white, satin dress as it waited inside its plastic, protective covering. The fancy dress fit for a princess.

Her breath rushed out. She'd dreamed of her wedding for so long.

A month out. One month to go until the big day.

The thick carpeting swallowed her steps as she made her way across the room. Her fingers trailed over the plastic bag. Then she reached for the veil she'd carefully arranged on the nearby table. Not the cheap veil she'd worn at Milo's bar—the fake, party one she'd put on Wren's head for just a quick moment.

No, this one was the real deal. Ridiculously expensive. Gossamer and—

Slashed?

She frowned at the cuts in the veil. "What in the..."

The door closed behind her. A soft click. She'd...she'd left the door open. Tom must have woken up, and if he saw the veil like this, he would freak out.

She spun around and shoved the veil behind her back even as she pasted a smile on her face. "Tom, I..."

It wasn't Tom.

He rushed toward her even as the veil fell from her fingers.

Chapter Thirteen

Loud, angry thuds woke Wren the next morning. Her eyes cracked open even as she heard a very disgruntled, *"What in the hell?"* from beside her.

She blinked away the sleepiness and saw Jake lunging out of the bed. He jerked on black sweatpants to cover that very nice ass of his and then he grabbed a gun and bolted for the bedroom door.

Then he grabbed a gun and—

"Jake!" Wren lurched upright as her heart raced in her chest.

The furious pounding continued.

Jake held a gun in his left hand. She realized his right hand now held his phone.

She leapt out of the bed, too. One of his T-shirts was tossed onto a nearby chair. She grabbed it, tugged it over her head, and crept toward him even as her heart thudded in her chest. The pounding was coming from his front door, and she had no idea what was happening. Who was out there? She only knew that someone needed to cover Jake's back. She was the only someone there.

His eyes narrowed on the phone's screen. Understanding clicked for Wren. He had one of those doorbell cameras at his front door. He'd be able to see their visitor from his phone. She exhaled and tried to take a frantic second to calm her racing heartbeat.

The furious pounding continued, seeming to echo through the house.

Their *angry* visitor was not giving up. "Jake?"

His head whipped toward her.

"Who is it?" Her bare feet inched forward.

"A pain in my ass." His nostrils flared. "I'll handle him. Everything is okay."

Her arms wrapped around her stomach. Things did not sound okay. It sounded as if their visitor was trying to break his way through the door.

Jake tossed his phone onto a chair. He did not put down his weapon. Instead, he kept the weapon and yanked open the bedroom door. Jake charged down the hallway.

She charged right after him.

Jake rushed into the den. Then to the front door. He flipped the locks and yanked it open.

No alarms beeped. Jake must have disengaged the alarms from his phone. Why would he—

"Do you know what damn time it is, asshole?" Jake snarled.

"Of course I do," came the immediate response. "Do *you* know what sort of shitstorm is heading *your* way, asshole? Because I'm thinking not."

"Hunter..." Jake growled.

"Let me in. The serial killer's daughter is about to be in for a world of hurt."

"The fuck she is!"

She backed up a step. Her hip hit the nearby table. Sent

a lamp to wobbling. She grabbed it. No, dammit, not fast enough. The lamp toppled, and her attempt to grab it actually just wound up making the lamp roll right off the edge and shatter when it hit the floor.

Shatter.

Jake whirled toward her.

Her breath shuddered in desperate heaves.

"Ah, there she is," the man in the doorway proclaimed. "Hello, serial killer's—"

Jake grabbed the man speaking and hauled him inside. Slammed the door. In a flash, Jake had the stranger pinned against the wall, and Jake's gun was far too close to the guy's face. "Don't say another word," Jake ordered, voice lethal.

"But...she's about to get cut."

A savage growl from Jake.

"No, seriously, her feet are bare, and she's about to cut herself and you need to—"

Jake whipped his head toward Wren once again. Then he was swearing and letting go of the stranger and charging toward her. Before she could question him, Jake swooped her into his arms and carried her toward the couch.

The stranger whistled. "She's got really nice legs. Cute toes, too. It would be a shame if—'"

"Fucking keep quiet, Hunter, or I will be breaking your face." Jake gently lowered Wren onto the couch. Then he checked out her feet. "You aren't hurt." A statement, not a question.

"I'm not hurt," she still replied because he seemed to need that assurance.

He grunted. "Good. Now let me go hurt *him*."

But she grabbed his wrist, stopping him. "Who is he?" Low. "And how does he know about *me*?" More specifically, about the biggest secret of her life? Pain curled around her heart. "Jake, did you tell him?" When she'd gone to sleep in his arms, she'd felt safe. But...had he just left her? Snuck out of bed and told this—this man all about her painful past?

Jake's eyes narrowed. "Who is he? He's an annoying bastard, that's who he is."

"That hurts, man. Hurts." From the stranger. "Oh, wait, not really. Sticks and stones hurt. Kinda, anyway. Words just amuse me."

She craned to look around Jake's form to get a better look at the uninvited visitor. When she did get that better look—wait. "I know you." He wasn't a stranger. At least, not completely. She'd seen him before. At Marley's wedding. "You're friends with Declan Flynn, aren't you?"

"I—" he began.

"The jerk is Declan's *best* friend," Jake groused. He had one hand on the couch behind her. "Hunter McQueen. And, no, I did *not* tell him anything about you. I made some calls last night, yes. I needed help on the case. I had to get people to start digging so I could figure out who is trying to hurt you. I did *not* share anything personal you revealed to me. I wouldn't do that."

"He didn't need to tell me," Hunter piped up to affirm. He whistled. "You would not believe the intel that Declan can access with a few clickety-clicks on his keyboard. And as soon as Declan realized just what was going down, he sent me to do cleanup. Or be backup." A shrug of one shoulder. "Probably more like both."

"I would not betray you, Wren," Jake said. "Know that." His gaze held hers.

She nodded. The vise around her heart loosened. She also tried to tug down the hem of the T-shirt because she'd rushed out and had not put on anything under the shirt.

"Good." He kissed her. Then straightened and glared at

Hunter. "Do you not have a phone? Why the hell are you pounding on my door? You understand that you could call first, like a normal human being? Call or text before you start trying to break down my front door?"

"I was *pounding* because Declan said you needed backup. As in, you needed someone to be here with you. Thus, I had to get inside your fancy beach house. And if I'd just called, you probably would have played hero, said you didn't need anyone, and ignored me." He began to stroll around the den. "Seriously, this is a nice place. All open-concept and what-not. Didn't even realize you had a home here. No offense, but you don't really strike me as the beachy type."

"*Hunter*. What is happening?" Each word seemed gritted. "And since when did you get so damn chatty?"

"I was trying to be reassuring." Hunter sighed. "Marley tells me I can be...intense sometimes." He crossed his arms over his chest and let his gaze sweep between Wren and Jake. Then back to Wren. He studied her in silence for a moment.

She took that moment to study him, too. Tall, about the same height as Jake. With broad shoulders. Though she thought Jake might have shoulders a bit broader. Golden, tawny skin. Hard features. Dark eyes.

"You don't look like a monster," he told her.

Her mouth dropped open.

Hunter winced. "Yeah, that's why I should avoid the attempts to be chatty. I do tend to say the wrong things. Being quiet and grim works better for me."

"I am going to *kick your ass*," Jake vowed. He thundered toward Hunter.

She jumped from the couch. Then grabbed a big pillow

from the couch to cover herself because the shirt was not enough. "Jake, no!"

"Yeah, Jake, *no*." Hunter didn't even flinch as Jake barreled to a stop in front of him. "This is not the way we respond when people come to help us. We say thank you. We show our gratitude. We do not—" He ducked a punch, but it had just been a trick attack.

Jake nailed him with a blow to the stomach. The real hit.

The air whooshed out of Hunter. "Yeah...*dammit*."

"You don't eye-fuck my lady, understand? And you never, ever refer to her as 'the serial killer's daughter' again. Her name is Wren. Say it with me...*Wren*."

Hunter rubbed his stomach. "Hi, Wren."

She kept the pillow in place. "Hi, uh, Hunter."

Hunter exhaled on a hard breath. He stopped rubbing his stomach and straightened fully. "The secret is out."

She inched closer.

"The Ice Breakers were working on the Sweetheart Slasher cases," he revealed. "FYI."

Wren flinched. The press had loved calling the murders the "Sweetheart Slasher" cases. The pictures of the poor couples had been splashed everywhere. Sweethearts who had been savaged by the killer. *The Sweetheart Slasher*. Her father had hated that moniker. Had thought it was insulting. Ridiculous. That it undermined the work he'd been doing.

What work? He was a twisted killer. He took lives without remorse. He was the monster. The slasher in the dark.

"The Sweetheart Slasher was positively ID'd recently. Jonathan Wales, former psychology professor turned psycho killer." He grimaced. "The guy killed seven couples, but the Ice Breakers suspect there could be more that were never linked to him. They'll probably be showing up at your door next, by the way. Everyone will want to pick apart your brain. After all, you're the person who knew the killer best."

Like plenty of shrinks had already tried to pick apart her mind. Back when she'd been younger, the Feds had sent her to talk to shrinks and counselors again and again. They'd wanted clues to find her father.

Not like she'd really been able to open up to them. Considering her own father excelled at mind fuckery, she'd never trusted the so-called experts enough to reveal her secrets. Besides, she'd had no idea where her father had gone. After the night he'd sliced into her, he'd vanished.

"Someone leaked your identity last night," Hunter continued.

She shook her head because she must have misheard him.

But he nodded. "It happened on the web. On some of those true-crime sites. Then it was posted in group chats. Things exploded from there. Declan picked up the chatter, of course, because that man always picks up intel. He figured you were in for a clusterfuck as soon as people figured out where you were hiding—especially with the shooting that happened yesterday. That bit was shared, too, I'm sorry to say. So expect your bloody past and present to be front page news, STAT."

This couldn't be happening. "No one knows about my past." No, not true. Uncle Milo knew. Honey knew. Jake—

"Your secret is out. The world knows. Or, as they are waking up right now, more people are finding out. Your dad has been tied to the murders of seven couples."

Seven couples. Fourteen individuals. So much blood.

"He terrorized the world for years before he vanished. Hell, not often a killer like him goes dormant, but he did. Somehow."

Did he? She'd always feared he hadn't stopped, but Uncle Milo had been watching so carefully. Constantly looking for vics who had fit her father's profile.

"The infamous Sweetheart Slasher's death is going to be big news. And the fact that his daughter—long presumed dead—was recently attacked? Come on, the story is killer. You know the old saying, if it bleeds, it leads."

She did not know that old saying.

"There's blood all around you," Hunter bluntly informed her. "Your story will be the lead everywhere."

And that would be her world, exploding into a thousand pieces. "Excuse me." Her voice was wooden. Brittle? "I need to get changed." She cleared her throat. "Especially if every reporter in the area is about to be at the door." Hadn't he said they would figure out where she was hiding? "Can't have them interviewing me while I just wear a shirt. What would the world think?"

That I'm the serial killer's daughter. That I'm as twisted as my father. That I'm a monster.

"I'll be back in just a moment." After she got her control back in place because she did not want to shatter in front of Hunter. With that, Wren turned on her heel and marched back down the hallway. One careful marching step at a time. And as she fled, the truth burned through her. Something she'd always known, deep down inside. A reckoning had come.

I knew I couldn't hide forever.

But she'd still hoped that she somehow could...

* * *

Jake surged after her.

"Yeah, how about no?" Hunter curled a hand around his shoulder. "We need to talk, man. Now."

What he needed was to make sure Wren was okay and—

A fist hit his side. The air shoved out of him, and Jake spun toward Hunter with a glare.

Hunter smiled lazily at him. "Even."

"You are a crazy bastard."

"So I've been told." He rocked forward onto the balls of his feet. "Someone just blasted your lady's real identity all over the web. That someone wants her to have no place to hide. Declan told me you have an enemy trying to use her against you."

"Yes." He couldn't see her any longer. Had she been crying? She'd better not have been crying.

"How did your enemy find out about her past? Because there are all sorts of personal details leaked. Like the fact that she lived with her fake 'Uncle Milo' in Hilton Head and that she got here when she was a teen. That she was present for her dad's killings. Pictures of her were included. Hell, some of them looked like freaking selfies of her and several other women. One of them even had a bridal veil on her head. What was up with that?"

He had to unclench his jaw. "The damn phone!"

"Excuse me?"

"The bastard after her took Wren's phone yesterday. He used it to call me. If there are selfies in this leak—pics of Wren and her friends at the bachelorette party—they probably came from her phone."

Hunter nodded. "And maybe also on that phone, she might have had confidential texts with Milo?"

Probably. Shit. "A phone is a person's life. He could have found out all kinds of intel on her."

"Intel that he couldn't wait to share with the world because he's trying to wreck her life. Her anonymity is gone. I came here first thing because—one, I was already in the area."

"What in the hell were you already doing in the area?" Jake exploded.

"Your brother sent me."

Jake could not have been more shocked. "Eb?"

"He's a bossy bastard, you know that?"

Yeah, he and his brother were both bossy bastards.

"He told me that you and your Wren needed help. Eb sent me in to keep an eye on you, but I'm barely in the area and then I start getting frantic phone calls from Declan saying I have to make immediate contact and give you backup, STAT. Thus, the pounding at your door." He looked at his watch. "I figure I've beat the pack of salivating wolves by a bit. We can get your lady, get her the hell out of here, and then stash her someplace else. Declan has plenty of safe houses you can use. Trust me when I say *plenty*. Your brother-in-law has put them all at your disposal."

Wren hadn't wanted to lose the life she'd worked so hard to build.

Before Jake could speak, his phone rang. The peal came from the bedroom because he'd left the phone back there. "Don't move."

"We all need to damn well get moving. Not like we have time to just sit and shoot the breeze and—"

The phone was still ringing.

Jake rushed down the hallway. The door was ajar, but he shoved it fully open. Wren stood by the bed, still wearing his shirt, and she had his phone in her hand.

"It's Honey," she said, her worry clear as she offered the phone to him.

He hurried forward, snagged the phone, and heat rushed through him when his fingers momentarily tangled with hers. *Every time I touch her, I feel that surge.* Always had. Always would.

He put the phone to his ear. "Honey..."

"We have a problem." Grim words.

They had several. They had a clusterfuck. "Not exactly the news I was hoping to hear first thing this morning."

"Is Wren safe? You got her with you?"

Wren watched him with her wide, deep eyes.

"I have her," he said. *And I'm keeping her.*

"Makayla Lane is missing."

The news was so unexpected that he shook his head in automatic denial.

"Her fiancé discovered that she was gone this morning. I'm at her house now, and there are signs of a struggle. A struggle—and blood."

Shit.

"A lot of blood," Honey added quietly.

Wren grabbed his arm. "What is happening?" Terror lurked in the darkness of her gaze. "Jake?"

And he had to tell her even as he knew it was going to break her heart, "Makayla is gone."

Chapter Fourteen

GONE—GONE WHERE? THAT HAD BEEN HER IMMEDIATE response because Wren just couldn't understand. But Jake's dark features had told her the rest of the story.

Something happened to Makayla. While Wren had been safe in Jake's arms, someone had taken her friend.

Where was Makayla? And was she even still alive?

"I'm heading to Makayla's place—now!" Wren had dressed as quickly as she could. Fresh jeans. Blouse. Tennis shoes. All items that had been in her travel bag. She changed and was rushing for the front door at Jake's beach house, but he moved into her path like the immovable object he tended to be.

Only there wasn't just one immovable object in her path. There were two. Hunter stood right beside him.

Hunter cleared his throat. "I think the plan is for you to go to a safe house. You go with Jake, and I can try to find out what is happening with your friend."

Her chin angled toward him. "What's happening is that Makayla is missing. Makayla—a woman who has never hurt anyone in her entire life—is gone." She'd felt dread settle in

163

her stomach the minute she'd seen Honey's name on the phone's screen. The nightmare wasn't over. It was just getting worse. Only now, Makayla was involved.

"You don't know that her disappearance is related to what is happening to you," Hunter pointed out. "Hell, maybe the woman just got cold feet and decided not to get married. That happens, you know. Brides run away. Pretty sure there have been movies about that very scenario."

The faint lines near Jake's mouth deepened. He shook his head. "The woman didn't run away. Honey said there was blood at the scene. Signs of a struggle."

Hunter sucked on the inside of his cheek. "Okay. So, yeah, that looks bad."

She gaped at him. "It looks more than bad! It looks like my friend has been abducted, and I'm not just going to sit here and do nothing to help her!" She lunged around the men.

Only her lunge didn't get her particularly far because Jake caught her by the shoulders and stopped her. "What are you going to do, Wren?" Soft.

"I'm going to the scene." Step one. Not like she had a whole drawn-out plan yet. "I want to talk to her fiancé, to Tom." That seemed like a good starting point. "I want to see what evidence Honey discovered." All good things to do, right?

"I can do all of that," Hunter offered. "And you can go with Jake. Go get tucked away in a nice, secure safe house. I'll report back as soon as I know anything."

They wanted to tuck her away. Check. Got it. But this was her friend, and running while Makayla was in danger seemed like one really shitty thing to do.

Her father would have said it was a normal move. *Survival.* And you always had to put your own survival first, according to him. Friends would turn on friends. Lovers would turn on lovers.

Screw you, you bastard. "I'm going to Makayla's. And unless you two are planning to kidnap me," she jerked away from Jake, "you will not be stopping me."

Hunter nodded. "Okay, kidnapping is an option we can put on the table. Not my first choice, of course, but if it gets the job done—"

"You're not touching her," Jake snapped out. His gaze didn't leave Wren's face. "Where you go, I go." His nostrils flared. "Let's see what we can learn about your friend, but you never leave my sight."

"This isn't some big trap," she threw at him. "Taking Makayla would not do anything to you. Her disappearance doesn't hurt you in any way! She's *my* friend." This wasn't about him.

"Yeah, and you're pretty much his everything." Hunter shrugged. "So I can see where this goes straight back to Jake."

"What?" The man was delusional. Had to be.

"Shut the hell up," Jake groused to Hunter. "And just follow us to the scene, would you? Stay sharp. Maybe this is an attempt to lure us all right out in the open."

"Exactly, and that's why we should not just go trotting right out into the open, but you clearly have a problem telling the woman no. Dude, just say no. Watch me do it. *No.* See?"

Wren squinted at him. "Do you have issues we need to know about?"

Hunter waved a hand toward Wren even as he told Jake, "She offered to let you kidnap her. It is a viable option, especially if her safety is what matters the most to you. Take her away. I'll help you."

She realized that Hunter was completely serious. He thought Jake should kidnap her and they should what— abandon Makayla? "Who are you?" she demanded.

"Clearly, the only one with sense here." Hunter crossed his arms over his chest. "If you were mine, there wouldn't be a discussion. You'd be over my shoulder and in the car as I got you the hell out of here in record time."

She had to pick her jaw off the floor.

Jake moved her, deliberately tugging her to his side. "Hey, asshole," he said, voice pleasant—well, pleasant only if *pleasant* could cut like a knife, "she's not yours. She's mine. *Mine.* And we're going to find out about her friend because Makayla matters to Wren. What matters to Wren matters to me. Got it?"

"Got it." A twist of Hunter's lips. "Let's just hope this doesn't explode in our faces. My orders were to get you two in a safe house. Not to parade around town, but sure, whatever, let's do things your way."

Enough of this. "We're wasting time." She barreled for the door.

Jake beat her, of course. He went out first, checking the area. No one was around. No danger lurking. No crowd of reporters intent on dragging out her twisted past for the world to see. Though, if Hunter was right, the throng of reporters would be showing up soon enough.

They jumped in the Jeep. She grabbed her seatbelt and clicked it into place.

Jake reached out and curled his fingers under her chin. His touch was careful. "If danger comes at you, I will kidnap you in order to keep you safe."

"No, you wouldn't." He was bluffing. She wouldn't buy it.

"Yes, sweetheart, I would." He didn't even blink. "If it

meant protecting you, I'd do anything. Even if you hated me for the choices I had to make."

* * *

CHAOS. That was what she found at Makayla's house. Deputies rushed everywhere. Honey stood on the porch. When Wren rushed toward her, she realized that Honey was holding some sort of plastic bag in her left hand. White fabric—darkened to red in spots—filled the inside of that clear bag.

"I need a crime scene team," Honey shouted into her phone as she pressed it to her ear with her right hand. "Hell, yes, I get that I'm not FBI any longer. I don't care. I want the best you can send. I've got a woman missing. I've got blood. I've got an abduction that happened while her fiancé slept in the same house with her. *Get me resources.*" Her eyes locked on Wren. Widened. She ended the call, shoved the phone into her pocket, and thrust the plastic bag at the deputy to her left. "What in the hell are you doing here?" she demanded of Wren.

Wren's gaze lingered on the plastic bag. "Is that a veil?" It looked like a wedding veil inside the bag. A bloody wedding veil.

"It was in the bed with me this morning." Tom's wooden voice.

Tom sat on the second porch step. Wren hadn't even noticed him until that moment. She'd been too intent on reaching Honey. Tom's hands dangled between his knees, and his shoulders bowed forward as he hunched. "I reached for Makayla when I woke up." He swallowed. His Adam's apple bobbed. "I touched it. Felt like a big spider web beneath my fingers. I opened my eyes, and the veil was

167

there, and then I saw the blood." Another swallow. "I shouted for Makayla. She didn't answer." He blinked. Looked at his hands. "She didn't answer."

"Wren, you shouldn't be here." Honey was adamant. "This is a crime scene, and I—"

"I want to go inside."

Honey snorted. "And I want a million dollars for Christmas, but that shit ain't happening." She bustled forward. Hopped down the steps. "Crime. Scene." A wave toward Jake. "You know this stuff. You know how it works. She can't just parade inside when I need a team to look and find out what happened to our vic. She should not be here."

"I tore through the house," Tom cut right over Honey's words as if she hadn't been speaking. Maybe he hadn't even realized that anyone was talking.

Wren thought he seemed lost in shock and grief.

"The room where she'd been storing her wedding dress..." He licked his lips. "There was blood all over her wedding dress. The thing was slashed to pieces." His eyes squeezed shut. "*Is my Makayla slashed to pieces? How did I sleep through all of that? How did I not hear something?*"

"Good damn question," Honey muttered.

Wren caught the mutter. But then, she thought maybe Honey had wanted her to catch it.

Honey mouthed, *Be careful* to Wren and Jake.

Surprise rolled through Wren. What was happening? Hold on, did Honey think Tom could be involved in Makayla's disappearance? Tom could be uptight, prickish, sure, but he loved Makayla.

Love is a lie. In the end, we all put ourselves first. Another lesson from her father.

Her gaze lingered on Tom.

His head suddenly shot up. His eyes—bright blue—

locked right on her. It was as if he'd just realized she was there. "This is your fault." He jumped to his feet. Tom flew off the steps and came right at her, stabbing his index finger in the air toward Wren. "You did this!"

Jake stepped right in front of her. "You need to settle your ass down."

Tom drew up short.

Wren peeked over Jake's shoulder at Tom.

"Wren did not do anything to Makayla," Jake stated very, very definitely. "She's here because she's worried about her friend. I happen to have some expertise in the area of kidnappings—worked more than my share of these scenes. I can look around and see if anything stands out to me. I'm here to offer my help. Wren and I are both here to help."

Tom's ragged breathing sawed in and out. "Wren was the target."

What?

His head tilted as he peered around Jake to see her. "She told me—you were attacked *twice*. If someone is after you, then why is my Makayla gone?"

I don't know. But we will get her back. They had to get Makayla back.

"This might not be related to the attacks on Wren," Honey informed him, voice brisk. "It's far too early to make any sort of assumption. I told you that already. Now, listen. *Listen.* I'm pulling in my contacts at the Bureau. We are going to conduct a thorough investigation. We will find Makayla."

A shudder shook Tom's long, lean body. "But will she be alive?" He raked a hand over his face. He wore blue pajama pants. Nothing else. Even his feet were bare. "Is she alive?" He licked his lips once again. "Hostage rescue."

Another heavy breath. "Yeah, yeah, I know that's what you do, Jake. Maybe someone took my Makayla hostage. You have to rescue her." Now he grabbed Jake. "Go in the house."

"That's what I was damn well trying to do," Jake rumbled.

Wren stepped to the side so she could see everyone a bit better. Was that—was that blood on Tom's pajama pants?

"Search the house. Find clues," Tom pushed Jake forward. "Scooby-Doo that shit. Whatever you need. *Get Makayla back.*"

Honey cleared her throat. "This is a crime scene. Jake isn't going inside because he's a civilian. He's staying out."

"I want him in!" Tom's face mottled.

"It's not really about what you want," Honey returned, hands on her hips. "It's about doing things the right way. Making sure that Makayla has every advantage. And that we don't mess up the investigation."

Tom whirled on her. "It's about bringing her *home!* He does this stuff, right? He just said he did! I've read stories—heard the tales in town! He brings people *back.* When the authorities give up, he gets them home! I want my Makayla home."

"This isn't *exactly* what he does," Honey mumbled.

"Let him look," Tom urged, words almost feverish. "Let him just see if he can find something to lead us to my Makayla. Please." A gulp. "I'll donate as much money as you want to the sheriff's department. I will do anything you need. Just—*I need Makayla back.*"

"Are you trying to bribe me right now?" Honey wanted to know.

"*Please!*"

Honey glanced over at Jake. Then Wren. She motioned

for the nearby deputy to get lost. He did. Then, huffing, she said, "You come in with me. You touch nothing. You see something that stands out, you tell me." Another hard huff. "Come on, now. Before sanity asserts itself again and I change my mind."

Jake tangled his fingers with Wren's and hauled her toward the house. As soon as they crossed over the threshold, Honey very firmly shut the front door.

Silence.

Honey stared at Jake. Then Wren. "Did I make that scene look grudging enough? Trying not to look too eager, you know."

Wren frowned at her.

"I'm former BAU, I clearly know my crime scenes. Damn well don't need anyone else's eyes on it to give me a profile or an idea of what went down." She rolled *her* eyes. "I *do* need techs to dust for prints and collect DNA. So seriously, don't touch shit." She rubbed the back of her neck. "But I wanted you to take a look, to make sure I'm not going completely crazy..."

She bustled past them.

To the right.

To the room that Wren knew housed Makayla's dress because Makayla had excitedly shown it to her just days before. Honey pulled on gloves near the door. Then she swung that door open. Jake stepped forward.

"No." A sharp denial from Honey. "I want Wren in first. She's the one I need seeing this, not you, Jake. Not that I don't think your hostage skills are top-notch but...again, I know how to create a profile. I'm no amateur. That's not what this little tour is all about."

Wren's stomach twisted as she stepped inside. The first thing she saw was Makayla's beautiful wedding dress. Not hanging up so lovingly any longer. On the floor. Sliced to pieces. Splattered with blood.

Her hand flew to her mouth.

"Don't faint on me," Honey warned. "Do some deep breathing or shit like that."

She wasn't going to faint. At least, hopefully, she would not. Wren inched inside the room.

"Tom admitted to knocking over the table. Said he even grabbed her wedding gown. Or what's left of it. That's why he had blood on his fingers and his pajama pants."

"Is that why?" Jake asked, no emotion in his voice.

Wren glanced back at him. "You can't suspect Tom."

"He was in the house. Didn't wake up despite all of this." Honey waved her hand around. "Jake isn't the only one with Tom on a suspect list."

Wren's gaze slid back to the dress. Makayla had been so excited about that dress. She'd flown to New York in order to buy it.

"Maybe Tom saw an opportunity," Honey mused. "All the trouble with you...maybe he figured he could use it to his advantage and get rid of an inconvenient fiancée."

Wren crept forward. "She's not inconvenient. She's the woman he loves."

"Didn't think you believed in love," Honey noted.

"Love makes you weak," she said, the words coming as if by rote. "Or, at worst, it makes you crazy. Just like my fa—" Wren stopped. Blinked. Because she'd just caught the light on the windowsill. All of the breath left her in a sudden surge as she lurched toward that light.

Makayla's ring. The rock that Jennifer had envied. It sat there, nestled against the base of the window as it perched on the windowsill. Sunlight hit the big diamond and made light burst out like a shooting star. "Oh, God." This couldn't be happening. Wren shook her head. "No."

"Her ring was left behind," Jake said. "Okay, guessing it will be bagged and tagged just like everything else in here. Maybe all of the blood isn't hers. Could be that her attacker nicked himself in the fight. Good call on pulling in the FBI's crime scene analysts. They'll push through the work one hell of a lot faster than any local team ever could. Maybe you'll get a hit in the system."

Wren couldn't look away from the ring. "He always left the rings behind. That wasn't in the papers. The authorities kept it out deliberately." Another lurching step toward the ring. "Uncle Milo told me once that it was his signature. My fa—the killer said it was his way of showing the world that the relationship was over. That it was never real in the first place. The rings bind, but now they've been severed." Her eyes squeezed closed. "He cut off their fingers. That was what he always did. That's what happened here, too. That's what happened to Makayla. Why there is so much blood." She whirled. Glared at her *friend*. "You knew it was him, Honey. You spouted that crap about suspecting Tom, when all the while you knew it was—"

"It's not your father, Wren." Soft. Honey's features showed her sympathy. No, her pity. "He's dead, remember?"

Dead. Dead. "I need to see his body." Something she'd wanted to do from the first moment she'd heard he was gone. "Maybe there is a mistake." Her gaze jumped to a watchful Jake. "This is him." Jake would believe her. "You and Eb were wrong. What's happening is about my past. It's about my father." It had never been about the brothers. She rushed toward Jake. "He would leave the rings behind. When my father took his victims, he left their rings. *Her* ring is left behind. All of this blood—he cut off her finger. That's what he did." Sucking in a breath, she fought the nausea that boiled through her blood. *I will not faint. I will not faint.* "The general public never learned about this part. The Feds kept it quiet. It has to be him—don't you see? He's not dead. He's here. He's been playing with me. He took Makayla. *This is him.*"

Chapter Fifteen

"YOUR FATHER IS DEAD, WREN." HONEY'S VOICE WAS very certain. "Milo doesn't make mistakes. He went to the scene to verify everything himself. That's where he's been—where he *is*. Look, there was...a lot of decay with your father's body. DNA had to be used for the identification process. *Your* DNA. Your father's DNA that was collected after you were put in witness protection. The remains are his. Jonathan is not still out hunting in the world. But someone who knows what he did may certainly be."

The pain and horror on Wren's face gutted Jake.

"Your story was leaked on social media," Honey added.

Wren didn't react.

Because they already knew this bit, courtesy of Hunter's early arrival. So it wasn't exactly a shocking reveal at this point.

"It was posted on an assortment of true crime groups, too." Honey heaved a disgusted sigh. "The daughter who should be dead but was 'living it up along the beach.'"

Now Wren did flinch.

"Someone knows who you are, Wren." Honey edged closer to Wren. Lifted her hand as if she'd give Wren a reassuring pat on the shoulder but stopped before actually touching her. "Someone knows a great deal about you and your father. Someone with a whole lot of intel. Too much intel, to my way of thinking. This is stalker level."

"Wren's phone was taken." With an effort, Jake kept the emotion out of his voice. He even managed to unclench his fists. "I'm thinking the killer could have scrolled through her device. Accessed her private emails. Her texts. Learned a ton before he dumped the phone at the hospital."

"This wasn't on my phone." Wren was adamant. "Or in my texts. I *never* talked to anyone about this. Not about how he left rings behind. How he severed fingers." She rubbed the back of her neck. "The FBI team investigating knew those details. My father knew. I knew."

"And what about the families of the vics?" Jake asked. He needed to learn more about these old cases. But, hell, the Sweetheart Slasher had never been on his radar when he'd been younger. The bastard certainly was, now. "They had to notice missing fingers on their loved ones."

Wren flinched again.

Yeah, he'd just displayed zero tact. Story of his life.

"There were an assortment of injuries on the victims," Honey explained into the uncomfortable silence. "Some premortem. Some...post."

Hell.

Wren's hand left her neck and fell back to her side. She swayed as the color seemed to drip from her face. He wrapped his arms around her. *Don't faint on me, sweetheart.*

"I'm not going to fall," she whispered.

"You sure as hell aren't." He pulled her closer even as

his gaze swept over the room. Of course, Honey knew her crime scenes. The woman probably had a profile spinning through her head, and he wanted to hear it. Right then. "Talk to me, Honey. Tell me what you see."

A brief pause and then... "Copycat. It's what I see. It's what my gut tells me."

He nodded. "Same." His exact thought. And like there was really any other option. No way was the dead killer strolling through Hilton Head.

Honey paced a bit to the right. Hummed. "Our perp overpowered Makayla with minimal effort. After all, Tom said he heard no screams. I'm thinking male, fit, someone who knows how to get in and out of houses without alerting homeowners. Probably started B&Es when he was younger and worked his way up. There was no sign of forced entry along any of the doors or windows. He has his craft well honed." She seemed almost admiring. "If he was good enough—and I think he was—Makayla might not have even realized he was in the room with her until it was too late. He would have done a swift overpower job on Makayla. The woman is five-foot-four and a breeze could knock her down." Honey turned away. Moved near the dress. Her head angled toward the blood spatter on the floor. "He got her here. Took her out. She—"

"She would have screamed when he cut her finger off," Wren insisted. Her chest rose and fell quickly. Too quickly.

But Honey shook her head. "Not if she was already knocked out. Maybe he drugged her. Would have made moving her body easier. It's always easier when they don't fight."

Jake nodded. He'd figured all the same things. But a few things about the scene bothered him. "There are no blood droplets through the house. It's just right here. If he cut off her finger, then hauled her out, he would have left a trail." He'd paid careful attention to the floor on his way to the room.

Nothing had been there. Something should have been. Violence was messy. Blood was a bitch to clean up.

Honey looked back at him, a frown tugging her brows low. "He made sure there was no blood trail."

Jake had another question that needed to be asked. "Wren, what did your father do with the, ah, the fingers?"

She turned her head to stare up at him. "If he...if he took one partner first, he left the severed finger for the second victim to find."

Fuck. If that was the case, then Tom was going to lose his mind when he discovered Makayla's finger.

"I'll get my deputies to start searching," Honey announced.

There was a sudden flurry of voices from outside the house. Honey hurried toward the window. Peered out. Swore. "Reporters. Hell. I knew we'd only keep them away so long. Vultures swooping in over prey." She slanted a glance back at Wren and Jake. "You two need to go, now."

There was nothing in the room that could lead him to Makayla. "Where is the vic's phone?"

"Tom turned it over to me already. It was in the bedroom. Her car is still in the drive. Her keys and purse are all here at the house. I'm pulling up feeds from all nearby traffic cams to see if we can spot her in any vehicles, but, hell, you know that stuff is spotty. We'll be lucky if we turn up anything in that footage." She adjusted her badge. "Got to give a statement to the Press. Do *not* mention the Sweetheart Slasher out there, understand? Let's try to keep this to a minimum shitshow level."

That seemed like an impossible task. Jake was pretty sure they were already at maximum shitshow level.

But it was time to get out of there. Jake did one more sweep. The blood-spatter trail nagged at him. Truth be told, the whole scene nagged at him. The ring had been left as almost a—a deliberate taunt to Wren.

A mind fuck.

Jaw locking, he led her back through the house. At the front door, Honey exited first. He waited, knowing she would work to pull the attention of any reporters her way. He'd considered slipping out the back door, but he knew if he did that, they could still be spotted going to his Jeep. So he was opting to take the shortest escape route.

"She had to be terrified." Wren's low voice.

Yes, her friend had probably been afraid.

"She's still alive."

He hoped so. But he wasn't going to lie and swear that she was. He didn't want to lie to Wren.

"My f-father never killed victims right away. Certainly not until he had the full couple together." She glanced toward the partially open door. "We should make sure Tom has protection."

He wasn't convinced Tom was the next target.

It keeps coming back to Wren. Everything circled back to her.

"Keep your head down," he advised her. "Odds are the reporters will spot you no matter what, but it should just be the local crowd here now." No heavy hitters...yet. "We get in the Jeep, and we get the hell away." Hunter would be out there, watching and waiting. Once they arrived at the promised safe house, they would figure out their next plan of attack.

And Jake was chomping at the bit to attack. Playing

defense wasn't his style. Even back in high school, he'd been on the offensive line. He lived to attack. Not to sit on his ass and wait for the battle to come his way.

He saw that Honey had led the reporters to the side. Time to move. He opened the door fully and hurried out. He made sure to keep his arm around Wren's shoulders and to press her tightly against him. Questions were being fired at Honey, one right after the other, but near his Jeep, a small group had gathered.

Not local reporters. At least, he didn't recognize them.

"There she is!" An excited cry from a woman in a red dress. "Margaret! Margaret! Over here!"

Wren flinched.

"What's it like to have a serial killer for a father?" the woman asked.

A short, balding man with small glasses and brown eyes that matched his muddy shirt squinted at Wren. "Did you see what he did? Were you there for everything?"

"Get away from my ride," Jake ordered them. "*Now*."

The man scampered back. The woman didn't. And another male was with her. Thin and tall.

"Did you ever try to save them?" the woman demanded. "Or did you even care?"

"I'm sorry," Wren began.

Yeah, fuck this. He scooped her into his arms. Got her to the passenger side and deposited her in the seat. Then he whirled for the growing crowd. Who in the hell were these people?

"She should have died like the victims!" This cry came from the tall, thin male. The one with sun-bleached blond hair and a phone gripped in his hand as he filmed the scene. "Margaret, what do you have to say to the families out there? All of the families of the victims who never got to hug their loved ones again because of your father? What do you want to say to them?"

Jake got right in front of the phone, blocking the camera. "Who told you to be here?" he demanded. He recognized an ambush when he saw one.

"Her dad took someone else!" From the woman in red. "Did she help him, *again*? Was Margaret in on it?"

That woman needed to stop screaming in his face. "Did you hear about the attack and this location on a police scanner?" Was that how they'd known to be there?

"No." The woman's chin notched up. "It was posted on our local crime loop!" She pointed at Wren. "We know all about you! You can't hide! We know what you did!"

Declan had better use his tech and find out who the hell was posting Wren's business everywhere. "She did nothing. Now get the hell out of the way."

But the woman in red was smiling. And she'd just pulled something out of her bag.

The reporters were looking their way because the little group was freaking loud. The woman in red darted closer to the Jeep, and she lifted a bottle toward Wren. She started to throw the contents at Wren.

Oh, the hell she would.

He grabbed her arm before the woman could throw the bottle. Red liquid jostled over his hand. Onto his clothes. "Are you fucked in the head?" he demanded.

The woman glared at him. *"She's the devil's daughter! She'll always have blood on her hands!"*

Okay. Clearly, this was a big day for the screaming woman.

And the reporters were rushing over because the lady

had obviously wanted a scene and her fifteen minutes of fame. She'd even come with her own special effects—a bottle of red paint and her filming buddy who would no doubt be loading everything onto social media, if he wasn't already streaming live.

Jake tossed the bottle to the side. The woman was already reaching into her bag for another bottle. Seriously? Her gaze was lit with fierce intent. He studied her with a cynical eye. Full makeup. Carefully styled hair. A body-hugging red dress. Because she had to be camera ready for the big show, didn't she?

You aren't touching Wren.

He blocked the woman's path. She could throw paint all over him. She was not touching Wren.

"Not today." Honey grabbed the woman's wrist this time. "*Not today.*" Honey jerked her head toward the Jeep. "Get her out of here, Jake. Go on, now."

Damn straight. But before Jake left, he made sure to take note of every face in the crowd. From the shadow of a nearby tree, he spotted Hunter doing the same survey. Only Hunter had his phone up and was recording the scene.

Maybe even broadcasting the thing straight back to Declan Flynn?

Their own livestream. Nice.

Without another word, Jake headed around the vehicle and jumped into the driver's seat. He reached for the steering wheel.

Wren caught his hand. "You have paint on your fingers."

Yeah, he did. His fingers were a glaring red. Like blood. He swiped his fingers over his shirt. Red remained on his fingers, but he grabbed for the wheel anyway. So what if he smeared some paint? Getting Wren out of there was his goal.

"She was going to throw the paint on me."

He reversed the Jeep. Whipped them out of there. The tall and thin jerk—the lady in red's filming buddy—still had his phone up and was recording. *Oh, I will be seeing you again.* He drove down the road, hurrying from the scene, because the sooner they were far away from those people, the better he would feel about her safety.

Silence filled the Jeep.

The motor growled. The Jeep ate up the empty road.

"You got hit with the paint instead of me. I'm sorry, Jake."

"You're not the one who threw the paint. You have *nothing* to be sorry about." Jake bit off each word through clenched teeth, then his head turned as he glanced at her. "Margaret?"

She grimaced. "Yes. That was me. In another life."

"Name never would have worked. You're Wren. You're—"

A black truck barreled from a nearby driveway. It erupted straight out with a snarl of its engine and hurtled for the Jeep. Straight for Wren's side of the vehicle. "Wren!" Jake bellowed even as he grabbed the wheel and tried to spin them, desperate to get her away from the point of impact.

The other driver didn't stop. The front of the truck slammed into the Jeep, and the vehicle hurtled, bounced. Metal crunched. Wren screamed.

The truck reversed.

"Jake?" Wren's desperate voice.

She reached for him.

The sonofabitch driving the truck hit them again.

Air bags deployed in the Jeep, and a cloud of white surrounded him. He shoved at the bags even as the other vehicle's engine growled and snarled and came at them the hell again.

Again.

His head slammed forward. Then back.

Then the bastard hit them *again.*

Chapter Sixteen

A KNIFE FLASHED BEFORE HER. WREN DIDN'T EVEN have the breath to scream. Something wet dripped down the side of her face.

The air bag that had been pinning Wren in place deflated with a hiss. The knife came at her. A fast slash as she tried to turn her face away.

Nothing I can do. It's going to cut me.

Only it didn't slash her in the face. It slashed away her seatbelt.

The Jeep was on its side. She blinked blearily. Jake? Was Jake cutting her free? She tried to angle her head toward the driver's seat.

Another air bag was in her way. She reached out, pushing against it.

"Say goodbye," a voice growled.

Then hard hands were grabbing her and hauling Wren out of the vehicle. And those hands weren't Jake's. Because she'd just seen Jake beyond the airbag. Slumped. Unconscious? "Jake!" she screamed.

"You're gonna pay," the man told her. The knife was

gone. Where had it gone? He dragged her out of the Jeep. What was left of the Jeep. Smashed and crumpled. Broken. The way she felt. Her feet kicked out over the street. She heaved in his hold and twisted.

"Help!" Wren cried.

"The hero can't help. No one can help. You are—"

A dark SUV flew down the street, coming right toward them. The man hauling her swore. His grip slackened for just a moment, and Wren tore free.

Only she didn't get far. He grabbed her again. Whirled her toward him. She punched at him, as hard as she could.

He hit her back. A fierce upper cut to the jaw that had her seeing stars and weaving on her feet.

"Get away from her!" A roar. A roar that had come from the SUV. Dazed, she glanced toward it. Saw...

Hunter? Yes, Hunter. He'd been following them. He'd help. He'd—

The man who'd just hit her yanked a gun from the side of his coat. He fired toward Hunter. Quick blasts.

"No!" Wren yelled. She threw her body against the shooter. He staggered beneath the impact, but didn't fall. Instead, he just grabbed her with his left hand and with his right, he shoved the gun against her side.

"Come with me or die here."

You were never supposed to go to a secondary scene. How many times had Honey drummed that important fact into her? Wren knew her odds of survival would plummet if she left. She'd never see Jake again.

She shook her head. *No.*

"Fuck it then." He smiled at her. A round, soft face. But his brown eyes glinted with hate. "Die here." Sweat trickled down his temple. He licked his lips.

"*She's not dying.*" A bellow from Jake.

Her breath shuddered out.

Jake had made it out of the Jeep. Jake was okay. Everything was going to be okay.

Um, or, judging by the fact that she had a gun jabbing into her and she was still seeing spots from that punch to the jaw, maybe...not?

"You're surrounded, bastard," Jake thundered as he stalked closer. Her gaze skated to the left. Jake paced forward, and he had his gun up. His paint-splattered fingers held the gun in a rock-steady grip and his face—ice cold and terrifying. "You've got me here and you've got my buddy coming in behind you."

The shooter stiffened. "No one is behind me."

"Yeah, he is. My friend Hunter is closing in. You missed him with your shots. Now you have me and you have him to deal with, you dumb prick. And we're both pissed and planning to shove bullets into your brain. So there's that fun future waiting for you."

A siren wailed. They hadn't made it very far from Makayla's crime scene. *Makayla.* "What did you do with her?" Wren whispered. If Hunter was closing in, she had to keep the jerk distracted. She also had to help her friend.

The attacker's brows whipped up. "What in the hell are you talking about? Do with who?"

"Makayla," she breathed her name. Her jaw ached from where he'd hit her. "Is she still alive? Please..." The tremble in her voice was real. "Makayla hasn't hurt anyone. Let her go."

"I don't know who the hell Makayla is," he yelled back as spittle flew from his mouth, and panic filled his eyes. "I'm here for you! You and that freak father of yours killed my sister! You are going to pay! You are—"

"Freeze, bastard!" Hunter snarled. "What you feel right

now? It's a gun pressed to the back of your head. So much as twitch, and the trigger gets pulled and that means—*bam*. Your brains go everywhere, though I'm really not convinced you have a lot of those."

The attacker's eyes widened. A spattering of freckles covered his nose, and his pale skin seemed to whiten even more. "She has to pay." His red hair was tousled, as if he'd raked his fingers through it again and again.

Jake grabbed Wren and wrenched her from the other man's hold. Then he put himself in front of her, shielding her with his body. "For my crimes?" Jake demanded. "Screw that."

"For what she and her father did! They took Carrie! She has to pay!"

Carrie. The name clicked for Wren. Carrie Carpenter. Wren stumbled back. Carrie Carpenter had been that terrible, final victim. Wren had put her hands on Carrie's neck, and she'd tried to stop the blood flow, but it hadn't helped. Carrie had been staring at Wren as all the blood left her, and Carrie had been trying so desperately to talk. To form one final word. But her throat had been savaged, and she'd never voiced another sound. Her lips, though, they'd formed... "Adam?" Wren rasped the name.

Adam was Carrie's brother. I know...because I had to research her. I had to know more about her. The woman I couldn't save...

Carrie's husband had died before her, killed as part of the sick experiment. Carrie's final thought hadn't been for the man she'd married. The man whose cold body had been dumped near her. It had been for the young brother she'd left behind. Her final thought had been of Adam.

An inhuman shriek burst from the attacker when Wren

said his name. He flew forward, trying to shove past Jake so he could take aim at Wren and shoot her.

Jake didn't speak. He just grabbed the redhead. Twisted the man's arm fast and hard and something near the man's shoulder seemed to pop, and in the next breath, Jake had him on the ground. One of Jake's feet was planted at the base of the man's head, and he had the guy's arm extended up in a wrenching position that was making the guy—*is this Adam?*—howl in pain.

The attacker's gun had fallen to the ground. Hunter grabbed it and tucked it into the waistband of his jeans. Then Hunter was in front of Wren. "You good?"

No. She'd just been hit by a freaking truck and her jaw ached. Her friend was missing, and the howling man had tried to kill her. Not a good day.

Hunter winced when he looked at her face. "Jake will freak out when he sees that." His left hand lifted, and, carefully, he raised her chin.

She flinched.

The wailing siren was close. Super close, and when she pulled away from Hunter and turned her head to the side, she saw the cruiser rushing toward them. Not just a cruiser, though. Other cars were following in a parade-like line.

Wren stepped back. The man on the ground was screeching and twisting, but there was no way he was getting out of Jake's hold.

"I called the cops when I realized what the hell was happening," Hunter revealed. "The bastard was lying in wait. As soon as he spotted the Jeep, he tore for it."

For her side of the vehicle. Her body ached and fear had her heart racing far too fast. She scrambled toward Jake and the struggling man.

Hunter grabbed her from behind and held her back.

"How about we don't go running for the man who just tried to kill you? Great plan, huh? Am I a genius or what?"

The man looked up. Tears streamed from his eyes. "I hate you!"

Yes, she believed that he did.

"You should be dead. Carrie should be alive! Carrie should be here, not you! Not you!"

Jake wrenched the man's arm up higher. A high-pitched shriek of pain erupted from the guy.

"Where is Makayla Lane?" Jake demanded.

"Who the...*ah, my arm!* Who the...who the fuck is M-Makayla?"

"She's the woman you abducted last night. The bride to be." Jake's voice was flat. "You broke into her house, and you kidnapped her."

The cruiser screeched to a stop. Wren didn't even glance that way. She couldn't take her eyes off Jake. And the panicked man in his grip.

"I didn't kidnap anyone!" The man heaving on the ground shook his head. "Just came for *her.*" His head angled up so he could glare at Wren. "Got the call that you would be here. Came for you. Waited. Saw you drive in. Knew you'd come out. One long road in, one long road out. So I waited. *I waited.* All this time. All these years. Only no more waiting now. You're going to die!"

"The hell she is," Jake told him.

"*Let him go!*" Honey's sharp order. She slipped forward, with her gun drawn. A deputy shadowed her movements to the right. "Jake, let that man go and back away!"

"This bastard just tried to kill Wren! He plowed into my Jeep. Hit us again and again." Jake wrenched the guy's arm up a bit more.

Another howl.

"*Let him go.*" Honey didn't lower her gun, but Wren realized it wasn't aimed at Jake. It was pointed at the man on the ground. "I've got him," she promised, "and I am not going to let him hurt anyone."

Jaw locking, Jake slowly let go of the man. Jake took a step back. Honey crept forward.

The man who'd been on the ground leapt to his feet. With an inhuman scream, he flew toward Wren.

Hunter's grip tightened around her stomach.

"Freeze!" Honey bellowed.

The man didn't freeze.

Jake launched at the man's fleeing back. He tackled him, even as a thunder of gunfire exploded. Jake and the redhead hit the ground.

Honey wrenched her head toward the deputy. "What did you do?"

He'd fired his weapon, that was what he'd done. Had he hit Jake with the bullet? Wren tore from Hunter's grip and hurtled forward.

But Jake was already moving. He shoved back and up and flipped over the attacker. Then Jake's fist flew into the man's face. One hit, two, a third and—

Wren stumbled to a stop. "Jake?" Was that blood on him? Or the paint from before? *Be paint. Be paint.*

Hunter blew past her. He caught Jake's fist and stopped him mid-blow even as Honey and the deputy swarmed in.

"He's out of commission," Hunter said. "Get your control back, man. Now."

Jake's breath sawed in and out. But he nodded grimly and rose to his feet. Instantly, his eyes locked on Wren. And that blazing gaze narrowed.

Honey and the deputy bent near the fallen figure.

Jake came straight to Wren. His gaze drifted over her. Locked on her jaw. "Baby..." Lethal. "You're hurt."

Her hand skimmed over her jaw. It ached, but nothing was broken. "He, uh, hit me when he pulled me out of the Jeep, and I was trying to get away—*Jake!*"

Jake had whirled away and stormed back for the man she fully believed was Adam. Jake knocked the deputy out of the way. Adam balled up his fist and tried to take a swing at Jake.

Bad move.

The blow missed, and Jake pounded at him with fast and furious hits. Adam screamed and blood flew from his busted lip. Adam fell back even as Honey surged between the two men.

Jake froze with his hands fisted.

"I am *taking it* from here!" Honey blasted. "Jacob Jones, you get back. You hear me? You get back! You go to Wren, and you protect her." She pointed at the deputy who lurched to his feet. "Timothy, cuff this bastard!"

Timothy hurried to cuff the bastard.

Jake drew in a deep, shuddering breath. Then another. His glare remained on the attacker. One moment. Two. Three. Then, slowly, his head lifted. His head turned. His eyes found Wren.

Another deep breath. He strode toward her. His hand rose, and his fingers lightly skimmed over her jaw.

She caught his hand. "I'm okay."

His gaze burned down at her.

"I am." A little bruised, but this was hardly the worst she'd been in her life. Giving in to instinct, she closed the last bit of distance between them and wrapped her arms around him. He was warm and strong and when he pulled her tightly against him, some of the hard terror around her heart finally eased.

"Where is Makayla Lane?" Honey demanded to know. "You tell us right now!"

"She should die!" Adam cried out. "She should die for what she did!"

For just an instant, Wren squeezed her eyes shut. But there was no hiding from some things in this world, no matter how much you tried. And she'd tried hiding already. For such a very long time. She pulled from Jake. At first, his hold tightened, as if he wouldn't let her go.

But then he eased his grip.

Wren stepped back. "Makayla has done nothing wrong!"

"Not talking about her! Don't *know* her!" Blood dripped from Adam's busted lower lip. "You! You should die! You're the one I'm after! *You should die!*"

Jake twined his fingers with Wren's. "That's not ever gonna happen."

Honey grunted.

"This SOB slammed his car into my Jeep," Jake stated in a chilling voice that promised retribution would come. "He tried to kill us both."

"Just her!" A shout from Adam. "She is evil! She doesn't get to live! She doesn't—Carrie is dead. We buried her and all I get is a cold headstone. She doesn't get to live while my sister is gone!"

Jake's fingers squeezed her hand. "After the crash, the bastard took Wren. He hit her. He attacked her, Honey."

Honey's stare slid over Wren's face. "I see the bruise coming already."

Adam had already been cuffed. Timothy stood behind

Adam, and when he gripped the suspect's right shoulder, the redhead screamed in pain. "Be careful!" Adam cried.

Timothy's jaw tightened. Hunter watched from just a few feet away. Silent. Menacing.

But, glancing over her shoulder, Wren saw that Hunter wasn't the only watcher. More cars had been following Honey from Makayla's place. That whole would-be parade. Not just other deputies. The woman in red was there. And the guy who'd been filming Wren before—he had his phone up and was recording this whole scene.

Timothy and Honey started reading the suspect his rights, but he went right on screaming over them.

"*She has to die! I won't stop until she is dead!*"

There was such hate in his voice, and, when she looked back at him, the hate filled his eyes, too.

He stared straight at Wren, and he promised, "I will kill you."

Chapter Seventeen

Jake wanted to kill the bastard.

He glared at the suspect who'd been cuffed to the table and left in the small interrogation room. Not like this area was a hotbed of crime. The sheriff's station in Hilton Head was small. The staff mostly young, inexperienced.

Except for Honey. Honey knew exactly what in the hell to do with violent criminals. She knew how to make anyone break. Something he admired about her.

Honey stood beside him now in the observation room at the station. They surveyed the suspect through the one-way glass. The station had two interrogation rooms, and the perp was in the biggest one. All eight feet of it.

"Do you think you beat the shit out of him enough?" Honey asked, voice mild.

The man—Adam Rule—had a face that looked battered to hell and back. EMTs had checked him out. No serious injuries. But he was going to hurt for a while. The blood on his face had been cleared away. His right shoulder had been dislocated. Yeah, Jake knew he'd done that to the jackass. The shoulder had been treated, and Adam's left hand was currently cuffed to the table. A sling immobilized the right shoulder.

That shoulder would hurt for a while. So would the bruises.

You bruised Wren, you sonofabitch. You hit her. I should break your face for that attack. Even better, I should break you.

"Jake?"

"He punched Wren." His voice came out completely flat even as rage poured through every cell of his body. "He aimed his truck at her side of the vehicle. That man is lucky to be breathing right now."

"It's, ah, good that he's breathing," she replied, sending him a quick side-eye glance. "Because people who are breathing can make big confessions. They can tell us where missing brides are. They can tell us just how they came to be waiting to ram a truck at you and Wren. They can answer all kinds of pertinent questions like that, whereas a dead man can't tell anyone jack."

He forced his jaw to unclench. "Let me in the room with him."

"Why? So you can finish the attack you started?" Honey snorted. "I don't think so. That would be a horrible idea."

"Then let me go in." Wren's quiet voice.

Jake stiffened. "Sweetheart..." The endearment rolled from him. Deep. Low. Dark. "You think I intend to let you anywhere near that bastard again?"

"Sweetheart..." Her voice was soft and husky and sent an ache right through him. Her soft steps padded closer to him as she came forward to join them at the small observation window. "You think I'm just going to stand here and do nothing while my friend is missing? I have to help her."

His head turned toward her. When he saw the darkening bruise along her jaw, hot fury exploded through him all over again. He took a lunging step for the door.

Wren sidestepped to block his path. "I'm okay."

She kept saying that. She wasn't okay. The prick had slammed into *her* side of the vehicle. Jake had tried to turn the Jeep so he could take the impact, but there hadn't been enough time. And the jerk had hit them again and again. Jake's head had bounced all over the damn place—especially when the Jeep flipped to the side—and for one freaking, stupid moment, he'd actually blacked out.

As soon as his eyes had opened, he'd reached for Wren. He'd shoved away the remnants of the air bags around him, but when he'd been able to see clearly, Wren had been gone.

Gone.

He remembered roaring her name and feeling like the whole world had just gone dark around him.

"I think it's a good idea," Honey mused. "And probably one best executed while I'm still in command."

Jake whipped toward her. "What? Why the hell would you lose command?" And *how* was it a good idea to let Wren into that room with the attacker?

"Oh, come on." Honey rolled her eyes. "The Feds are blasting their way here. We've got an abduction in our quiet town. We've got the newly discovered daughter of a serial killer. This story is gonna be big, and there is no way a small-town sheriff gets to stay in charge of anything this big. Especially not since I hit them up asking for their help on the Makayla Lane crime scene already. They're only gonna *help* if they get to be in charge. Feds never play nicely with others."

"You can handle a case better than anyone at the Bureau. Hell, you *were* the Bureau," Jake pointed out.

"Once upon a time. Yep. Sure. Now, though, I'm a small-town sheriff who is looking hard at complete retirement. I won't be in command of this investigation for much longer. Just stating facts. I know how the Feds work." She waved toward the glass. "He confessed to the attack on Wren. He did not confess to taking Makayla. When he is near Wren, the guy loses control. Starts spouting everything in his head. If we want to push him more, before the Feds storm my station, then I say we send her in. Of course, you can also go in as the fierce guard that you are."

Damn straight he'd go in. *If* Wren went inside.

"I don't think he took Makayla." Wren seemed very certain. "I know him."

Jake waited. She hadn't said anything about the perp before. But *before* had been a clusterfuck. People filming them in the street. Deputies swarming. EMTs poking and prodding and that jackass in the interrogation room? He'd been raging at Wren the whole time.

"I knew him as soon as he mentioned Carrie's name," she added. "Carrie was my father's last victim." Her gaze darted to Honey. "She was the one—"

"The one *you* tried so hard to save," Honey finished. "You still had your hands on her throat when I found you, Wren. Your father had slashed your shoulders to hell and back, but you were trying to save that woman. And for your efforts, her brother just came and tried to kill you."

Wren shook her head. "He doesn't know what I did."

Jake needed to know more. Every single detail about the Sweetheart Slasher and Wren. And to think, he'd once foolishly believed he knew her so very well. Every day, new secrets emerged.

Wren's attention focused on the man who sat on the other side of the glass. "That man in there—I think he came for me. I don't think he's involved in what happened to Makayla, and I think the longer we focus on him, the more time we waste." Wren straightened her shoulders. "So I'm going in there, and I'm talking to him."

Honey nodded like it was the best plan ever.

What the hell? Were the women trying to drive him insane?

"He's cuffed," Wren reminded him. Like he needed the reminder. "And his other arm is out of commission."

The whole guy should be out of commission.

"Go with her," Honey directed him. "You've been her shadow every moment as it is."

He'd been *guarding* her. Where she went, he went. So, hell, yes, if she was going in interrogation, he was, too.

"But don't kill him, Jake." Honey's admonishment was mild. "No matter what provocation he may give. Like I said, dead men can't answer questions, and I would sure hate to have to lock you up. It will be awful hard for you to shadow Wren if you're locked up because you killed a guy who was cuffed."

She wouldn't be locking him up. And no one would be keeping him from Wren. Ever.

"We are losing time." Wren's deep, dark eyes were on him. "Makayla is losing time."

Hell. "Let's do this." But if the guy moved to attack, Jake would stop him in the most brutal way possible.

* * *

HER KNEES SHOOK. Her jaw ached. Her stomach knotted. She wanted to turn around and run out of the station, but instead, Wren opened the interrogation room door. She walked slowly across the threshold. Her gaze landed on the man seated at the small table.

"*You!*" Adam Rule tried to bolt to his feet.

But Deputy Timothy Hernandez stood nearby. He surged forward and pushed the guy back down. "Are we going to have a problem?" Timothy demanded.

Wren figured they probably were.

Especially because Jake followed her into the room. Adam's gaze immediately jumped to him, and fear flashed on the man's face. "Keep that bastard away from me!" Adam shouted.

Jake leaned against the wall on the left. "Do you often go around attacking women and plowing into random Jeeps? Or was today special for you?"

Adam hadn't asked for an attorney. He hadn't asked for anyone. Actually...he had.

He asked for me.

While she'd been watching him from the observation room with Jake and Honey, Adam had shouted Wren's name, over and over. Well, not her current name.

Margaret.

A name she hadn't used in so very long. Because Margaret had died. When her father attacked her, when he tried to see wings beneath her skin and Margaret had begged and pleaded, but he'd just kept cutting, that girl had died.

"She has to die. Carrie died. Carrie *died*."

"I know," Wren said. She wanted to keep emotion out of her voice. To be calm and cold. Honey and Jake could do that. They could stay in control, no matter what. But she wasn't them. And she was so tired of pretending.

What was the point in keeping her mask? The world had discovered her secrets. Or else the man currently cuffed wouldn't have come for her.

"I know," Wren repeated. "Because I was there when she died."

Another surge upward.

Timothy pushed him right back down. "Uh, Wren, don't know why you came in, but you should go back out—"

"Honey sent me in." It was the only idea Wren currently had. She pulled out the chair across from Adam. Sat down. It was either sit down or her knees might give out and she'd fall. "Your name was the last thing to pass from Carrie's lips."

Adam shook his head.

"She couldn't speak then." Wren put her hands on the table. "My fa—" Wren stopped. Squared her shoulders. "My father had slit her throat. Blood was everywhere. I tried to help, but there wasn't anything I could do. She looked at me, and she mouthed your name. You were her last thought."

"You fucking bitch," Adam breathed as tears filled his eyes. "I am going to *kill* you."

Jake stalked away from the wall. He, too, put his hands on the table. But only so he could lean in toward Adam. "You don't know who I am, do you?"

Adam didn't look his way.

But, no, clearly, he didn't.

Adam has nothing to do with Jake's past. This is all about me.

"I'll educate you, quickly. Wren belongs to me," Jake said.

And—wait, his voice wasn't flat and cold. Not unemotional at all. It seethed with rage. With deadly intent. "Anyone who tries to hurt her? They have to go through me. I will *annihilate* those who try to hurt her. If the authorities hadn't arrived on that scene earlier, you'd be a dead man right now."

Adam finally looked at Jake. Fear made him look.

"Hi, there," Jake said with a shark's predatory smile. "I'm the man you need to fear for the rest of your life. Me. You see, Wren? The woman you hurt? She's kind. She feels pity for you. I don't. I think you're a grown-ass man who tried to hurt *my* Wren. You used your fist on her. A man doesn't ever raise his fist to a woman. I don't care how much grief you're feeling. You don't do that. So I think I'm looking at a fucking prick who deserves to get the hell kicked out of him. And the more you threaten my Wren? The more I intend to rip you apart. You need to realize that there won't always be a deputy close by. One day, it will just be me and it will just be you."

"Uh, Jake..." Timothy began. "Uh, I don't think you're supposed to—"

"Who told you my real identity?" Wren asked. She would not waste more time.

Adam's head whipped back toward her.

"You were waiting because someone told you who I really was. You've been angry for years. Understandable. You lost your sister. Grief can twist you up and it can destroy you from the inside."

"That's no fucking excuse," Jake snapped.

Adam hunched back in his chair. "Got a call last night. Then a text. Your picture. Said—said everything about you. That you were in on the crimes with your father—"

"*She was a kid!*" Jake thundered.

Definitely still high on emotion.

"*She was a victim! You think he didn't hurt her, too?*" Rage boiled in Jake's words.

Adam blinked.

"You got a phone call," Wren said as she tried to get things back on track. Her hands pressed hard against the wood of the table. "And a text. Was the caller a man or a woman?"

"It was some—some stupid robotic voice. I hung up the first time, thought it was a joke." He licked his lower lip. Winced. "Called back. Said—said the Sweetheart Slasher's daughter was alive. That I had to stop you because you were just like him."

She didn't react. At least, not on the outside. But inside? Her heart raced faster. The knots in her stomach got so much worse.

Jake leaned forward a bit more. "So you jumped in your vehicle, and you rushed here to *stop* Wren?"

"Wren?" Adam seemed to taste the name. "Is that who you are now?" Adam squinted at her. "You pretend you were never Margaret? That you're someone named Wren?"

That was exactly what she did. Pretended, over and over again.

"I drove in from Greensboro." Adam's breath heaved out. "You were five hours away from me all of this time." He shook his head, as if in wonderment. "Five hours."

Wren swallowed.

"Do you know what happened to my family? After Carrie? My dad drank himself into the grave. My mom cried every day until she died. And me? I was the helpless kid who watched his world collapse." His teeth snapped together. "I *hate* you. I hate your father. The caller told me he was dead, so I can't get to him, but I damn sure got to you." He smiled. "I got to you, and I am going to *kill* you."

The fury and hate in his eyes was terrifying.

Wren sucked in a breath. "I—"

The door flew open. "Enough of this bullshit." Honey stomped her way inside. Her right hand flew up as she pointed at Adam. "You think you're the only one in this world who knows pain? Like you get some damn monopoly on it?"

"I—"

"The woman in front of you tried to save your sister. Do you hear me? Let me repeat, just in case. *Save her.* And you know what happened for her trouble?"

"Honey, no," Wren whispered.

Jake turned to frown at Wren.

"She almost died for her trouble. Her father was going at Carrie. He'd sliced her across the throat, not deep enough to kill because he was a sadistic bastard who enjoyed screwing with his prey. Wren jumped between them. She fought her father. She was a freaking kid! Her dad turned on her. Used his knife on her."

Her father's voice barreled through Wren's head. *You're trying to save her? Margaret. Oh, my Margaret. You're the angel I've been looking for all this time.* His eyes had been so dark.

She had her father's eyes.

You must have wings beneath your skin, if you're an angel. Let's see if we can find those wings.

She rolled back her shoulders and swore she could still feel the pain from those old wounds.

"Your sister ran out and left her," Honey announced starkly. "She left a kid bleeding so she could escape."

Wren's gaze skittered back to Adam. "Your sister was just trying to survive. I *wanted* her to survive."

But there had been no angel wings beneath her skin.

Her father had found that out far too quickly. He'd tossed her aside. Gone chasing after Carrie.

Wren released a long breath. "But she didn't get to survive. He found her. She hadn't made it far enough. He caught your sister, and he brought her back, and this time..." She could taste the bitterness of the memory. "The wound on her neck was much deeper. I tried to stop the blood flow." She had *tried*. "I put my hands on the wound, and I applied as much pressure as I could. She mouthed your name. And..." Wren stopped.

Silence in the room. The thick uncomfortable kind of silence that she'd always hated.

But Honey stopped the silence. "We got a tip about the Sweetheart Slasher's location. Someone had spotted a car believed to be linked to him." Honey strode closer to the table. Her leg bumped into the edge. "I was FBI back then. We went in with a full team, and when we crashed down into that basement, I found a blood-covered kid crouched over your sister. At first, I thought they were both dead. Then the girl blinked."

She'd been too afraid to move.

"So don't you dare give me your bullshit about this woman needing to die." Honey curled a hand around Wren's shoulder. "She didn't hurt your sister. She tried to help her. She carries scars because of what she did, and you —you're a dumbass."

Adam shook his head.

"Someone is manipulating you," Honey continued fiercely. "Using all that hate and pain you got trapped inside of you. You're a weapon. The bullet in a loaded gun. They aimed you and pointed you at Wren, and you took off. Now you're in here, about to get locked away, and you don't even know that you were a pawn in someone else's game."

Adam started to lift his right arm. Winced.

"The phone call and text you mentioned getting last night." A muscle jerked along Jake's jaw. "That was you, being set up by the person we're currently after. A man who kidnapped a woman last night."

"H-he didn't say anything about a kidnapping!"

"Was it a he?" Jake demanded to know. "Because you said the voice was robotic."

"I-I don't know! It was robotic! He told me—told me who she was." His eyes latched onto Wren. "Told me that you'd be at that house this morning. That you would be on that road."

Honey swore. "He gave you the missing vic's address?"

"I..." Adam glanced at them all. A frantic sweep of his eyes. Then he shook his head. "I don't know what's happening! I was told the Sweetheart Slasher's daughter was going to be there—that she'd be in the black Jeep. I waited, and when she came down that road, I-I...hit her." He blinked. Then repeated, softer, "I hit her. Because...she's evil." His gaze fell to the table.

"There's not a mean bone in this woman's body," Honey declared.

Oh, but Honey was wrong.

There is plenty of darkness in me.

"You're being used," Jake told him. "You're just another means of attacking Wren. Another way to make her suffer." Jake shoved from the table. He shot a disgusted glance at Adam. "He's a distraction. While we're with him, the killer we're really after is making his plans. He's got Makayla, and he could be kill—" He stopped.

Too late.

Wren kept her spine straight. "He could be killing my friend."

Adam shook his head. "I-I don't know what's happening!"

She would explain things. Nice and slowly. "A woman is missing. Her name is Makayla Lane. She was taken last night by someone who seems to have been imitating my father." She didn't stumble over the word father. Not this time. "If you were told to be at that exact location today, told I was going to be there, then it's probably because the person who called you is the same individual who abducted Makayla."

"I don't know any Makayla!"

She believed him. "I don't think you do. But the killer knows you. He knew that you would come running to get your revenge on me." And the timeline wasn't adding up for her. If the killer had found out about Wren's identity through some sort of info on her phone...no, no, there wouldn't have been time to locate Adam. The killer must have known about him *before.* "Have you talked recently to anyone about the Sweetheart Slasher? Or about your sister?"

"Yeah." Slow. "Yeah, I posted in one of those online chats a few weeks ago. A true crime chat. It's for the families of vics."

"We're gonna need to know what specific chat," Honey insisted. "And we're gonna need full access to your phone, *now.*"

Some of the fury had faded from Adam's eyes. "There's really a woman missing out there? Like, like my sister was missing?"

"Yeah, asshole, there is." No sympathy from Honey. "And you're gonna help us find her. So cooperate, got me? Cooperate fully. Right the hell now."

* * *

THIS WAS A FUCKING SHITSHOW.

Tom had managed to get back in the house long enough to grab clothes. The place was a crime scene. And gawkers and reporters were everywhere. People were watching every single move he made.

He'd gotten changed out of the pajamas. Some deputy had said the pajamas were evidence. Tom had switched into khakis and a dress shirt and actual shoes. He'd snagged his phone and called his father. The old man had freaked. Said this was going to be horrible publicity for the family and the business.

Like Tom gave a shit about the publicity. He wanted Makayla back. Makayla and her sweet smile and her soft touches and the way she could just make him feel *good* when he was near her.

He'd slept while she'd been taken.

Slept.

How much of a failure could he be?

His phone rang just when he was preparing to march back up to one of the deputies. He didn't recognize the number, and he started to ignore the damn thing but...

Sudden instinct had him shoving the phone to his ear. "Hello?"

"Tom?" So faint. So soft.

His Makayla.

"Makayla." He started motioning toward the deputy. The woman wasn't looking his way. "Baby, are you okay? There was blood, and I've been so worried!" He bounded toward the deputy.

"Tom, I need you to help me."

"Anything!" He was almost to the deputy. She'd turned her back on him while she talked to some of the gawkers.

"You have to bring Wren to him."

He froze.

"If you d-don't, he's going to kill me." Fear broke in her voice.

"I'm getting the deputy—"

"*Don't tell anyone.*" Tears made the words barely understandable. "He's...hurting me. Tom, *please! Please!*"

He could not move a muscle.

The deputy turned around. She frowned at him.

"Please," Makayla rasped in his ear.

"Yes, Dad," Tom said, very clearly. Did his voice sound funny? Too sharp? He cleared his throat. "I'm still at the scene. They don't have answers. They don't know where Makayla is." He nodded to the deputy, then spun on his heel. He wanted to race away from the deputy and the people who'd been staring with wide eyes at him and the whole scene. Instead, he forced himself to move slowly. One step at a time.

"You have to bring him Wren," she said, the tears still clogging her voice. "If you don't, he...he said he will cut off more than just my finger. It's her or me, and, God, Tom, *please don't let me die!*"

"I won't."

"You love me, don't you, Tom? *Please, please...don't let me die.*"

Chapter Eighteen

"I DON'T LIKE TELLING ANYONE THEIR BUSINESS BUT...
this isn't a safe house." Hunter crossed his arms over his
chest. "It's a bar."

Jake flipped off the other guy. He damn well knew
where they were. Not like he was thrilled about the
situation, either. But after the scene at the station, Wren
had refused to go to the safe house.

And, honestly, he didn't exactly blame her. He was
chomping at the bit because he wanted to go on the attack.
So when he'd gotten the text from Eb, asking to meet at
Milo's bar, he'd switched gears. "Eb is coming here." His
twin should be arriving any moment. If the tricky bastard
wasn't already lurking around somewhere. "Since you two
have been in close contact, figured you would already know
that. Can't believe your new bestie didn't text you."

Hunter shook his head. "Haven't talked to your brother
today. Been kind of busy stopping you from committing
murder in the street. You know, as one does. I've just been
busy, busy, busy."

Jake grunted. He was not apologizing for the attack in

the street. That prick had deserved to get the hell beaten out of him.

"Those knuckles of yours look a little bruised," Hunter noted. "Did you hurt them when you slammed them into the guy's face over and over again?"

"He hit Wren. With a fucking truck." Then the jerk had punched her with his fist. The man was lucky to still be breathing. Come to think of it, if Hunter hadn't been there, maybe the jerk wouldn't be breathing.

Dead men can't answer questions. Honey had been right on that score. Though, so far, they hadn't turned up a whole lot of useful intel from Adam Rule yet.

"That truck will live on in my nightmares." A chair leg screeched as Wren pulled the chair back and then sat down near a small table. The bar had been dark when they first arrived, but now illumination flooded through the building. The place didn't open until seven on a normal night. This was hardly a normal night.

She pushed back her hair. The sight of the bruise on her jaw enraged Jake.

"Do you still think this is all about you, Jake?" Wren asked. "Because it sure seems heavily centered on my past."

He parted his lips to respond.

Then his twin sauntered out of the back office. Figured that he'd snuck in the back door. Typical Eb. Locks never kept him out.

"Oh, it's definitely about us," Eb assured her. "This time, we're not just being narcissistic assholes. The attacks are because of what we've done."

Wren's head turned toward him. A wide smile curled her lips as she jumped to her feet. "Eb!" The weariness that had been on her features moments before had vanished.

A matching smile stretched across his brother's face.

And then Eb rushed to Wren. Hauled her against him and hugged her tightly.

"Aw, man." Hunter sidled close to Jake. They stood beside the long bar. "If you could see your expression right now." He released a soundless whistle. "Settle down. I am not in the mood to stop you from killing again. Once a day is gonna be my limit."

Not like he'd ever kill his brother. But Eb could stop hugging Wren any minute. Any. Minute.

"Jealousy issues, check. You have them."

How much longer was the hug going to continue? Jake took a step forward.

Eb finally let Wren go, but just so his hand could rise up and curl under her chin. His eyes narrowed, and then he launched a look of fury Jake's way. "I told you to *protect* her," Eb fumed. "Why in the hell is she bruised? You had one job, man. Like...one. 'Protect Wren.' Easy. Done. Finished."

Jake took another step away from the bar. A bigger, close-to-lunging step. "Easy? She had two attackers trying to abduct her on night one! I'd barely arrived in town when I had to jump in to get them the hell away from her!"

"Okay, you're gonna kick his ass." Hunter plopped down on one of the barstools. "Check. Have at it. Told you, once a day is my limit. You will get no interference from me."

"Easy?" Jake almost choked on the word as he repeated it yet again. "Let me make sure you understand the full picture here. After I saved her on the beach and we went to her uncle's house the next day, a prick was lying in wait for her there. I killed him." Jake marched toward his brother. "*Easy?*" Oh, but that one word pissed him off. "A fucking truck came at us today in an ambush. Did you hear that? A truck."

Eb stormed right at him, too. "Yeah, I said *easy*. It's Wren. Just eliminate the bastards after her and save the day. Done."

Jake threw a hand in Hunter's direction. "The dumbass backup you sent wouldn't let me kill him!"

"Well, damn." From Hunter. "When you're both glaring, I truly can't tell you apart. Hey, Wren? If we spun them around in circles, would *you* be able to tell which one is the evil twin and which one is the good one with just a glance?" Mocking words.

"Yes." From Wren. Simple. Truthful. "I can always tell them apart. But *neither* twin is evil."

She was so wrong on that score. The truth was that they were both evil, and they both knew that fact. But time to get down to the one thing that mattered... "Who is after Wren?" Jake gritted out.

Eb's jaw tightened even more. "Considering that you and I eliminated a lot of very bad people over the years, our suspect list tends to be a bit long," Eb threw back. "But I'm narrowing down our possible choices. Slowly but surely. Figured it has to be someone we took out together."

They had taken out some real bastards in their time. Drug runners. Human traffickers. Domestic terrorists. One particular creep had been a cult leader. He'd been intent on getting all of his followers to obey his commands—and kill themselves. Jake and Eb had stopped him just before he served up poisonous drinks to everyone, including the kids.

Eb glanced toward Hunter. "Thanks for covering my brother and Wren until I could arrive in town."

"You were busy with an undercover operation." A

casual roll of one shoulder. "I was bored. Declan and Marley insisted I take a holiday. Screw that. Not like I wanted a typical vacation, anyway." He slumped casually against the stool. "Don't know how up to speed you are on current events, though. Someone want to give him the quick and dirty version? Or should I do the job?"

"My father was a serial killer." Wren lifted her bruised chin. "Someone found out my secret and has been blasting it everywhere."

Eb blinked. Then winced. "Yeah, sorry, baby."

Jake's shoulders stiffened. "Sorry? That's all you've got?" He'd certainly expected more.

"Oh, what? Was I supposed to be more dramatic? Can't be. I've known that news for a very long time." Eb reached out to touch her shoulder.

"Wait, you *knew*?" Wren's shock was clear. She batted Eb's hand away before he could touch her. "*For a very long time?*"

Jake felt the same shock pouring through his body. "Why the hell didn't you say something? Why didn't you tell me?" What the actual hell?

Now Eb frowned at him. "Uh, maybe because it wasn't my secret to share? Maybe because I didn't know how you would react, bro? Maybe because you usually growl when I bring up Wren's name in any way, and I didn't want to say or do anything that would make you turn into an even moodier SOB where she was concerned."

Jake drew back his fist for the punch.

"Jake." Wren shook her head. "Don't."

But he wanted to deck his brother. Too much rage and adrenaline and, fine, *fear* still poured through his veins. The aftershocks of that wreck, of nearly *losing* Wren, had pushed him to the edge—and then right over. If Hunter hadn't been on the street, Jake knew he very well might have killed Adam Rule.

No one hurts Wren in this world.

She put her hand on his chest.

"You thought I couldn't accept Wren's past?" Jake knew his voice sounded funny. Too hard. Too flat. Too guttural. "Wrong, jackass. I will accept every part of her, always." He stared into her eyes. Those beautiful, dark eyes. Eyes he loved. The woman he loved.

"Uh, yeah." Eb cleared his throat. "Let me clarify here. I didn't worry about you accepting her. Not a concern at all. I worried about you losing your absolute mind. When it comes to Wren, rational behavior is not your friend."

He should look away from Wren. Tell his brother to screw off. He didn't. He kept right on staring at what mattered. Wren.

"Case in point," Eb sighed. He edged closer. Poked Jake in the side. "I didn't tell you because you would have gone out and tried to hunt down her father."

Yes. Definitely.

"You would have wanted to kill him."

Where was the problem with that? Jake didn't see one.

"And it wasn't my secret to share," Eb repeated.

Wren's head turned toward him.

Without those deep, soul-stealing eyes holding him in place, Jake blinked.

"How did you find out the truth?" Wren asked.

"Milo never stopped looking for the Sweetheart Slasher. One day, I might have...interrupted a private call between him and some of his federal buddies. By interrupted, I mean I was somewhere I shouldn't have been. Eavesdropping my diabolical heart out." A shrug. "I just got bits and pieces from that conversation, but I'm a bulldog. I started digging. This was very close in time to our sister Marley's attack."

Wren backed away from Jake and Eb. Immediately.

"Yep." Eb nodded.

Hunter just watched them all silently.

"That was what happened." Eb pointed at Wren. "You and Marley had always been friends. Granted, you were closer to me and Eb, but I know you've always adored Marley."

"Marley is great," Wren mumbled as she shoved back a heavy lock of hair. "Everyone adores her."

"Especially Declan." Hunter cocked his head as he added that tidbit about the billionaire. "She's his obsession." He paused. "Probably his sanity, too. Obsession and sanity. They balance each other out, so there's that."

Once upon a time, Jake might have laughed at those words. The idea that a woman could be both a man's obsession and his sanity? Ridiculous.

But, uh, yes...*true*.

His gaze swept over Wren.

Yes. She is my obsession and my link to sanity.

Because if anything happened to Wren, his control would be annihilated. His sanity would be next. And the bloodshed that he would leave in his wake as he utterly destroyed the fools who had taken her? Who had hurt her? Oh, it would be terrifying. Devastating.

"You cared about Marley, you hated what had happened to her, but you were afraid to go around her after Marley's attack. Got me to wondering *why*." Eb tapped his chin as he continued to study Wren. "You aren't the type to abandon a friend in need. I mean, sure you showed up for her. You always show up. But you were so hesitant. So careful. Not at all your normal self. I was gonna talk to Milo about it, and that's when I happened to hear something I shouldn't." His eyebrows pulled low. "What did you think? That if Marley found out the truth, she wouldn't want you near her?"

"The truth." Wren pressed her lips together. "Yes." A nod. "Yes, I thought that Marley had been attacked by a serial killer. She had to face evil up close and personally. And there I was, pretending to be her friend, when the truth is that I'm probably just as twisted on the inside as her attacker ever was."

"Bullshit." An immediate response from Jake.

Everyone looked at him. Good. Wren's head had snapped toward him the fastest.

Now that he had everyone's attention, Jake said it again, "Bullshit." He reached for her hand. Brought it to his mouth. Kissed her knuckles. "There is nothing twisted about you. You're the best thing in my world. You are not your father, Wren."

"I was there. I *was there*. I don't have wings." She blinked quickly to get rid of the tears that filled her eyes.

"You do to me. You're my angel, and you always have been." He used his grip on her hand to tug her closer. "The guardian angel who saved me when I was sixteen." His head lowered, and his lips brushed over hers.

"*Ahem.*"

Eb seemed to be choking. Someone should probably help him. Maybe Hunter would step in for the job. He could slap Eb on the back. Or just deck him. Jake let the kiss with Wren linger.

Until she pressed lightly against his chest. "Jake?" Her mouth pulled from his. Her eyes searched his.

"*Ahem.*"

From Eb again.

Jake turned his head. His gaze met Eb's.

A deep furrow cut between Eb's brows.

Hunter's sigh drifted across the bar. "This would be why I said someone needed to give the man a quick and dirty rundown of events. Let me help out?"

Eb's furrow deepened. "Did you just kiss Wren?"

Damn straight, he had.

"Yep. I'll help out," Hunter declared to no one and everyone. "Get the focus on the big events. Ready? Here we go. Wren's friend Makayla was abducted last night. The scene at her house was set to make it look like a copycat of the Sweetheart Slasher's attacks." Hunter rose and headed closer to them. "After leaving the scene of the abduction, Wren and Jake were ambushed. This would be where I utterly failed in my backup duties, by the way. Sorry about that. Didn't exactly expect a truck to come barreling at them. Hard to plan for that particular scenario."

Eb blinked. "A truck?" Then he motioned between Jake and Wren. "What is this? This kiss?"

"You have focusing problems," Hunter told him. "Let's stay on the truck. The perp driving it seems to be a family member who lost his sister to the Sweetheart Slasher." Hunter thrust back his shoulders. "Declan said someone was spreading the truth about Wren online. Obviously, that person was digging up her past as a means of wrecking her current life. The homicidal driver today, he was another means to that end. He had so much anger and hate boiling in him. All you had to do was point him in the right direction." His gaze landed on Wren. "Her direction." His mouth tightened. "Now he's in jail, we're here, and how about you tell us exactly who is at the top of your suspect list, huh, Eb? Drop the leaving-us-in-suspense routine. Because I like to know what sort of threats I'm facing, so that, you know, things like barreling trucks don't catch me by surprise. I hate surprises. Personality quirk."

"I do *not* remember you being this chatty before," Eb muttered.

"What can I say? Danger makes me talkative. It also pisses me off. Or maybe I'm still bitter about the surprises."

"Yeah, well, I hate them, too," Eb agreed. The furrow remained. "Who was the truck driver?"

"Adam Rule," Wren replied to Eb. "His sister Carrie—she was, um, the last known victim of the Sweetheart Slasher."

"And I think the bastard playing this game with us knew Wren's secrets for a while. He had all of this set up. This is no discovery that just happened." Jake was certain of this. "He's trying to destroy her life completely."

"He's trying to destroy me because of what my father did!" Wren's face flushed. "Again, going back to this being all about me, not you two—"

"Wren, I got emails with your pictures. Texts saying I would pay. That Jake would pay." Eb's voice was uncharacteristically grim as he cut through her words. "They came in via a secure system. Tracing them is almost impossible, even with tech master Declan Flynn helping me out. Hell, the only thing we've been able to discover so far is that the messages did come from this area. They bounced all over the world, but Declan has finally narrowed down the source. And the source? The texts? He swears they came from a computer in *this* bar. Or somewhere within a hundred-foot radius of the bar. But seeing as how plenty of people pour in and out of here each day, it's not exactly the smoking gun that we need."

Wren's lashes fluttered. "You've been specifically *told* I'm being used to make you pay?"

"Yes," he confessed. An exhale. "There was more, actually." He darted a glance toward Jake. "Don't flip out, okay?"

"Can't promise that." Wouldn't promise it.

"There was more included in the messages I received. Only, I was in the middle of a damn firefight with a small sect of terrorists in a country I cannot name. A CIA operation that was going south faster than you can blink."

She blinked. Jake thought she'd blinked pretty fast.

Jake also thought that if his brother didn't spit out the rest of this story immediately, he would be flipping out.

"I was told that Jake and I had destroyed this person's entire world. And because of that, your world would be destroyed, Wren. You'd lose all your friends."

She inched back a step from Jake.

"You'd lose your business."

Another little step.

"Then you'd lose your life."

"*Not happening*," Jake vowed.

"Yeah, well, that would be the reason I told you to haul ass here and *protect Wren*." Eb blew out another long breath. "Because we destroyed this person's world, this jackass intends to destroy *our* world."

"I'm not your world!" Wren exploded. "This is *my* life! What happens to me doesn't change *your* world!"

"Are you shitting me right now?" Eb squinted at her. "I love you."

His brother always said those damn words so easily and—

"So does Jake," Eb revealed. Ever so casually. Like he'd just said the sky was blue. Something everyone should know. "Only I love you like the incredible friend you've always been to me. Jake loves you like the insane obsession that you are to him."

Wren's mouth dropped open.

"Tact," Hunter mumbled, "you should have more of it. And here I mistakenly thought you were the charming twin."

"No time for charm." Eb's focus didn't leave her face. "You're being used against us, Wren. It's bullshit and it's not fair, but it's happening. Jake and I have wrecked a lot of lives. The people we hunted were criminals. Not talking about some jaywalker on the street. They were sadistic, powerful, and far too dangerous. These people often had networks that stretched wider than you can imagine. Eliminating all their ties can be impossible. Tracking down all the loose ends is like searching for the old needle in the haystack. But that's what we are currently doing. Searching for that needle. Declan is helping. Milo's Fed contacts are helping. The CIA personnel who owe me are helping."

Wren had been retreating, but now she surged toward Jake. She grabbed his arms. "It's not true." She searched his gaze.

"Oh, it's true," Eb rolled right on. "And we know the hunter right now has to be someone who was close to one of the individuals we eliminated. A friend, a family member, a lover. You don't go to these great, dramatic vengeance lengths unless there is a powerful, emotional attachment."

"You don't love me," Wren told Jake.

His back teeth ground together.

"You...want me," she added.

"Uh, I'm trying to talk about the sadistic killers who we've got on the suspect list," Eb interrupted. "Are you listening to me?"

"You don't love me," she said again to Jake. "It's okay. I don't expect you to love me."

"Why the fuck not?" Jake demanded.

Her eyes widened.

Yeah, his brother had finally shut his mouth. Time for Jake to do some talking. "You're the most lovable damn woman I've ever met."

Her mouth opened. Closed.

"And, hell, yes, I *love* you." There. Done. Said. And it felt so good to say it. But he jerked his gaze off Wren and glared at his brother. "How the hell did you know?"

"That would go back to the part I said before...when it comes to Wren, rational behavior is not your friend. If she so much as stubbed her toe back in high school, you tended to go batshit. So, yep, I get that everything happening now must have you on the verge of exploding."

Understatement. His stare slid back to Wren.

"You...love me?" Wren asked. The words were as dazed as her expression.

This was not a conversation he wanted to have with Eb and Hunter staring at them. "Wren..."

A hard, desperate pounding shook the front doors of the bar. His head whipped toward the booming sound. He'd locked those doors after they'd arrived. He'd also thoroughly searched the place and locked the back doors.

But Eb had managed to get in, no problem.

"That doesn't sound friendly," Hunter murmured.

Understatement.

Eb was already pulling out a gun.

The fierce pounding continued. Only it was followed by, "*Wren!*" A fierce yell. "Wren, it's Tom! Are you in there? Wren? Jake! Jacob Jones! Please, be in there! *Wren, I need you! I need you!*"

"What in the hell?" Jake began stalking for the front doors. Wren followed right behind him. So did an armed Eb. And Hunter.

The door shook again.

"He's pounding even harder than you did when you showed your happy ass up at my place," Jake said to Hunter.

One of the doors groaned. Trembled.

"That man is not knocking." Hunter was definite. "Sounds more like he's ramming the door with something? What in the hell is he doing, plowing his shoulder into the door?"

Jake opened one of the two big, entrance doors. Tom rushed inside. He'd been running, and, yes, apparently banging his shoulder into the door in a wild bid to knock the heavy door open. Without the door in position any longer, he shot forward, stumbled, and fell onto the floor.

"Tom Hadden?" Eb frowned down at him. "You look like shit."

Tom tossed back his head and glared at Eb. Then he rose to his feet. His hair jutted at odd angles, as if he'd been pulling at it. Lines cut across his face, and his eyes were lined with shadows. "Tell me how you look after someone takes the woman *you* love." His breath heaved. Then he pointed at Jake. "You."

"Me...what?" Jake peered outside of the bar. Saw no one. It *appeared* as if Tom had come alone. He shut the door. Bolted it.

"You specialize in hostage rescue. You pull people out of hellholes." His hand shot through his hair. That hair jutted out even more. "I need you. You have to get my Makayla back."

Jake exchanged a long look with Eb. Then he focused

on a practically vibrating Tom. "That's the goal we all want."

"Yeah, well, it's more than a goal for me. *It's a necessity.*" A ragged exhale. "And I know where she is. Only I don't know how to get her free. That's where you come in." His shoulders squared with intent. "I will pay you any amount of money, but you have to go now. You have to get my Makayla out of hell. *You have to save her.*"

Chapter Nineteen

Jake loved her. Eb had known about Wren's past for a long time. And Tom knew where Makayla was being held. The shocks just freaking kept coming.

Wren sucked in a deep breath. *Focus.* Her friend—Makayla was alive. They could save her. They could stop this nightmare. Makayla wouldn't wind up like the others. She would make it home.

She had to make it home.

She's not like the other victims. Not another vic that will never come home because of the Sweetheart Slasher.

"You need to call Honey," Jake said to Tom, his voice adamant. "Get her and the deputies, and we will storm the place where Makayla is being held."

"No!" Almost a scream from Tom. His fingers were shaking. Correction, his whole body seemed to be shaking. "You don't get it! The caller said—said if he saw any cops or deputies or any of that type of shit, then Makayla would be dead! Dead! I can't take the chance that they'll be spotted. I can't risk Makayla's life. *You* have to do it. You know you can. You do this thing for a living all the time! You sneak in, you get the victims, and you sneak out. Done. Dammit, done. *Please.*" His voice broke. "I am begging you here. Makayla is my world. I need you to get her out. I know where she is. I will tell you everything. You can save her. You can take down the bastard who took her. *You can do it all!*"

"Slow down," Hunter advised him. His stare was hooded as it swept over Tom. "Take some breaths. You look like you're about to pass out. What did you do, run all the way to the bar?"

"I searched all over freaking town for Jake and Wren! Couldn't spot his Jeep!"

"Yeah, that's because it was totaled. Again, you need to take some deep, calming breaths."

"Fuck breaths! My fiancée is going to die if we don't act!"

Wren's heartbeat drummed in her ears. "Did you...did you find her finger?"

"*What the fuck?*" Tom blanched. "What kind of person asks questions like that?"

The daughter of a serial killer.

Obviously, Honey had not yet told Tom to expect that particular calling card.

"I got a phone call. *A phone call.* The voice was—" Tom stopped. Shuddered.

"Robotic?" Jake asked softly.

Tom's eyes narrowed. "Y-yes."

Jake nodded.

"I heard Makayla, though. I *talked* to her. She's alive. I know where she is. And you can get her out. The voice...h-he gave me the address, but I'm not freaking superman. If I rush in, we're both dead. I know it. *I know it.* I heard some of those people talking at Makayla's house." His gaze darted to Wren, then wrenched away, as if he couldn't stand to look at her too long. "Those true-crime freaks who showed up out of nowhere. They said that her dad—he took couples. Killed them both. Lured one out to be with the other. I get that this is a game. A twisted-ass game. If I go rushing in, then Makayla and I will both die. *Makayla can't die.*" He surged forward and grabbed the front of Jake's shirt. His hands fisted in the material. "I will pay you. Just like your other damn clients! I'll *pay anything!* Just go and get my Makayla. Save her. I am begging you."

* * *

"I don't like this," Eb said, his voice carrying just to Jake's ears. They were still in the bar, but Jake wasn't going to be there for long.

He had a hostage to save. A killer to take down. A nightmare to stop.

"I need to go with you," Eb added.

Oh, hell, no. Jake secured his gun. He'd strapped a knife to his left ankle. The gun he'd just secured went into the holster that he'd pulled over his shoulder. The handy thing about Milo's bar? In the rear of the bar, nestled in a private room, Milo kept a secret safe well stocked with a variety of the best weapons money could buy.

Legal and illegal weapons. Jake was helping himself to the all-you-can-take-buffet. He put another holster on his right ankle. Tucked a small gun inside it before lowering the leg of his jeans.

"Jake, I'm the best backup for you, and you know it."

True. There was no one he trusted to have his back more than his twin. And since Eb was the best, he stared him in the eyes and simply said, "Protect Wren."

"Fuck."

"I can't walk out of this bar without knowing she has the best guard by her side. You have to stay. I'll take that prick Hunter with me. He's good in a fight." They both knew exactly what dark violence waited in Hunter's past.

"Hunter isn't me."

"No, but he'll do. We'll go in, eliminate the threat, and bring the bride home." Done. And by eliminate the threat, yes, Jake meant permanently. He intended to take out the mastermind behind this plan. "Two men tried to take Wren the first night on the beach. I never saw the guy Wren spotted behind me."

"And the other attacker is on the slab in the tiny morgue in town, check. Understood. Exactly where he should be."

Jake grunted. He grabbed one of the bulletproof vests from the safe. Good old Uncle Milo. "Honey is running down all of the dead guy's contacts and aliases. She's already had fingerprint hits on him. Looks like he is some thug for hire. Name is Colin Miller. He did lots of B&Es, had a history of assaults. She told me at the station that she thought he was the type you hired when someone wasn't paying a debt." Info she'd revealed before the interrogation. *You want a message sent? Some pain delivered? Colin Miller was your guy.*

Only he would never be delivering any other messages.

"I get it." Eb knew the type, too. Clearly. "Hired muscle who follows orders but doesn't have any real power?"

"Yep. So that makes me wonder if his partner is also hired muscle or if he is the ringleader."

"Let's assume, for the moment, that he's hired muscle. He's one person. The leader is the second. Probably has more guys waiting in the wings because he's obviously a planner and he's coming after *us*." Eb quirked a brow. "We're not easy targets."

Nah. "Easy is boring."

"Damn straight." Eb sucked in the side of his cheek. "So basically, you could be walking in to face a full army. We have no idea how many people will be waiting for you. And you want me to just sit here with my thumb up my ass while you and Hunter go out to do the fighting."

Jake put the bulletproof vest on a nearby table and moved to stand directly in front of his brother. He looked straight into those identical eyes and ordered, "Protect Wren."

"Fuck," Eb said again as his shoulders slumped.

There were more things that needed to be said, but there wasn't a lot of time. Not while a woman's life hung in the balance.

Tom swore he had the exact location for Makayla, but the guy hadn't shared those specifics yet. He kept stalling on that part. Waiting to make sure Jake wasn't going to call in Honey and her deputies.

So far, he'd revealed that the abductor had contacted him. Said Tom had to trade himself if he wanted Makayla to go free. Even good old Tom realized that was bullshit. There would be no trade. There would just be death.

And that was why Tom searched so desperately for me. The guy hadn't possessed Jake's number. He'd driven to Jake's house, then to the bar...

Where he was ready to knock down a door in order to get to me and Wren.

"I thought you wanted Wren," Jake said. He should have held those words back. Definitely not the time for this talk. He got that. But... "I was gonna fight you for her, just so you know."

"Of course, I fucking wanted her." But then Eb jerked back when Jake lifted his hands. "Easy, bro. *Wanted*. Past tense. Wanted not want. As in, I was a horny teenager and she always smelled like vanilla and honey, and when she looked at me with those big, dark eyes of hers, I pretty much wanted to run out and slay dragons."

Don't kill your brother. Do not kill your brother.

"I used to think *you* hated her," Eb added.

Jake swallowed at that admission from Eb. "I could never hate Wren."

"Yeah, time and maturity made me realize that. Sometimes, when you want someone so much and you think you can't have the person, the rage and the need twist in you, don't they?"

"Thought you wanted Wren," he rasped again. "So I kept my hands off her. I was the good brother."

Eb snorted. "Try that shit again. If you kept your hands off her, it wasn't because of me. Cute try."

"I fucking love you, dumbass. I would never want to hurt you."

Eb grabbed his shoulder. Squeezed. "Stop saying nice things. You need to go out and kill someone so that the woman we *both* love gets to be safe *and* gets one of her best friends back." But he didn't release Jake. "You didn't want to hurt me because you're the good one."

Despite the situation, Jake laughed. "Bull. Everyone knows that you're the—"

"The one who lies with a smile?" A warm smile curved Eb's lips. The smile never reached his eyes. "The one who can fit in with a crowd and laugh and joke but still stay ice cold on the inside because all he's really doing is mimicking everyone else?"

Jake frowned.

"The one who got damn lucky because *you* are his brother, and you accept me and all my twisted parts, and you were even willing to sacrifice your own chance at happiness...to stay in the shadows because you were seriously afraid of hurting *me*?" A shake of Eb's head. "Let me tell you a few quick things. Because, though I love you to hell and back, you can occasionally miss out on social cues. Mimicking was never your strong suit. You just told the world to fuck off and went about your business. Always admired the hell out of you for that, by the way."

Eb admired him?

"Envied you, too, but that's a story for another day. When there is no ticking clock." Brisk now, Eb said, "I sent you to protect Wren because I knew you would. You always protect those in your life. You would sacrifice for those you love, and like I said, experience and maturity made me see that what I might have thought was hate—hate in the way you would never stand too close to Wren, the way you wouldn't be alone with her, the way you would watch her with such cold eyes...ah, brother, you were dying of love for the woman, but you didn't tell her. Maybe it was because you didn't think she'd love you back. You've always thought you were the dark one. The one who thrived too much on violence and danger, but, bro, you're the one who left the CIA. You're the one who became the hero and helped the people who were being forgotten. You make a living saving hostages. You're the one who rescues." A pause. "And Wren loves me like a friend, but *you* are the one who owns her heart."

Wren hadn't said she loved him. There had been no time. She'd just stared at him in shock and—

"Go save the day, hero. Then come back and claim the woman you love. You deserve to be happy, and so does she."

Jake opened his mouth to reply, but the door to the back room swung open.

"*Jake.*" Wren's voice. Her angry voice.

He spun toward her.

Hunter stood behind her, appearing vaguely sheepish as he peered over her shoulder. "There was no stopping her. She wanted to see you, so she's seeing you." But he sidled around Wren and went straight to the safe. "What is this bit of wonderment?" He started poking in the safe. "Oh, I want this." He took out a big, serrated knife. "And this." A Glock. "And I'll need one of those." He helped himself to a bulletproof vest. "I noticed the one on the table, so I figure if Jake got one, I get one, too, right?" He nodded toward the table where the other bulletproof vest waited.

"Right. You both get bulletproof vests." Wren strode toward Jake. Her glinting gaze shot fire at him. "The better to not get killed. And you are absolutely coming back without a scratch anywhere on you, understand me, Jacob Charles Jones?"

Uh, oh. She'd used his full name. Random fact? Jake's parents had been obsessed with *A Christmas Carol.* Especially his mom. Every year, one of his favorite traditions as a kid had been curling up with her while she read the holiday story to him. And every year, she'd cry and smile and tell him that God had blessed her because she had such a wonderful family.

He'd been named after Jacob Marley from *A Christmas Carol.* Technically, he'd split the character's name with his sister, Marley.

Eb? Well, that was short for Ebenezer.

But his mom hadn't just stopped with naming them after the characters...She'd been a huge fan of the author so...

Jacob Charles Jones. His middle name had come from the first name for the author of *A Christmas Carol.*

Eb, oh, poor Eb. He'd really gotten screwed. His full name was actually Ebenezer Dickens Jones.

A real dick, that was what Jake had often said about his brother.

And his mom had yelled at him every time he'd teased his twin.

I loved my mom so much. She made every holiday special. She made everything in the house better. Then, when we lost her, things in my life went dark.

Wren poked him in the chest. "Not a scratch, understand me?"

He'd been at his darkest when Wren had stopped him from getting hit by that truck at just sixteen. Something he'd never told her...or anyone...not even Eb...Something he'd denied over and over, even, sometimes, to himself, but...

I saw that truck coming.

That one moment when Wren grabbed him—that moment had changed everything. Every single thing. "I might get scratched." Full disclosure so she would not be surprised. "But I'll come back. There is nothing in this world that will stop me from coming back to the woman I love."

Her lower lip trembled. "You are an asshole."

Eb shoved at Hunter. "Stop digging in the safe. Can't you see this is a romantic moment? Come on. Let's give them some privacy." He nudged Hunter toward the door.

"Makayla!"

Only Tom was in the doorway, blocking their exit. Frantic, desperate Tom. "You have to get Makayla! There is no time to waste!"

No, there wasn't time. Not enough time to tell Wren all

the things he wanted to say to her. Or, at least, there wasn't time now. There would be, after.

You are an angel. My angel. So what if you don't have wings? You saved me that long ago day. Saved me when I was lost because I couldn't handle the grief that came from losing my mom. Everyone else seemed to be able to keep going. Eb and Marley—they didn't give in to the dark. Even my father adjusted. But I couldn't. And then, there was you.

The sunshine in his darkness.

"I'll be back, Wren." It was a vow. "And I'll bring Makayla. The threat to you will be eliminated, and you will have your life back. Your business. Everything will be protected."

She shot onto her toes. Grabbed the nape of his neck and hauled him toward her. Wren's lips planted against his in a hard, desperate kiss. She kissed him with passion and hunger. Need and—

Love?

Wren pulled away. Glared. "Fuck the business," she said bluntly.

"Dirty mouth," Eb chided. "What would Uncle Milo say?"

"Fuck the business," Wren repeated. "And I don't want the same life back. I want a new one, with you. So don't you dare get hurt. You come back, and we start again. Got me?"

I will have you forever.

There would be more time, later. Time to tell her all of his secrets. Time to confess that he'd been watching over her for far too long. Needing her, for far too long.

But he had a job to do. An enemy to eliminate.

His fingers brushed carefully along her bruised jaw. He hated that bruise. "I've got you," he said. Finally, he had her. He didn't intend to ever let go.

"I'll protect her," Eb swore. "Count on me."

"No!" A sharp cry from Tom. He pointed to Eb, then Jake. "You both have to go! Makayla needs you!"

"I'm going with Jake," Hunter explained. "He'll have backup. Don't worry about that score."

But Tom's eyes widened with terror. "He needs *more!* Eb, you have to go, too! You know Makayla! You know how sweet and innocent she is and—*the guy said he would cut her up! Would kill her!* You both have to go!" He hurried to stand in front of Wren. "I'll stay with her. I swear, I won't leave Wren's side. I will stay with her every moment."

Yeah, no. Not happening. "No offense, Tom," Jake told him though he didn't actually care if Tom did take offense, "but I want my brother protecting Wren."

"You don't trust me?" Tom's seemed stunned.

"It's not about trust. It's about the fact that I know Eb would die to keep Wren safe."

Tom blinked, owlishly.

"I would," Eb agreed with a nod. "Though I prefer to kill in order to get the job done. Not to die. Dying is not the thing, you know?"

A tremor shook Tom's body. "You're both crazy." He scampered away, frantic steps. His shoulder rammed into the side of the large safe. His head whipped from one person to the next to the next. "You're *all* crazy."

"We're the crazy ones who will get your bride-to-be back," Jake pointed out. Really, was hurling insults the way to handle the situation? Tom was not making friends. But then again, he'd been a prick back in high school, too. "Now give us the address."

"I-I don't have it...yet. Not exactly, anyway."

"What?" That had not been what the man said before.

Jake was sure as hell not in the mood for games. Or deception.

Tom shoved his hand into his pocket. "I was just told to get over toward St. George Road. I'm being given directions, piece by piece. That's what the caller told me. Said to be ready. Th-the first direction just came to me. My phone just dinged." He hauled the phone from his pocket. "That's why I rushed back here to get you. You need to go, now. A new direction is supposed to come in approximately every five minutes from here on out. You have to follow every direction. *Hurry!* You have to get over to St. George and be ready for what happens next! Hurry!"

Jake stalked toward him. He swiped the phone from Tom. "You stay at this bar with Eb and Wren, understand?"

"I just want Makayla back," Tom whispered. "That's all."

"And I'll get her back." Though he wasn't gonna say the task would be easy. "For the last time, let's call Honey. It's what we need to do."

"*No! Makayla will be dead if you bring in the authorities!*" Panic had Tom's voice breaking.

Grimly, Jake nodded. "Give me the password on your phone."

Tom did.

Jake studied the texts that Tom had already received. His head angled toward a watchful Wren. What would he be doing if she'd been taken? If she'd been the one to leave a bloody dress behind for him to find?

I would destroy anyone and everyone in my way as I fought to get to her.

He had to go back to Wren. Once more. He closed in on her.

"*We are wasting time!*" Tom choked out.

Jake pulled Wren into a tight hug. His mouth went to her ear. "Stay near Eb." Eb would protect her.

He eased back.

"You stay alive," she told him.

He planned to do just that. After all, he had far too much to keep living for.

A life with Wren waited.

* * *

"I'm walking him out," Eb announced. "Then I'm securing the bar. We'll stay here in this place until we hear back from Jake and Hunter."

Wren wrapped her arms around her stomach. She'd been through plenty of horrors in her life, but watching Jake walk away pretty much gutted her.

He loves me. He's heading straight into danger.

And I haven't gotten the chance to tell him that I love him, too.

Why hadn't she said those words? So what if they'd had an audience? She'd wanted to shout the truth to the world.

But...

He was gone.

She hadn't said the words. And she was so terribly, horribly afraid.

"Is he gonna bring her back?" Tom's voice. Low. Scared.

Her gaze darted to him. He stood right beside the large safe, looking too pale. When his arms moved a bit, she saw the deep imprints of sweat in his pits. Sweat also beaded his brow.

"If anyone can bring her back, it will be Jake." *I should have said I loved him.* Why hadn't she? *Why?*

Because my father drummed it into me that love isn't

real. That in the end, people will betray the ones they swear to love. That we can only protect ourselves in this world. Love is a lie.

Love is a lie.

So when Jake had confessed, she hadn't responded because she was still trapped in the hell her father had made. "No more."

"What?" Tom asked.

She hurried for the door. She had to get to Jake and tell him. She couldn't—wouldn't—be afraid any longer. Her hand grabbed for the door handle and Wren wrenched it open.

A tall, broad-shouldered male stood there. Intense, topaz eyes. Thick, dark hair. A jaw made of granite and a face built for sin.

The wrong twin. She didn't need to look down at his clothes to know she was staring at Eb. She knew just by gazing into his eyes.

I've always been able to tell them apart just by how they look at me.

"I need to tell Jake something," Wren rushed to say.

"He's gone, Wren."

Her heart squeezed in her chest. She'd been too late.

I'll have the chance again. This isn't some ending. I'll be able to tell him how I feel. She would. *I will be able to tell him...*

I love you.

* * *

His Jeep had been totaled, so Jake headed for Hunter's SUV. His feet crunched over the gravel in the lot. He wanted to glance back at the bar, but he kept his focus forward. He had to stop thinking about Wren. Concentrate on the job.

She knows I love her.

And he intended to spend each day for the rest of his life proving that love to her.

Hunter hopped into the driver's seat. Jake took shotgun. They tossed their bulletproof vests into the backseat.

"Let me make sure I've got this mess right…" Hunter's index finger tapped against the steering wheel. "We're just going to blindly follow directions that are sent to us on that guy's phone? That's the plan?"

"No." One hundred times, no, they weren't doing that bullshit. As far as he was concerned, that was just some trick that the kidnapper had been using on Tom. Keeping him distracted and busy and chasing his own tail. Jake wasn't dealing with that BS. "*You're* going to get Declan Flynn on your phone right now. He's going to use that tech magic of his and all his shady connections—and he's going to trace the number that is sending the texts to Tom." Did it look like Jake was in the mood to blindly do any damn thing? This wasn't some freaking scavenger hunt. This was life or death. "We're going to get Declan to pinpoint the sender's address, and we will go in with guns blazing."

Hunter's lips curled in a slow smile. "I knew you were the twin I liked better. Knew it from the very first time we met."

Jake grunted. "Get your best friend on the phone."

Hunter got his best friend on the phone. And then they started tracking their prey.

Chapter Twenty

"WHY—WHY ARE THERE SO MANY WEAPONS IN THAT safe?" Tom's eyes were huge as his head craned, and he peered inside the cavernous space. Uncle Milo would never go for a small gun safe. The mere idea would insult him.

"Her Uncle Milo is a collector of weapons," Eb responded as he continued to block the doorway. "Everyone needs a hobby, am I right?" He smiled. One dimple winked. An exact copy of Jake's rare smile. "Don't worry, Tom, we're not stealing anything from Milo. We texted him. He gave us permission to borrow a few supplies—when he was giving us the safe combination."

Wren eased out a low breath. "I wish you'd gone with Jake," Wren told Eb.

Eb's jaw hardened. "The bar's entrance and exit have been secured. We'll stay here until we hear back from Jake." He sidled around her and headed for the open safe. Tom's neck was extended as he studied everything inside that he could spy. "Uh, excuse me?" Eb asked, voice pleasant.

Tom jumped as if a snake had just bitten him.

"I need to close this. Though, first, don't mind if I do..."

He pulled out a Glock. "The old standard. Jake took one. Only fair that I have one for myself. I'm sure Milo would want me to keep one close."

Tom shoved his hands behind his back and hurriedly retreated as he watched Eb load the weapon.

"Police love this gun," Eb explained to him. "I own several just like it." He studied the weapon. "Always gets the job done."

"Oh, God." Tom sat down, rather heavily, on a nearby, wooden chair. "Have you killed a lot of people?"

Eb kept staring at the gun. "Define 'a lot' for me, would you, Tom?"

"Oh, God."

"That's a pretty bad definition. Want to try again?"

* * *

DECLAN FLYNN DID NOT DISAPPOINT. By the time the perp sent the next set of directions to Tom's phone, Declan was on the line with Hunter giving an exact address for the SOB.

They rushed right to the location, cutting through roads and racing toward the low-end motel that waited just on the edge of town. There were only two cars in the lot. One was a top-of-the-line, gleaming white Benz that stuck out like a sore thumb. A convertible Benz.

The other was a beat-up work truck.

The convertible sat in front of room number seven. All the rooms were accessible from the outside. Bright red doors. Windows to the right of each door.

The work truck was in front of room thirteen.

Jake's gaze locked on the convertible. "I fucking know that car," he said. He reached for the door handle.

"Bulletproof vest!" Hunter snapped. He grabbed the vests from the backseat and shoved one at Jake. "We brought them for a reason! We don't know who the hell is waiting in there."

Actually, Jake thought that he did know…

* * *

THEY STALKED BACK into the main section of the bar. Wren found herself standing on the small dance floor. It had been just a few days ago when she'd been in practically that same spot with her friends. Jake had walked inside the bar, moving with that predatory grace of his as he cut through the other dancers. As soon as she'd seen him, she'd been unable to look away.

Then she'd kissed him. Again, practically in that same spot. One kiss that had completely changed her world. Because after that kiss, she'd fled. He'd followed. Saved her.

Kissed her again.

"Are you getting a drink?" Tom asked, the words holding a note of surprise.

She looked toward the long bar counter on the right. Eb stood behind it.

"This isn't for me." Eb held up a bottle of whiskey. "I thought you could use a glass, Tom. You're not exactly having the best day, you know?"

Tom almost tripped in his haste to get to that bar.

"A little liquid courage?" Eb mused. He put the bottle on the bar top. Grabbed a glass from beneath the counter and pushed it toward Tom.

With shaking fingers, Tom poured the glass full of the whiskey. He downed it all in one gulp. The glass clinked when he put it back down. "I needed that." His shoulders hunched as he leaned toward the bar. "I'll take whatever courage I can get."

* * *

"So, how are we gonna handle this?" Hunter glanced at room number seven and then at number thirteen. They'd slid the college kid at the front desk fifty bucks, and he'd confirmed these were the only two rooms with guests. He'd also provided them with descriptions of the occupants.

"I say we knock on the door." Jake stalked straight to room number seven. With zero hesitation, he lifted his foot and kicked in the door. The wood shattered. The door flew inward, and Jake charged over the threshold. "Knock, knock."

Jennifer Kent screamed as she leapt off the sagging bed. Her eyes were huge and horrified, and she clutched a phone in her hand.

Jake aimed his weapon at her. "Found you."

"*No!*" She stumbled backwards. Tripped. Fell on her ass. "Don't shoot me! Don't!'

"You have one loud-ass knock," Hunter noted as he ambled inside. He also had his gun up and ready. He frowned at Jennifer. "She's the mastermind? Her?"

"*I'm not! I'm not! I'm not the mastermind!*" Jennifer dropped the phone, put her hands up, and remained on the floor. "Tom just asked me to help him—he had these instructions that I was supposed to send to his phone. H-he told me what happened to Makayla. Said he needed my help to get her back, and I just—I felt so *guilty* that I had to help him."

Jake did not lower his gun. "Why do you feel guilty, Jennifer?'

Her head sagged forward. Her chin almost touched her chest. "Because Tom and I hooked up a few months ago. We were both drunk. At least, the first time, we were."

Was this BS for real?

"Makayla never found out or...I don't think she did." She bit her lower lip. "Now she's gone, and I'm a shitty friend, a super shitty maid of honor, and I just—I wanted to help get her back, okay? To make amends. Tom called me earlier. He...he asked me to come here and meet him. We, um, we met here when we hooked up..." The words trailed away miserably. "When I arrived, he told me what was happening. Asked me to send some texts. He said he had a plan to get her back." Her eyes lifted to the gun. "Don't shoot me."

A plan to get her back.

"Oh, I'm thinking Tom had a plan all right," Hunter mused.

Fuck. Yeah, the bastard sure did have a plan. The tricky sonofabitch. Jake whipped out his phone and called his brother.

* * *

"I love Makayla," Tom said with a determined bob of his dead. "I'd do anything for her." He released the glass. His hand fell back to his side. "*Anything.*"

A phone rang.

Wren jumped at the sound.

Eb tugged a phone from his back pocket. "It's Jake." His brows pulled low as he stared at the screen. His thumb swiped across—

"*I have to get her back!*" Tom suddenly yelled. He

244

lunged over the bar top and shoved something against Eb's chest.

Eb shuddered. Jolted. A guttural growl tore from him even as Wren screamed.

The phone fell from Eb's fingers.

And Tom kept shoving the taser in his hand right against Eb's shaking chest.

* * *

Eb answered on the second ring.

"Eb," Jake snarled before his brother could say a word. "Tom is lying to us, watch out for—"

A guttural growl—then a scream, Wren's scream—filled the line.

Jake's heart stopped beating.

A clatter. More yells.

Silence.

"Eb?" Jake said his brother's name even as fear curled around his heart. "*Eb, talk to me.*"

But Eb didn't talk to him. The line had gone dead. He immediately tried to call again, but the phone rang and rang.

"What is happening?" Hunter demanded. He stood right beside a crouching Jennifer.

Jake stared straight at her.

She shook her head. "I-I was just told to send the texts. To do it every five minutes. He said it would help—that we had to bring Makayla home, no matter what it took."

No matter what it took...

"The bastard is a dead man," Jake vowed. "Bring her," he told Hunter with a jerk of his weapon toward Jennifer. Then he whirled for the door.

* * *

WREN JUMPED on Tom's back with a shriek. She wrapped her arms around his neck and heaved back. The taser finally fell away from Eb's chest, but his eyes had closed, and he fell behind the bar.

Tom threw her off him. Wren hurtled and slammed into a table. It crashed beneath her, and she hit the floor.

Tom spun toward her. He still had the taser clutched in his hand.

Would the taser work again? She hadn't gotten a good look at the one in his grip. She couldn't be sure without knowing what type of taser it was.

She just knew that Tom was closing in.

"I don't like guns," he told her.

Her searching fingers grabbed a broken chunk of a table leg.

"I saw this inside the big safe. Grabbed it." He looked down at the taser. "I'm sure Eb will be okay."

"He just took a ton of voltage *to the chest*. You aren't sure of anything!" She staggered to her feet. Gripped the table leg like a baseball bat. "Why are you doing this?"

"Because I have to get Makayla back." He sucked in a deep, heaving breath. "It's you or it's her, Wren."

"What?" Was Eb okay? *Please be okay, Eb.*

"I got a phone call. That part of my story was true. I heard her. My sweet Makayla. She can come home." He took a lurching step toward her. "But only if I trade you."

Wren shook her head.

A phone was ringing behind the bar. Eb's phone? Her own phone was still in Honey's custody.

"I have to trade you. She's not the one he wants. This is about you. You...you're evil, Wren."

No, no. "Stay the hell away from me."

But he took another step toward her. "I heard all the people talking about your father at Makayla's house. All the things he did. All the things you had to see. My Makayla—she's never hurt *anyone*. But can you say the same?"

"I am going to hurt the hell out of you if you take one more step toward me." Because who had taught her how to swing a bat so long ago? Eb and Jake. They'd played varsity baseball. She'd gone to their games. Watched as they hit home runs. Eb had teasingly shown her how to make a quick hit one night after a big win. Then Jake had painstakingly gone through the process with her again because he'd said what Eb had shown her had just been bullshit.

She gripped that table leg and got ready for a home run swing.

Tom kept clutching the taser. "I love her. Don't...don't you love her, too? Isn't she your best friend?"

"Yes, she's my friend, and I—"

"Trade for her," he said. Begged. "Prove that you care. Just take her place. You know that Jake will come for you. He'll save you. I have to save her. This is the only way I can do that."

Wren shook her head.

"I'm sorry," he told her. Then he lunged straight for her.

Wren screamed again. She swung the table leg, and it shattered against his shoulder when it made impact. Tom bellowed in pain, but didn't stop his advance. He shoved the taser at her, jamming it into her side, but it did nothing.

Wren had no weapon now, so she fought with her hands. Her feet. But she couldn't stop him. He threw down the taser, and his hands went around her neck. He drove her back with his hold, and they barreled into another table, then a wall and then...

He pinned her against the wall. Her hands clawed at his grip. Too tight. Too painful.

"I'm sorry, Wren," he said, and it sounded as if he meant those words. "But I choose her."

Chapter Twenty-One

Jake burst into the bar. "Wren!"

He could hear sirens in the distance. He and Hunter had called Honey on their way back to the bar. He'd hoped Honey and her team could get there before him, but when he'd pulled into the lot, it had been empty.

No cars at all.

Only...Tom's silver Lexus had been there earlier.

His gaze landed on the broken table. The shattered table legs. His breath heaved in and out. "Wren! Eb!"

A groan caught his attention. It came from behind the bar. Jake leapt over that bar and slammed down on the floor right beside his brother.

Another groan as Eb's eyes fluttered open. "J-Jake?"

"Where is Wren?" He heard Hunter's footsteps. They'd zip-tied Jennifer's hands and left her in the backseat of the SUV. He knew Hunter would be searching the bar. *Find Wren. Find Wren alive.* "Eb, where is our Wren?"

"I'm so...s-sorry..."

No. *No.*

* * *

HE CARRIED her up the stairs. He'd duct-taped her hands in front of her. Duct-taped her feet. Dumped her in the backseat of his car, and when she'd screamed—well, surprise, surprise, Tom had slapped duct tape over her mouth.

For someone who kept apologizing about what he was doing, Tom sure had zero hesitation when it came to kidnapping.

Her body bounced against his shoulder as he climbed the stairs. He grunted and swore but still got her up the familiar steps. She knew the steps all too well. Knew the house well. After all, it was her Uncle Milo's place. The place she'd lived in for her last two years of high school.

The yellow police tape flew in the wind when he tore it in half and lurched with her toward the back door. "I've got her!" Tom called out. He shifted a bit, left one arm locked around the back of her thighs as he kept her over his shoulder, and his other hand knocked against the closed door. "Let Makayla go! I brought Wren—"

The hinges groaned as the door opened. "Get inside." A low, snarling order. A man's voice. One she did not recognize.

Tom hurriedly rushed over the threshold, then he dropped Wren onto the floor. Her elbow rapped into the wood, and her ass hit hard. She shook her head, sending the hair flying out of her way so she could see just who it was that she faced.

Only as her gaze lifted, it collided with Makayla's. Makayla's stunned eyes as Makayla sat in a chair near Uncle Milo's kitchen table. Makayla's arms were behind her back. Her nightgown stained with blood.

"Makayla!" Tom held his arms out to her. "Baby, you're safe, let's go—"

The man stepped between Tom and Makayla. A few inches shorter than Tom. Maybe around five ten? Muscular build. Black hair. Hard eyes. A faint scar slashed over his left cheek while a spider tattoo crawled up the right side of his neck.

"Where do you think you're gonna go?" the man asked.

Tom didn't back away. "I brought Wren to you. You said it would be a trade. Wren for Makayla. You said—"

The man's hand moved in a flash. It flew up, and he sank a blade deep into Tom's chest. Behind the duct tape, a scream trapped in Wren's mouth.

Blood poured from the wound.

Tom glanced down at his own chest.

"I lied," the man with the spider tattoo said. He yanked the knife out of Tom's chest. Tom's hands slapped over his chest as he tried to stop the blood flow. Only the blood pumped right through his fingers. It soaked his shirt. Covered his chest. Tom fell onto the floor beside Wren.

Blood poured from him.

And Wren realized Makayla had just watched the entire scene, and she hadn't said a word. Makayla had not screamed in horror and fear.

But...but Makayla was smiling.

She was also rising from the chair. Wren had thought that Makayla's arms were tied behind her, but they weren't. They slid to Makayla's sides, and...

She still has all ten fingers.

"You lied, too, Tom," Makayla announced. She took the bloody knife from the stranger. Then she bent in front of Tom. Crouched between Tom and a bound Wren. Makayla shot a disgusted glance at Tom, then peered at Wren. "Do you know what he did?"

He'd done all sorts of shitty things so far. Makayla would need to be a whole lot more specific—

"He fucked that cunt Jennifer. That bitchy cunt with the bad, bottled hair. A woman who pretended she was my friend."

Not the big reveal Wren had expected.

Makayla put the knife to Tom's throat. "You said you loved me, but you fucked my friend."

His breath heaved. In...out...In...

So much blood.

"You lied to me," Makayla said. She pressed the knife against his throat a bit harder.

"I...l-love..."

"You love me?" Makayla asked him. She smiled at him. "Prove it. Die for me."

He blinked. His lips parted.

Makayla slit his throat. Pretty, sweet, bubbly Makayla *slit her fiancé's throat.*

* * *

"I'M NOT GOING in a damn ambulance!" Eb shoved away from the EMTs who were trying to force him onto a stretcher. "I'm finding Wren. *Now.*"

"Your heart needs to be examined," one of the EMTs stated as he stubbornly held his ground. A hard task in the face of Eb's glower, but Hayden Washington had always been up to the challenge of facing off against Eb, even in their high school days. "You said you blacked out."

"*Because I was fucking tased!*"

"Right near your heart!" Hayden fired back. "We need

to make sure you didn't suffer a cardiac incident, that you are stable, that you are—"

"Trust me, I am exceedingly *unstable* at the moment." His hands had fisted. "I'm going to find Tom Hadden, and I am going to kill the bastard. He'll be begging before I am done with him."

"*Ebenezer*," Honey snarled. "*You get your control back, and you get it now.*"

Jake didn't move. He didn't say a word. He was battling a rage that threatened to swallow him whole. Wren was gone. He didn't know where Tom had taken her. He didn't even know if Wren was still alive.

She has to be alive. The world wouldn't still be turning if Wren wasn't alive.

At least, his world wouldn't be. His world would stop.

"I've got an APB out for Tom and his car. Every deputy I have is on the hunt. We will find the man, understand?" Her glare bounced between Jake and Eb. "You two should have called me immediately. As soon as Tom appeared pounding at the bar." She waved away Hayden. "Eb's not going to the hospital because he's too freaking stubborn! I need to talk to the twins alone, *now*."

Hayden reluctantly backed away.

Eb and Jake moved closer to her in the bar.

Her glare grew hotter. "You left me out of this."

Jake didn't speak. He couldn't. Too much rage choked him.

"What did you think would happen? That you'd find the mastermind and kill him, so you didn't want to involve a sheriff who might stop you from going off the deep end?" Her low voice quaked with her anger. "What. The. Hell?"

Jake one hundred percent intended to find the mastermind and still kill him. Done deal. The only question was...how much pain would Jake administer before he sent the SOB to the devil?

"You can't pull this vigilante crap with me," she snapped.

They had. They were. They would. "When I find the bastard who has Wren, he's dead." Simple fact.

Her eyes widened. "Don't *say* shit like that to me." She whacked him on the back of the head.

Jake blinked at her. "Did you just hit—"

"A sheriff assaulted you," Eb agreed before Jake could even finish his question. "I saw it. With my own eyes."

"A woman who loves you idiots like a mother just tried to whack some sense into you. *Don't announce your intentions.* That's called premeditation." A long exhale as she looked anxiously around. "Feds made it to town about thirty minutes ago. They are gonna be putting their noses in where they don't belong. You can't screw up in front of them." The diamond studs at her ears winked as she turned her head to take in the scene again and to make sure the wrong people couldn't hear their conversation. "Don't leave evidence behind." Even lower. Just for their ears. "If it needs to go down as self-defense, make sure that is the way the scene reads, you got me? You hear what I'm telling you?"

Jake understood exactly what she was saying.

"I got a hit on a potential partner for the dead guy in the morgue," she added. "I was coming to tell you about that development when the world blew up in our faces. The guy in the morgue? Colin Miller? Turns out, he generally tends to work with a partner. A partner higher-up on the food chain. His buddy Vander Henley is a suspected hitman. Pay him the right price, and he'll eliminate your problems. Colin had been texting Vander.

He'd tried to delete the messages, but they were recovered."

Vander could have been the second attacker on the beach. "So who is paying them?"

"Got people digging into their bank accounts now. Have to be careful. Not exactly going through the *legal* channels," she muttered. "Aw, hell, look alive. Company's arriving."

That company was just Hunter. Exactly the man Jake needed. "Vander Henley," he immediately announced the man's name when Hunter closed in. "We think he might have been partnering with the bastard I took out at Milo's place, Colin Miller. We have to get Declan on the line and have him use his people to tear into Vander's and Colin's bank accounts. Someone is paying them, and we have to know who that person is."

"Uh, excuse me..." Honey growled.

"Declan's *non-legal* channels are a hell of lot faster than yours." Declan had his tech stretched out like tentacles in the world. With a few clicks, the man could find any information. And he could destroy just about anyone, too.

Case in point, he took out the killer who tormented my sister Marley. Erased him from the world with barely a blink. Meanwhile, Eb and Jake had been working for months in order to get close to that particularly savage SOB. Eb had even pulled strings to be sent into the prison undercover, just so he could get close enough to take out the predator who'd hurt Marley.

But Declan and his tech had beaten them to the kill.

Literally.

Hunter immediately pulled out his phone.

"The fucker *tased* me. Bad enough that I once let Hunter get the drop on me. At least he's a former Ranger."

Eb rolled back his shoulders. "But Tom? Freaking Tom Hadden? He's a pencil pusher, dick neck, pain-in-my-ass who couldn't even make the JV team back in the day. And I let him tase me. Never even thought that he might have swiped something from Milo's safe. Oh, I am going to make that guy pay."

Hunter had sidled away.

And Jake was standing there, doing *nothing*.

Fear and fury rolled through him. He had to think. *Think*. The first attack had come just outside of this very bar. Wren had been on her way back to Milo's place. The pricks had been lying in wait for her.

They'd escaped by boat.

Are they somewhere with a boat right now? Because that would be a nightmare. They could be out on the water, and they'd be putting more distance between Jake and Wren with every second that passed. Or, fuck forbid, they could dump Wren's body in the water. She'd sink beneath the waves, and he would never, ever see her beautiful face again. Never hear her voice. Never stare into her eyes and find his heaven waiting.

"What are you thinking right now?" Eb wanted to know. "Because you look like you're ready to murder someone."

Jake spun and drove his fist into the wall.

The second attack. It had come *inside* Milo's house. And Wren had said—she'd said that the prick told her his partner was waiting at Milo's bar.

Why were all the attacks centered around places that belonged to Milo? Jake's fist hit the wall again.

"I don't know what that particular wall has done to you," Honey muttered. "But, yeah, sure, kick its ass if it helps you feel better."

If Wren hadn't gotten away from her attacker at Milo's beach house, if she hadn't managed to get out and signal to Jake, she would have died in that house.

Died in Milo's house.

Milo.

Milo...who was a former Fed. Milo, who knew all about Wren's past. Who'd hidden her for so many years.

Milo...who had worked with Jake and Eb a few years ago on a special task force case that had come up in the area. Some assholes had been drug smuggling in Hilton Head. Jake had just stopped working for the CIA back then. He'd been bumming around before getting heavily involved in hostage rescue. And Eb—Eb had signed on to help because the man loved danger. They'd teamed up with Milo and a firefight had erupted. Turned out the bastards on the boat had been bringing in weapons and guns and...

Three of the bastards on the boat died. He didn't even recall all their names.

The whole thing had mostly been covered up because one of those guys had been the nephew of the governor. The man had been running for re-election and had tolerated zero scandal. More BS that Jake hadn't been in the mood to stomach. The governor had been Andrew Tate, and the nephew? Gregory. The leader on the crew they'd taken out. Jake definitely remembered him.

The bar's front door flew open and banged against the wall. "What in the hell is happening here?" A big, redheaded bear of a man stood in the doorway. His curly hair shoved back from a broad face, a face lined with a thick, red beard along the jaw. His green gaze took in the scene. Seemed to count the people, the faces he knew...

Honey.

Eb.

Jake.

"*Where is my niece?*" Milo O'Shaw bellowed. Fear flashed on his face. Milo wasn't a man given to fear.

As Milo stalked toward him, Jake understood exactly what had been happening all along. "It's not just about hurting me and my brother. It's about hurting you, too."

"Where is Wren?" Milo demanded.

Because Milo O'Shaw loved Wren like a daughter.

That's why she was chosen. She's the link that the three of us share. The one way to destroy three men, all at once. The plan had been to kill her at Milo's. To leave her body there and maybe Milo would have found her, if Jake hadn't arrived in time to stop her attacker.

Only Wren had been taken again.

Where would be the perfect place to hide her? The perfect place to, God forbid, hurt her?

The answer was right there. Spinning through Jake's mind. A place that was *already* a crime scene. A place the cops wouldn't be searching right now.

A place...where Milo O'Shaw could eventually find Wren's broken body. "I know where she is."

Milo's bright green eyes narrowed. The lines on his face deepened as he asked, "Then why the hell are we just standing here? And, somebody, give me a fuckin' gun!"

Chapter Twenty-Two

"ARE YOU GOING TO PUT YOUR HANDS ON HIS NECK?"
Makayla stood with the knife in her hand. Blood dripped
from the tip. "Try desperately to save him the way you
attempted to save that woman so long ago? I believe her
name was Carrie, wasn't it? Carrie, the beloved older sister
of Adam Rule. That guy just never got over his sister's
death. Such a terrible shame."

The blood had almost reached Wren. She jerked her
bound hands back.

Makayla laughed. "Oh, come on, there's plenty of blood
on your hands already." But she motioned to the man with
the tattoo. "Get her in the chair."

He grabbed Wren's arm. Yanked her up. Slammed her
down into the same chair that Makayla had used moments
before. Wren's duct-taped hands flopped uselessly in her
lap. With the tape also bound so tightly around her feet,
there was no way she could run.

"You tried to save her—Carrie, I mean. And how did
that work out for you?" Makayla looked down at her
dripping knife. "I think, for your trouble, her brother tried to

kill you, didn't he? Crazy how fate works. Especially when fate has a little help from someone like me. Someone who knew exactly what Adam would do if he ever found out about you and your fake life."

Wren muttered behind the tape.

"What's that?" Makayla's head tilted back. "Can't hear you. Van, be a sweetheart and rip that tape off her mouth, will you?"

He was a sweetheart. He ripped the tape off her lips with a merciless snatch of his fingers, and Wren screamed because she was pretty sure he'd ripped skin away, too.

Makayla laughed. "The serial killer's daughter." A shake of her head. "I think the world believes you are tougher, scarier than you actually are." She closed the distance between them. Kept her dripping knife. "Of course, I did embellish a bit. When I contacted Carrie's dear, grieving brother. When I posted about you in those true crime groups. When I was weaving my web and wrecking your world, I insinuated that you were involved in all sorts of wicked things with your father." She raised the knife. Pressed the bloody tip to Wren's chest. "That you were just as evil as dear old dad."

The pounding of Wren's heart echoed in her ears. "How did you...find out about my past?"

"It was actually through Milo. That sonofabitch. I was looking for a way to completely rip his life apart, only when I went tearing into his life, I discovered—ready for this shocker? Milo had no family. Zero. Zero blood family. Certainly not some half-brother who'd supposedly fallen hard for a gorgeous Spanish lady during his time studying abroad. There was no fairytale couple that had left behind their daughter for Milo to raise. There was just Milo's past with the Feds. And rumors that he was still hunting one particular serial killer who had always eluded him. The Sweetheart Slasher. Of course, that killer was at his peak when I was a kid. *You* were a kid, too, so you know that. But I got curious about the monster who had become Milo's obsession. And I discovered that Jonathan Wales—Dr. Jonathan Wales—was one of the individuals strongly suspected to have *been* the Sweetheart Slasher. A man who'd vanished. Along with his daughter."

Wren tried to jump out of the chair, but the goon with Makayla had moved behind Wren. He clamped his hands around her shoulders to hold her in place.

Makayla lifted the knife and let it press into Wren's throat. "If I am following the story correctly, your dad began by cutting Carrie's neck. Not too deeply, though, at least not at first..." The knife cut into Wren. A graze, then, harder.

"You're my *friend*," Wren gasped out. She ignored the pain from the cut.

Makayla blinked. "You were the girl who gave me a spot at her lunch table the first day I walked into a new high school." She smiled at Wren and stopped cutting her. "That was really sweet."

Wren was afraid to breathe.

"But you know what *wasn't* sweet?" Makayla's face twisted. "When those asshole twin brothers who follow you around like freaking puppies *killed* the man I loved! When your annoying *uncle* set a trap for Gregory and they launched an attack, and there was nothing left of him. One minute, Gregory was there, planning for our future, saving money so that we would have enough cash to do whatever we wanted. So I would never, ever have to worry again." She leaned in close to Wren. "That rich uncle of his turned his nose up at Gregory and at Gregory's mom—called her an addict. Said she was gonna bring down the family, so he just cut them both off! But Gregory was so smart. So strong. We fell in love and our lives were going to change." She pulled the knife across Wren's throat in a long slice. Not deep, just long. One side to the other.

Wren felt the blood slide down her throat. She pressed her lips together to stop a cry of pain from escaping.

"Gregory was running drugs. Guns. Smuggling." Makayla made the announcement as if she'd just confessed that he was a car salesman. Or an accountant. "So Gregory had some flaws. Who doesn't? But that interfering Milo saw a deal that he shouldn't have seen. Nosey jerk. I guess you can take the Fed out of the Bureau, but you can't take the Bureau out of the bar owner. The dumbass took it upon himself to play hero—along with those prick twins. They took out my Gregory. No one knew that Gregory and I were involved. No one even knew I was there, that I saw every terrible moment that night." Her nostrils flared. "I saw the man I loved die."

Wren's gaze jumped to Tom. A Tom who appeared very dead. "And what was he?"

"Convenient," Makayla responded. "Far more convenient than I anticipated. To think, I first walked into that bank looking for a loan because I needed cash to pay for a hit." She finally pulled back the knife.

Wetness coated Wren's throat. Blood.

"Not like Vander is cheap, and your twins have a reputation. People don't like going against them, so I had to really make things worth his while."

Behind her, Vander grunted. "That bastard Jake killed my partner."

"Your partner..." Wren licked her lips. "He was in the process of killing me. Right here."

His grip tightened to a painful degree. Then his breath

was at her ear as he leaned in and told her, "You were going to be his first. The first time he stepped up and took a life all on his own." He bit her ear, hard, and she screamed. "You just never forget your first." Laughing, he let her go. Sauntered around to stand beside Makayla. "But the hero came rushing in to save the day." He gave a disgusted shake of his head. "And now Colin is gone."

"Jake is going to rush in again," Wren said. She ignored the throbbing in her ear and the blood on her neck. "He'll be here at any moment."

Makayla laughed. "*Why* would he be here? This is a crime scene. Why would a killer come here? Why would anyone bring you back here? Poor, broken-hearted Jake is going to think you were taken far away. Maybe you went out on a boat. Maybe you crossed state lines. He's not going to know." More soft laughter. "So, originally, my plan was for you to die. For the men who loved you to find your broken body. But that's not going to happen. At least, not right away. Because I realized something that would be even more painful."

"You're my *friend*. We had sleepovers in high school! We exchange Christmas presents every year!"

"You're a crappy gift giver. Spend more, would you?"

Wren's lips pressed together.

"I took your phone from this scene when you were being rushed away," Makayla confessed. "I knew your password because your dumb self gave it to me at the bachelorette party when I asked to use it for some pics, remember?" A shake of her head. "I scanned through your texts and emails, and then I called you because I wanted you and Jake to know that this wasn't over. It won't be over until you're gone."

"Makayla—"

"You're going to die, Wren. Don't get me wrong. And it's going to be extremely painful. But Vander is going to help me hide your body. Eb and Jake and your dear Uncle Milo—they will cling to hope when they don't find you dead. They'll think that maybe—just maybe—you're still alive somewhere. It's the hope that is the worst part, isn't it? Over time, that hope will dim. They'll hurt more. They will slowly break apart. And I will be there to watch." She sniffed and patted lightly near her eye, as if wiping away a tear. "I'll make sure I have a great, front row seat."

"Jake will know you're involved."

Makayla's hand dropped.

Wren's gaze went straight to that hand. "Problem one is that you still have all your fingers. Doesn't match with the whole scene you set up so that people would think a Sweetheart Slasher copycat was at work. You actually went a bit too far with that scene, I think."

"I'm not losing a fucking finger!"

Wren hadn't thought she would, or else the finger would already have been gone. "The fact that the Sweetheart Slasher cutoff fingers—that part was never released to the general public. What did you do, learn that from digging in Uncle Milo's files? His life?"

Makayla didn't speak.

"What did you do? Give yourself a cut somewhere so you could leave all of that blood at your place? Way to take a hit for your plan. But that isn't good enough, you see. You still have another problem. Problem two is that there is no bad guy. *You're* the villain. You're also acting as the victim. If you turn up, all hysterical and traumatized, who are you going to blame? Tom tased Eb at the bar. Eb knows that Tom lied to him and Jake."

"And that is what makes Tom the perfect fall guy!" A

pleased nod. Makayla smiled broadly. "He's also not going to be found, you see. How can Tom be found? He took you away. You'll both disappear tonight."

Vander glanced at Tom. "I'll take him out on the water. Cut him up and feed him to some sharks. Or, who knows? Maybe I'll save myself the bloody work and weigh his body down with something and dump him overboard. What the hell ever." He seemed utterly unconcerned.

Clearly *not* his first time to dump a body.

"They will have their villain," Makayla assured her. "I'll have my revenge for what they did. And, you know what? Maybe for some extra fun, I'll hook up with Eb or with Jake. Talk about fucking someone over."

"I don't think you're their type."

"I honestly thought you were fucking Eb until that scene in the bar with Jake. Imagine my surprise. Though, come on, curious minds want to know...have you fucked them both?"

She gazed at Makayla. Didn't speak. Just stared as ice slowly worked its way through Wren's body.

The smug smile on Makayla's face began to melt away.

"You lost the man you loved," Wren said. "A man who was a criminal. Who was smuggling—I believe you said drugs and guns? A real charmer, hmm?"

Makayla backed up a step. "It's easy to be on your high horse, isn't it? Because you think Eb and Jake are so perfect? They are *killers*, Wren! But then, I guess you do have a type, don't you? They say girls fall in love with men just like their fathers. Did you fall for a psychopath, too?"

"I'm staring at a psychopath," she replied.

Vander laughed. Then caught himself and coughed when Makayla glared at him.

"Sorry," he said, shrugging. "But she's *not* scared, and I like that."

A frustrated cry broke from Makayla as her attention snapped back to Wren. "*Why* aren't you scared?"

"Because you're nothing compared to what I've already lived through. Because I'm about to get out of this chair and I'm going to take that knife, and I'm going to plunge it into you."

The knife slipped from Makayla's hand and clattered to the floor. She instantly bent to pick it up.

"She's not scared," Vander murmured. "But you are."

"Scared of little old me?" Wren asked. She blinked. "Why? Could it be because while you were tearing into my Uncle Milo's life and making all your discoveries about the Sweetheart Slasher, you came upon some reports about me, too? Maybe some of the psychological profiles that were created when I was a kid who just couldn't, ah, attach, I believe it was called?"

"Are you like him?" Makayla breathed.

"You'll find out," Wren promised. The women stared at each other.

A tear leaked down Makayla's cheek. A real tear. "I loved him, and I want him back, but he's gone. Someone has to pay."

"And that someone gets to be me."

"It's all of them! The only way they can hurt is to lose what they love. You are the only thing all three love."

Jake had said he loved her. The best words she'd ever heard in her entire life. "That's why they are going to be storming the door any minute."

"They don't know where you are!" Makayla swiped away the tear. "They can't save you when they don't know!"

"Are you sure about that?" Wren shifted a little bit in

the chair. "Are you sure that Eb didn't fake getting knocked out by Tom? I mean, come on..." Her gaze slid across the floor. *Do not shudder. Do not flinch.* She'd worn a mask for most of her life, and she could damn well keep up the pretense a bit longer. She could keep acting like she was in control even as a helpless scream bubbled inside of her. "Come on, it's Tom. You truly think *Tom* of all people, you think he got the drop on Eb?"

And, for the first time, uncertainty flashed. On both Makayla's face and on her goon's face.

"We all knew Tom was lying when he appeared at the bar. Too nervous. Too shaky. So Jake and Eb had the idea to trick him. They talked about it while they were in the back room of Uncle Milo's bar. Jake only had a moment to give me the details. Said to go along with whatever happened. That they'd be right behind me." She smiled. "If you look out the windows, I think you might be surprised. Something tells me that they pulled Honey in immediately. Deputy cars probably have surrounded this place. They would have come in silently because Honey would want the element of surprise. While I've been talking and distracting you, Jake and Eb had been climbing the steps outside. One of them is about to come bursting in the front door. The other will come in the back door. Either they will kill you both or you will go to prison for the rest of your lives. Either way, you don't get your vengeance, but I do get away." There. Done. She'd almost believed her own words.

What she needed—what she desperately needed was a distraction. For one of them—maybe both, please both—to go and look out of the windows. Because then she could break free, grab a weapon, and try attacking. She wasn't going down without a fight.

They weren't using her.

Friends didn't fucking *use* friends in twisted vengeance games.

"You're lying," Makayla rasped.

Wren didn't deny the charge. She was, of course, lying. And bleeding. She just lifted her brows. "Am I?"

Vander swore. He whirled and stalked toward a nearby window.

So did Makayla. She spun. Hurried to a window.

Vander looked out first. "I don't see—"

Tom had made the mistake of duct-taping her hands in front of her. Her Uncle Milo had told her that most criminals would duct-tape you from the front. In one of his many, *many* safety sessions, he'd told her that, statistically, duct tape was used the most to kidnap people.

Her FBI bad-ass uncle had wanted to make sure that she'd never be kidnapped.

Well, look where I am.

"No one is out there!" Makayla chimed.

She started to back away from the window.

But Vander's hand flew out and curled around her wrist. "Wait..."

Wren rose to her feet. She lifted her hands in front of her body, then she kept raising them, moving up high above her head until she'd made what Uncle Milo had called a magic triangle. You couldn't pull apart duct tape from a standard horizontal angle. Uncle Milo had shown her that was too hard.

But if you had the magic triangle...

"Someone is coming!" Vander shoved up the blinds. "Shit!"

Probably just a random car passing down the road. Talk about perfect timing. Wren yanked her hands down from above her head and pulled them apart in the same, swift movement. Uncle Milo had always said that if it didn't look like she was elbowing someone who'd grabbed her, then she wasn't doing the move right. By the time her hands were sliding past her hips, she was free. Or at least, her wrists were free.

Wren glanced at her bound feet. Not like she could run far. But running wasn't necessary, not yet.

"Fucking hell," Vander snarled. "They're stopping. One car, two—"

Wren angled her feet in a V-shape. She shot down to the floor in a squat as fast as she could. That tape gave way. She could have just torn through it with her fingers, but Uncle Milo had been right—the squat was faster. Wren backed away, not making a sound as she headed for the kitchen. Uncle Milo kept a knife block set in his kitchen. His blades were always wicked sharp. Wren was uncomfortably aware that the knife Makayla had used on her had come from that kitchen block. She'd recognized her uncle's beloved eight-inch chef knife.

"They can't be here!" Makayla cried out.

"I'm not going down. Been to prison too many times already!" Vander twisted around. "What—where is the bitch?"

The bitch had made it to the kitchen. Wren heard his thundering footsteps behind her. She stretched for the block that waited on the counter. Her fingers almost reached it.

His hands locked around her waist. He hauled her back.

But she'd managed to grab one item from the block. Not the knife, though. The scissors that Uncle Milo kept nestled in the base of the block. She shoved her fingers through the open holes in the handle of those scissors—freaking 'comfort grip' as Uncle Milo had once proudly boasted—and she drove the sharp edge of the closed scissors into one of the hands that had grabbed her.

Vander let her go with a roar of pain. She spun around and she raised up the scissors in one fist. Wren plunged those scissors down at him even as he lifted his hands to try and block the attack.

"No fear!" Vander shouted, and he was shaking his head. "Fuck, yeah!"

Oh, she had plenty of fear. She just wasn't letting it stop her.

"Sorry, baby," he said right before he slammed his body into hers and they went flying to the floor. "Gonna be a shame to kill you." He grabbed her hand—the one that still clutched the scissors—and twisted. She knew he was going to break her fingers. She also knew she wasn't going to drop the only weapon she had.

Wren slammed her forehead into his. Or, that had been her intent. But the front door—a door Jake had previously broken and that had not been thoroughly fixed by the cops —came hurtling inward. The door thudded into the wall and Vander's head whipped to the right at the sound.

"Shit!" Vander snarled as Jake rushed into the beach house.

Jake's eyes locked on him. "Get the fuck away from her!" Jake. Big. Strong. Scary Hot. Wearing a bulletproof vest and with his gun locked in his hand. "Get away from Wren *now!*"

"No, man, I was paid to kill her. I *always* get the job—"

Boom. The gunshot didn't explode from Jake's gun. Instead, it had come from the left—from the back door that hadn't blown open with a crash. Even as Vander's body slumped to the side, Wren was wrenching her head toward the back door so she could see who'd just fired.

Uncle Milo had come in through that door. Opened it soundlessly. Jake had been his distraction, Wren realized.

"He told you to get the fuck away from my niece," Uncle Milo bellowed.

Vander growled. A guttural cry.

Wren scrambled away from him, doing a backwards crab walk even as her right hand clung tightly to the scissors.

Vander yanked at the gun near his waist, and he brought that gun up in a swinging arc toward Uncle Milo.

More gunshots. Two of them. Three? Four?

Wren crouched beside the counter in the kitchen. She was pretty sure that both Jake and Milo had both fired to take out the hitman. Vander's body twitched and blood spattered around him. His gun now lay a few feet from his outstretched hand.

"Wren!" Jake shouted her name.

She began to scramble upward. "Jake—"

But before Wren could get fully upright, Makayla grabbed her. Makayla fisted her hand in Wren's hair even as she put the chef's knife and its bloody blade against Wren's neck.

"No!" Makayla screamed back at Jake. "You don't get to save her! You don't get to rush in here and play the hero and go off and live happily ever after while my Gregory is *gone!*" The blade cut deeper.

Wren brought her scissors closer to her body. On her knees, she watched as Jake and Milo closed in. Both men kept their weapons up.

Eb and Hunter were right behind them.

And...

"*What in the hell is happening here?*" Honey demanded

as she rushed inside. "You idiots were supposed to wait for—"

"Everyone *out!*" Makayla's scream cut through Honey's words. "Out or I slit her throat right now!"

"You already have slit her throat," Jake responded, voice flat. "She needs medical care."

The wound wasn't that deep. Not yet.

"She's going to need a body bag unless everyone gets out!" Makayla screeched. "Now!"

Honey touched Eb, then Hunter. "Get out," she ordered.

They hesitated.

"*Out,*" Honey snapped.

They backed out. But Eb's expression showed his fury.

Honey sidled between Jake and Uncle Milo. "Milo..." An exhale from Honey. "I want you to step outside. You are a civilian. I can handle this scene."

"She's my niece." He did not lower his weapon. "And we both know that if we leave them alone, the first thing Makayla will do is kill Wren."

"You don't know that." Makayla's fist yanked back Wren's hair and head. The knife cut deeper. "I could decide to make a deal. But I won't deal if you don't get the hell out!"

Uncle Milo didn't move. Wren could see the struggle on his face.

"Shoot me," Makayla dared. "Bet I slice deep enough that she dies before you kill me. Bet you'll be the one shoving your hands over her throat and trying to stop all that blood, just like Wren did with Carrie all those years ago. And the result will be the same. Death. How does that *feel,* Milo? You feeling helpless enough? Do you hate what's happening? Do you wish you hadn't ever killed Gregory on that stupid boat?" A screech that hurt Wren's ears.

"Kill me," Uncle Milo said. He put down his gun. Held up his hands. "Wren had nothing to do with that."

"She had everything to do with it. *Everything*. She's the domino that made my life fall apart. If you hadn't adopted her, if you hadn't met her, saved her, then you would never have been in Hilton Head. You never would have settled down and tried to be a family man. Honey wouldn't be here because your lover wouldn't have followed you. Eb and Jake? Like they'd give two shits about this town if she wasn't here. The only reason everyone is here—it's Wren. She's the one who made you all line up. Who got any of you bastards to ever pretend you were good. Because of her, Gregory is dead!"

Uncle Milo took a step back. "I'm leaving." His gaze swept to Wren's face. "You are not your father."

Oh, he was wrong. "I am my father's daughter." A husky rasp because of the growing agony in her throat.

Pain flashed on his face. A pain that got worse when his gaze fell to her throat.

Honey shoved him back. "Leave! Now! Do you want to watch her die?"

He retreated.

Wren wanted to shake her head. To tell him to stay. The only end game here? It would be her death.

"Go," Honey told Jake.

"You'll have to shoot me and drag my ass out," Jake said. He still had his weapon aimed. "There is no world where I leave Wren to die. There is no world where I *ever* leave Wren."

"Get out, Honey." Makayla wasn't screeching any

longer. Instead, she sounded far too pleased. "Go call in some real Feds. You don't know how to handle business these days. They'll negotiate with me. I'm sure her life is worth so much…"

Honey retreated one step. Then another. But she didn't leave. Her hand went to her hip. To the holster.

"Worth so very much to the right person," Makayla finished. "Are you that right person, Jake? Tell me, what would you give if Wren could survive?"

"I'd give anything," he replied instantly.

"Because you love her."

"*Yes.*"

Makayla laughed with what sounded like real joy. "That's why I sent the messages to Eb, you see. Had to get some asshole tech kid to help so I couldn't be traced…but it's worth so much more when you *know* that you're going to lose what you love. When you know the pain is coming. I wanted to watch you and Eb try and stop it, but you can't… He can't. You're both helpless. Just like I was helpless the night Gregory died."

"He fired at us," Jake bit out. "He wouldn't surrender. He just kept shooting."

"*You killed him!* Now you're right in front of me, holding a gun…but you can't do a damn thing."

Wren angled the scissors. She looked down. Saw Makayla's bare foot. With Wren still on her knees, Makayla's foot was just inches away.

"Her father thought love was a lie. I've got an idea. Why don't we prove to Wren how wrong her father was? I want you to turn that gun of yours, and I want you to shoot yourself. Prove that you would do anything, even die—"

Wren drove the scissors into the top of Makayla's foot.

Makayla screamed. But she let go of Wren's hair. Let go of her hair even as the blade sliced—

Wren threw her whole body back to get away from that blade. She rammed into Makayla, took her down, and even as they fell, Wren twisted. She drove the scissors into her friend. Over and over.

"*Wren!*" Jake grabbed her. Pulled her back. Shoved her behind him.

Makayla lunged up with her knife.

Jake fired. Pretty much dead center on Makayla's chest.

Jake doesn't have to die in order to prove he loves me.

The man had already killed to prove that fact to her.

And he'd just done it...again?

Makayla's head made a horrible cracking sound when it slammed into the tile floor of the kitchen. Floor that Uncle Milo had painstaking placed just last summer. Blood poured from the bullet wound. From all the puncture wounds from the scissors.

Wren crawled forward.

"No!" Honey slapped a hand on Wren's shoulder. "Don't get near her!"

But Makayla wasn't a threat any longer.

Honey kicked the knife away. She grabbed her radio and called for backup. Only the backup was already there. Eb and Hunter and Milo hadn't gone far. They'd just circled around to come in again through windows.

They'd been waiting for their moment to attack. Like Wren hadn't known that they would all find a way back inside to help.

They loved her. Love was real. Love was something worth fighting for.

Even Makayla had loved, in her way.

"Wren, baby." Honey crouched before her. Put her hand over Wren's throat. "You're going to be all right."

Yes, she was. She tried to talk. "J-Jake..." Wait, did any sound emerge? Had she been able to say his name?

There was so much blood everywhere.

"You are gonna be all right, my sweet girl," Honey promised. There were tears in Honey's eyes. But Honey never cried. Never. Honey's hand pressed harder to Wren's throat.

So much blood. Everywhere. Wren could feel it covering her skin. Soaking her. Just like it had so long ago. Dizziness had her head spinning.

"Jake is right here. You stay with me, you understand?" Honey's voice shook. "Milo, get that stretcher up here!"

Then Jake was there. Right in front of Wren. Staring at her with a face that looked far too haggard. With fear surging in his eyes and with lines on his face that should not be there. "Wren..." Jake said her name like a prayer.

She was going to pass out. She knew it. The past and present were colliding. Blood was everywhere. Her fingers. Her arms. Her face. She could feel the stickiness on her skin, and it absolutely horrified her. She wanted it gone, gone, gone but she had to just sit there.

"Wren, God, don't you *dare* leave me," Jake ordered.

Jake and his orders.

"Where you go, I go," he snarled. "You remember that. Always. And I don't think heaven wants me yet. I need to redeem the shit out of my soul before they'll let me get past the pearly gates. And there is no way I'd ever drag you down to hell with me."

She was sliding down. Falling.

Or had she been down on the floor the whole time?

Wren just knew she was staring up at Jake. He'd put his hands over Honey's. They were both trying to help her.

"Angel, don't go anywhere."

Wait, was that Jake's voice? Or was it her father's? "No...wings..." Again, she didn't know if the words emerged. Or if her throat was too damaged.

"You don't need wings. *Baby, please...*"

Her eyes fluttered. She didn't hurt. That was probably good. Or was it bad? But there was something she had to tell him. Carrie had tried to get out one final word. Right at the end. She'd cried out for the person who mattered most.

Wren's father had been so wrong. People did love. They did fight.

"I...love you..." Wren said. Or tried to say. "Love...Jake."

* * *

HE DIDN'T LET her go.

Wren's blood covered his hands. His clothes.

The EMTs took her from the beach house. Loaded her into the ambulance.

Jake did not leave her. He did not stop holding her neck. Did not stop applying pressure. He got in the vehicle with her. Rode with her as the siren wailed and fear blasted through every part of his body.

His beautiful Wren was too pale. No color in her cheeks. No color at all except for the stark red that stained her neck.

He could hear the terror in Hayden's voice. The EMT knew how close to death Wren was.

Too much blood loss.

Too fast.

Wren, baby, please...I need you.

The siren wailed so loudly. They hit a massive pothole. The whole vehicle bounced. Fuck!

Wren's eyes opened.

For just a moment, she stared straight at him.

"I love you," he told her.

And his Wren...she smiled at him.

Chapter Twenty-Three

The blood was everywhere. Her fingers. Her arms. Her face. She could feel the stickiness on her skin, and it absolutely horrified her. She wanted it gone, gone, gone, but she had to just sit there. He'd told her to sit there. To not move. To not make a sound.

She had to sit in the blood and not move.

But it was so sticky. It was hardening on her skin. She could feel it. Smell it. Taste it. How long had she been there, covered in blood? How long would she be there?

A scream bubbled in her throat, and Wren knew it was going to break free. When the scream erupted, she would be dead. The monster had won. There was no happy ending. There was no love. There was no hope.

He'd won. And she would die.

"Where you go, I go, Wren." A low, deep voice. It pulled at her. Made her heart beat faster. "So where shall we go? What dreams are we gonna follow?" A strong hand gripped hers. "God, I have so many dreams that involve you. If you want the truth, *every* dream that I have focuses on you. I dream of us being married. Having kids with your eyes. I'd really like a daughter, one who looks just like you. Or, hell, could you imagine what it would be like if we had twins? Twin girls." A pause. His hand tightened on hers. "I dream about dancing with you at your Uncle Milo's bar. Being with you in front of the world and you not being scared. You not having to pretend. You being free and happy. That's what I want most, Wren. For you to be happy. Safe and happy."

Her eyelids fluttered open. Her lips parted.

"Baby, don't try to talk, not yet." Jake's eyes were right on her. "You're in the hospital, and I swear, you are gonna be fine. You just can't talk. Not yet. But you will, soon."

She blinked a few times. Frowned.

"What's wrong?" Jake immediately leaned toward her. "Are you in pain? What's happening?"

Her free hand reached up. Touched his cheek. It was wet. He'd been crying for her?

"Allergies," Jake said.

She felt her frown deepen.

"I'm allergic to the idea of anything ever happening to you." He pressed a kiss to her brow. "So you can't get hurt again, understand? If I have to surround you with pillows and guns and a fleet of bodyguards from Wilde, you will not ever be hurt again. You will be protected. You will be safe." Another kiss. "You will be happy."

She wanted to ask about Makayla. About the crime scene. About a thousand things.

But a heavy fog pulled at her again. There wasn't going to be time to ask about any of those things. Not yet. And she wasn't supposed to talk. So she just mouthed...*Love you.*

"I love you, Wren. I love you. Always have. Always will."

* * *

Three Weeks Later...

"We need to talk, Wren."

She stood on the beach, with the wind blowing her hair. Wren had draped a loose scarf over her neck even though the wounds had healed. Scarred, but healed. Still red now, but they'd fade with time. Pain tended to fade with time.

The scarf fluttered in the wind behind her.

At the hard, familiar voice, her head turned. "Hi, Uncle Milo."

Three weeks. Three weeks had passed since her friend had tried to kill her. Since Wren had been sent to the hospital with wounds far too similar to those inflicted by her father. The world knew all about the serial killer's daughter now. Though, instead of being a villain, she'd been given the role of victim, thanks to Makayla. The misunderstood daughter who'd just tried to escape the nightmare of her past. Only to be betrayed by a friend she trusted.

Wren hadn't lost clients. She'd gained them. She'd also gotten offers to do talk shows. To write tell-all books. To give interview after interview.

She'd turned down those requests. She wasn't quite ready to face the world and talk about her father. Maybe she never would be.

Jake had been at her side through everything. Steady and strong and ever-so-watchful. She was supposed to go and meet him inside Uncle Milo's bar that night. A big party. Uncle Milo's idea. A celebration to push away all of the pain from the past.

She watched as Uncle Milo approached her. He wore a black tux. This celebration was going to be a very fancy affair, or so he'd declared. Wren couldn't help but notice that Uncle Milo wasn't wearing shoes.

It was the beach, after all. A little smile tugged at her lips.

Uncle Milo didn't smile back. He just steadily closed the distance between them until he was right at her side. Big, towering Uncle Milo. The man who'd been her hero for so long.

I am my father's daughter.

She remembered having that thought when Makayla was attacking her. Only Wren hadn't been thinking about Jonathan Wales at the time. She'd been thinking about Uncle Milo and how he'd taught her to fight. To survive. How he'd told her about the legend of the clever wren and said it would be the perfect name for her.

"I'm selling the beach house," he announced.

She blinked.

"Oh, what, girl? You think I can walk in there without shuddering in horror every single time for the rest of my days? Nope. Not doing it."

"You love that beach house." Their house. The house they'd shared when she'd been an uncertain and terrified high school kid.

"I'll love a new place just as much." His gaze drifted to the water as the waves crashed into the shore. "Sometimes, you have to let go of the past. Move to the future. Otherwise, that shit will just drag you under. You'll be choking on the blood."

"Yes, I've, uh, been there and done that."

He swore. His head whipped toward her. "I didn't mean—"

"I love you." The words just came out. Normal. Her voice sounded normal again. The damage to her throat hadn't been too deep. She was all right. No, better than that. She was safe. She was happy. "I love you," Wren repeated.

His mouth dropped open. Shock completely slackened his face.

"In all of our years together, I never told you those words."

"You don't..." He sniffed. "You don't have to tell me. You think I didn't know?"

She smiled at him. "I love you."

"Dammit." He grabbed her. Hauled her close in a bone-crushing hug. As if Uncle Milo ever gave any other kind of hug. "Dammit."

Her face pressed to his tux. That fancy tux. He never did fancy, so this party was really special to him. Wren had a feeling she knew why.

"I love you, kid," he said.

She was far from a kid, and they both knew it. But Wren thought that she might just always be the kid he'd saved, no matter how old she got.

"You are my daughter," he added gruffly. "And I was proud as hell of you when you drove those scissors into that witch's foot."

She eased back. "I used the technique you taught me in order to get out of the duct tape."

"Figured you did. You never forgot anything I taught you, did you?" He let her go. Only to immediately grab the scarf that wanted to blow away. Carefully, he looped it around her neck. "You don't have to hide. Not any part of you."

Not anymore, she didn't. "Thought the scarf was stylish."

He raised a bushy brow. "You're always stylish," he said.

"That's why we're having a fancy party. You like fancy." He cleared his throat. "There's...something I need to t-tell you."

His stutter made unease slither down her spine. Uncle Milo never stuttered.

"The reason I didn't tell you about the discovery of the Sweetheart Slasher sooner..." A sigh. The waves crashed. Roared. Crashed again. "There wasn't a lot left. Mostly bones. Hair. You see, he'd been dead a very long time before his remains were found."

It wasn't overly cold, but chill bumps suddenly covered her arms.

"We wondered how he'd just stopped, how he'd gone dormant when he was...killing so frequently before." The wind tousled his red curls. "He was dead, Wren. All that time. You were afraid, but you didn't have to be. He died shortly after the attack on you all those years ago."

She shook her head.

"Self-inflicted," he added, voice thickening even more. "And, uh, there was an old note near the remains."

Another shake of her head.

"He thought you were dead. He bought the story we sold to the media."

Her breath came too fast. Her heart beat too hard.

"The note said...it said, 'I killed an angel. My angel. Margaret, forgive me.'"

Margaret. Only she wasn't Margaret any longer.

"If he could love anything in this world, it was you."

He hadn't believed in love. Because his heart had been broken. No, his mind had been broken. The heartbreak had just been an excuse. He'd been twisted and damaged and bent on so much destruction. Other lives had not mattered to him. Other people had not mattered.

But in the end, he was saying he'd regretted what he'd

done to her? Was that true? Or another mind game, a final one from her father?

Did it even matter?

He hadn't believed in love, but she did. She loved Uncle Milo. She loved Honey. She loved Jake and Eb and their sister Marley...

And she was going to love the life that waited for her.

This time, she was the one to give the crushing bear hug as Wren threw her arms around Uncle Milo.

* * *

THE BAR'S parking lot had been bursting at the seams. Filled with every sort of vehicle imaginable—from high end, luxury rides—because, of course, Declan Flynn had showed up with Marley and the man always drove in style—to sputtering classic trucks favored by some of the locals who were old friends of Milo's.

The interior of the place was equally packed because none of the locals wanted to miss this VIP event. They wore fancy evening clothes—tuxes would normally be way out of place in the dive bar, but this wasn't a normal night. A band played on stage, the bar was open, and laughter filled the air.

Jake had one mission. Only one. *Get to Wren.* He held a champagne flute in his hand and made his way through the crowd. Not a hard task because people tended to jump out of his way. Not Wren, though. His beautiful Wren just smiled at him as he closed in on her.

She wore a black dress, one that *glittered* when the light hit it just right. Small straps. Plunging cleavage. Diamonds winked at her ears. Faint red lines marked her neck, and he *hated* those lines because they reminded him of her pain. But the doctors had promised those lines would fade.

Jake wished that she'd never been hurt. Wished that he'd been the one covered in blood.

Wished that he'd gotten to her sooner. Wished that he—

"Stop it." Wren took the champagne flute from him. "Your glower is extra strong tonight, and you are scaring everyone." A soft chide. She clinked her flute against his. "If you smile, people will stop shuddering in their fancy clothes."

"You aren't shuddering." She was just glowing. Just being beautiful and perfect and his living dream. "I don't scare you."

"Of course, you don't. You delight me." She winked at him. "Because you love me."

"Yes." Just that. Stark. Maybe guttural.

"And I love you." Soft. Husky.

Yeah, they were getting out of that bar, STAT. He was getting her alone. He was getting her naked. He was getting *in* her. Jake reached for her left hand.

"Can I have everyone's attention?" Milo was on stage. In typical Milo style, he'd taken command of the microphone from the lead singer. Well, it was his bar, after all, so Jake figured the man could take control of a microphone if that was what he wanted. The lead singer slunk away even as Milo leaned toward the standing pole microphone and said, "Got some announcements."

Everyone turned toward Milo.

Honey stood on the side of the stage, looking absolutely resplendent in a bold red dress. She'd pinned her badge to her hip.

"Want to start by saying thank you." A bob of Milo's red head. "Thank you to Jacob and Ebenezer Jones. Boys..."

They weren't boys. Hadn't been in a very long time.

"Men," Milo corrected, as if realizing what he'd said. "Hell, hard for me to say that...I keep thinking of them as the sixteen-year-old punks who kept running after my Wren every chance they got...Tripping over themselves..."

Laughter came from the crowd.

"We did *not* trip," Eb groused as he appeared at Jake's side.

Jake wasn't so sure. He slanted a glance toward Wren. "Pretty sure I tripped a few times."

She smiled at him. Yep, that smile. He felt its impact all the way to his racing heart. He'd definitely tripped more than once over the years. With an effort, he focused his attention back on the small stage.

"Thank you for saving my Wren." Milo had a champagne flute in his hand. Though Jake was pretty sure that flute was filled with Irish whiskey, not champagne. "Though, I guess she isn't mine, any longer, is she?" Milo dead-eye stared at Jake. "Love her forever," he ordered, voice thickening.

"I will," Jake promised. And he made sure his voice was loud and clear and carried all the way across the bar.

Milo exhaled. "Good. Good." A deep inhale. "There's a woman here that I've also, well, I've loved for a very long time, too. But fear—fear's a real pain in the ass, isn't it? It can hold you back. Make you think that you can't ever have what you want most."

Honey suddenly started shifting very, very nervously on the edge of the stage.

Milo turned toward her. Bent down on one knee.

"Holy shit," Eb said.

Indeed.

"About time," Eb added.

Yep.

Milo held his hand out toward Honey. The hand not gripping the champagne flute filled with Irish whiskey. "Honey…" Milo began.

Everyone in the bar seemed to hold their breath.

"Will you marry a man who has worshipped the ground you walk on for over twenty years?"

A wide smile split Honey's face. She didn't say, yes, though. She rushed to him, kicking off her heels. And then they were hugging and kissing and everyone was clapping.

"I think that means yes." Wren sounded beyond delighted. She was even bouncing a little in her heels.

"Guess there will be a wedding in town after all." Eb drained his champagne. "And this time, the bride won't be homicidal. Always a bonus."

Jake had turned his head toward Wren. "Maybe there will be more than one wedding."

Wren stopped bouncing. She whipped to face Jake.

"Because I know how Milo feels. Fear can hold you back. It can make you think you're not good enough for someone, that you can't ever have what you want." Wren was what Jake wanted most. "I've worshipped the ground you've walked on since—"

He didn't get to finish. Wren had thrown her arms around him and was kissing him like mad. He kissed her back the exact same way.

"Well, damn," Eb exclaimed. Then… "*Hell, yes.*"

Hell, yes. Jake held Wren even tighter.

Mission accomplished…

Protect Wren.

Love Wren.

Marry Wren…

Chapter Twenty-Four

"Aw, someone looks like he just lost his best friend." Hunter sauntered closer. He was shadowed by a watchful Declan Flynn as they closed in on Eb.

Eb had just made it to the bar. He'd hoped for another flute of champagne. But, apparently, his plans were about to be derailed.

"Don't worry, you still have us." Hunter saluted Eb with a beer bottle. "We might not be wearing your face, but we still think we're pretty awesome."

Declan grunted in agreement. His watchful stare swept over the crowd, as if looking for a threat. Probably because he was. The man tended to *always* look for threats. "I'm amazingly awesome," Declan agreed.

"Uh, huh. Great for you, too." His fingers tapped across the bar. Why did these guys think he was depressed? He wasn't. "Didn't lose a best friend. She's just about to become my sister-in-law."

Declan began to smile.

"*Don't* go sharing that news yet. Well, fine, go tell Marley. Pretty sure you tell my sister everything."

"I do." A nod from Declan.

"But not anyone else. I don't think Wren and Jake are ready for a big announcement." He paused to consider the situation. *Had* she accepted? He was pretty sure she had. She'd seemed excited. She'd kissed his brother. Though she hadn't technically said the whole "yes" part as of yet. He turned his head, craning to look through the crowd. Honey and Milo were slow dancing in the middle of the small dance floor. Other couples were out there with them, too. Marley was taking photos.

Drinks were flowing. People were laughing. Life was good.

For everyone else.

This was the part where he was supposed to put the bright smile on his face. Be happy. And dammit, he was happy for Jake and Wren. He turned a bit more and rested his elbows on the bar top. "Glad my brother finally got the nerve to make a move on Wren. Pretty sure he's been in love with her since we were sixteen."

"And you weren't in love with her?" Declan asked.

Trust Declan to not care about tact and just jump right in with both feet.

"Maybe a little. Once upon a time." Wren was a whole lot like him. Through the crowd, he saw that she and Jake had just appeared near Honey and Milo. Wren hugged first Honey, then Milo. Jake hugged Honey before shaking hands with Milo. Then that hand of Jake's immediately returned to curl around Wren's hip.

Wren was close to Jake. Jake tugged her even closer.

An actual, real smile lifted Eb's lips. "My brother would walk through fire for that woman." *So would I.*

Silence greeted his statement.

His gaze swept toward the two men standing near him. "What?" Eb demanded.

"Someone is feeling sad," Hunter announced.

He'd just been *smiling*. How did that equal sadness? In what world? "Oh for fuck's sake..." His phone chimed with a ring, interrupting him just in the nick of time. The two pains in his ass needed to back off. "Got to take this," he said, without even looking at the screen. "Probably major confidential material. CIA stuff. Excuse me." He walked away, knowing it was probably just a bullshit call but not in the mood for more of Hunter's ribbing because, dammit...

I am feeling sad. Shit. His sister had married Declan, and Eb was absolutely thrilled for her. Marley needed to be happy. She was freaking light and joy and all those good things. She'd also been through hell. As for Jake, damn straight, Eb wanted his twin to live his best life. Sometimes, Jake worried him. Jake went too far into the darkness.

Wren will pull him out of that darkness.

Every now and then, Eb wished he had someone to pull him out, too.

But, then, other days, he liked the dark far too much.

He finally looked down at the phone screen. And it was someone from the CIA. Huh, how about that? Eb put the phone to his ear. "Yo, look, I'm not exactly in a secure setting..."

"Naomi Romano is not being charged for the murder of Hudson Wyatt."

Naomi's image flashed through his head. Golden, flawless skin. Dark hair shot with streaks of light. Dark, dark blue eyes. Lips made for sin. Body a perfect temptation. A woman who was...

A cold-blooded killer. "You are kidding me right now." His grip threatened to crush the phone. "The cops nailed her as their lead suspect. The DA was going after her with everything he had—"

"Charges are dropped. She's walking free. I know he was your former partner," the flat voice of his CIA handler told him, "so I thought that you'd want to know."

"She's guilty." He was certain of it. Absolutely certain. Hudson had loved Naomi. And she...

She murdered him. And now she's getting away with it?

"She might be guilty, but, again, she's not being charged. There isn't enough proof for the DA."

So she just got to walk away? Oh, hell, no. Not on his watch. Hudson had saved his life back in the day. The very least that Eb could do was make sure his killer paid for what she'd done. "I'll handle it."

"Uh, Eb? I'm not *assigning* you a case here. This isn't our—"

"Thanks for the info, boss." *Former* boss, technically. Though Eb hadn't gotten around to telling his family the news about his career change, not just yet. "I'll handle things from here on out."

"Those words inspire sheer terror within me."

They shouldn't. The only person who should be afraid? That would be the lovely Naomi. Because he was coming for her. Before he was done, he would make one hundred percent sure that she paid for her crimes. "I'll get the evidence to convict her. I'll serve her up to the DA on a silver platter. There will be no choice but to prosecute."

He shoved the phone into his pocket. Rolled back his shoulders. Returned to the two men who waited for him at the bar.

"All good?" Hunter asked him.

Good? Nah. Not even close. The world was full of evil. Naomi Romano was a woman who looked like the best kind of sin. She'd tricked his former partner into falling for her. Then she'd killed the bastard the day after their wedding. No, not *good* at all.

But he'd see that she got exactly what she deserved. And it might even be fun. Because, with her, finally, he'd be able to let out the darkness that he kept chained inside. "Fucking fabulous," Eb replied as a wide smile curved his lips. "How about another round of drinks?"

Hunter cursed. "That smile scares me."

Declan just watched with an unreadable expression.

Eb's smile grew a bit broader.

From the corner of his eye, he saw Jake and Wren slip from the bar. At least someone was going to get a happy ending.

And someone else...someone else was going to pay for the life she'd taken. Naomi Romano was guilty as hell, and he would prove it to the world.

Chapter Twenty-Five

THE WAVES CRASHED INTO THE BEACH. THE STARS glittered overhead. The man who loved her was at her side, with his fingers twined with hers. And there were zero bad guys waiting to abduct her on this stunningly perfect night.

What more could a woman want?

She'd kicked off her heels. Carried them in her left hand. Jake still wore his fancy shoes and didn't seem to mind the fact that sand was everywhere. He was big and strong and silent and it took all of her self-control not to jump the man right then and there.

Oh, why the hell not?

She dropped her shoes. Didn't even hear them when they hit the sand. Wren threw her body against his and pulled Jake's head down toward her. When their lips met, her mouth was open and eager, and she could taste the champagne on his tongue. Just kissing Jake was enough to make her feel drunk, but that had zero to do with the champagne and everything to do with the man who loved her.

And Wren believed that he did love her. With total and

utter certainty. He'd been with her through the dark times. He'd stared straight forward and never flinched.

There is no world where I leave Wren to die. There is no world where I ever leave Wren.

He'd said those words when Makayla held her. Wren had known that he meant them with every bit of his being. She'd seen the truth on his face. In his eyes.

There was no world where she'd ever leave him, either. Jake was it for her. But then again, she'd known that truth for a very long time, too. She'd just been afraid to admit it.

There was no reason for fear, not any longer.

It was time for hope. And happiness. And for finally letting go of the careful control that they'd both used to bind their lives for so long.

"Baby..." Jake breathed the endearment against her mouth. "I love you."

She would never get tired of hearing those words from him.

"I want you, Wren." Another kiss. Deep. Tempting. Claiming. The kind of kiss that made her knees weak even as her toes curled in the sand. "Let's get the hell out of here."

Wren pushed lightly against those broad, broad shoulders of his. "Why?"

"So that I can fuck you until you scream for me."

Oh, yes, please. But Wren shook her head. "No need to leave. We're the only ones on the beach." She'd checked, to be sure. The waves pounded. They'd walked far away from the bar. The stars gave them enough light to see that no one else was close by. Just them. "I've long had this fantasy," Wren began. "Where you and I are on the beach. And you are fucking me as if your very life depends—"

She didn't get to finish. He had her in his arms again.

Lifted her up against him. Such sexy strength. The skirt of her dress had hiked up more. Considering how short the dress had been to begin with, that additional hiking exposed her completely to him. As much as she enjoyed tasting him, Wren had to pull her mouth from his long enough to confess, "I'm not wearing panties." Because she'd had plans for the night, too. Seducing Jake had been at the top of her list.

He'd been treating her too carefully since she'd gotten out of the hospital. So gently. As if worried that she'd break with too much pressure. That wasn't her Jake. That wasn't her. She wanted the full onslaught of passion from him. She wanted him to go wild. Wren wanted that wildness for herself, too.

So Operation Seduce Jake had commenced. And, so far, it seemed to be off to a rousing success.

A tremor of need shook his hard body. His mouth slammed back onto hers. His tongue thrust deep. She pressed her core against him, rubbing lightly. She was already wet. Did he know that? She'd gotten wet from his kisses. Wet from wanting him. And he was—

Putting her down. Lowering her to her feet again.

Wren glowered. "Doesn't work this way, Jake—" Wren broke off when he shrugged out of his tux coat and spread it out on the sand. Then, in the next breath, he'd spread *her* out on that coat, too. "Okay, it works this way."

He laughed, then groaned, then had two fingers sliding into her.

She moaned. Wren grabbed him and her nails bit into his powerful shoulders through the expensive white shirt he still wore. The waves pounded. When she tipped back her head, she could see the stars that filled the sky.

"Missed this," Jake growled.

His head lowered. His mouth went straight to her clit. Working her. Licking and stroking, then dipping to dive inside of her. Her hips flew up to greet him. It wasn't just his tongue and lips taking her. His fingers stroked into her with a rough pressure that made her *wild*.

And she wasn't just looking up at the stars. She was flying with them as she came on a fast, brutal release. One that snapped her breath away and had her arching for him.

"Condom, dammit, baby, I don't have a condom!" He pulled away.

Nope.

She rolled with him. They rolled off that tux coat. She climbed on top of him. Straddled him. Yanked open his pants and realized she wasn't the only one who'd ditched underwear for the night. *Great minds do scheme and seduce alike.* The heavy length of his cock thrust toward her. She grabbed him with both hands. Stroked and pumped and then pushed the broad head of his dick right at the slick entrance of her body. "I want to have a family with you."

He went statue still.

"You're it for me, Jake. The man I want. The man I love. But maybe..." Uncertainty had her hands moving to splay over his chest. Goosebumps rolled over her skin. "Maybe you're afraid something bad is in my blood?" *Like father, like daughter.*

"You're the best thing in my life." He drove into her. A long, hard thrust that buried him balls deep inside of her.

Wren moaned. Gasped. Squeezed her eyes shut at the delicious fullness.

"Our kids...*I will protect them with my life. I will love them, just as I love their mother.*" His hands clamped around her hips, and he began to lift her. Up. Down. Up, down.

Her knees pressed into the sand.

"There is *nothing* bad about you." His grip tightened even more on her.

Her back arched as she ground her hips against him.

"You're mine, Wren, always *mine*."

One powerful hand left her hip. Snaked between them. His fingers strummed her clit even as his heaving thrusts had her hips bucking high. Had her coming again for him on an even harder explosion of pleasure.

He shot upward. Jake curled his arms around her and pulled her against his chest because she was pretty much collapsing against him. His mouth went to her neck. His lips feathered over the faint red lines that still marked her. He kissed her. He loved her.

He came inside of her with a roar. One that *maybe* the thunder of the ocean hid?

Or even if it didn't...

They were alone on the beach.

Alone, as her thundering heartbeat finally slowed. As her inner muscles still held him so tightly and powerful aftershocks of pleasure reverberated through her.

His head rose. He stared at her. Smiled at her. A real, warm smile.

And Wren knew that she would love this man for the rest of her days. Love him, laugh with him, protect him and the family they would have together.

Their kids would never know the terror she'd felt before. There would be no fear. No denying that love existed. That it was so very real. There would be no monsters who waited in the dark.

Wren knew that her life had now forever changed. There would be a family that surrounded her with joy. There would be Jake and Eb. Uncle Milo and Honey.

Marley and Declan. There would be memories. And there would be, above all...

Protection. Safety.

A happy ending that she'd been too afraid to ever dream of before.

She had it in her grasp now.

Nothing would be off-limits. No dream unattainable. Anything could happen.

Anything, even the best, brightest love in the world.

"We're getting off this beach," Jake rumbled. "And I am going to fuck you all night long."

Oh, she did like the sound of that. "Promises, promises..."

His laughter rang out, and it was the best sound she'd ever heard in her life.

THE END

Another Ice Breaker book is coming soon! Want to read Eb's story?

She is beautiful, charming, and guilty as sin.

Ebenezer "Eb" Jones is in the mood for deadly payback. He knows that Naomi Romano killed his friend and former CIA partner. The cops suspected her, the DA wanted to charge her, but the woman was far too smart for them. She slipped away from justice. Or so she thinks. He's about to make certain that she pays for her crimes. A life for a life. He will absolutely wreck her life. Promise made.

He's dangerous, conniving, and cold-blooded to the core.

Lying is second nature to Eb. Pretending to be someone else is as easy as breathing. So he works to slip past Naomi's guard. To learn her secrets. And he will learn those secrets. Even if he has to seduce them all from her beautiful, lying lips. Does that make him cold-blooded? Guilty as charged. It's a dirty job, but someone has to do it.

Another enemy is stalking his prey.

Eb isn't the only predator who wants justice. Naomi is being hunted, and Eb has to step in and shield her from a series of deadly attacks. Everywhere she turns, Naomi faces danger. He pretends to be the good guy, the savior that she needs. She breaks before him, desperate for help, and Eb realizes the woman is either one very fine actress...or maybe she's not the killer he thought.

Now she believes he is a hero and doesn't know that he is someone she should fear.

Eb succeeded in his mission of getting close to Naomi. Except now, his careful control is unraveling. He begins to want her. To need her with a desire that is more savage and primitive than any he's ever felt before. Two options— Naomi is the best liar he has ever met in his life...or Eb has made a fatal mistake. He's betrayed a woman who might own his heart, and if he's not careful, a jealous enemy closing in on them may rip her from his world.

She also might wind up hating him forever once she learns just how deeply his betrayal runs...

Passion can be lethal. And love? It will make heroes turn into monsters.

Author's Note: Time to solve another cold case with the Ice Breakers! Except...this case is far too personal for Ebenezer Jones. And when things get personal, rules will be broken. Control will be lost. And a man with an ice-cold heart man find himself lying—and falling for—a woman who is not meant to be his. A master of disguise, Eb can pretend to be anyone, anytime. Getting the truth from Naomi should be easy. Falling for her? That should not be part of the plan. Yeah...his plan is about to explode.

Personal Message

I wanted to take a moment and talk about one of the issues included in this book—suicide. Several years ago, I lost a very dear friend to suicide. I think about him often and wish I could have done something to help him. If you or someone you know is struggling with suicidal thoughts, you can call 988—it's a national number in the US for suicide crises (it's also for all mental health issues). You do not have to fight on your own. Sending hugs to anyone who may need them!

Author's Note

Thank you so much for taking the time to read FORBIDDEN ICE. I have enjoyed writing the Ice Breaker Cold Case Romance books more than I can say! Thank you so much for going into the cold case world with me. And there are more cold case adventures coming your way—Eb's book, ICE COLD LIAR is up next.

If you have time, please consider leaving a review for FORBIDDEN ICE. Reviews help readers to discover new books—and authors are definitely grateful for them! (Trust me—we are super, super grateful!)

If you'd like to stay updated on my releases and sales, please join my newsletter list. Did I mention that when you sign up, you get a FREE Cynthia Eden book? Because you do!

By the way, I'm also active on social media. You can find me chatting away on Instagram and Facebook.

Again, thank you for reading FORBIDDEN ICE. Thanks for enjoying romance books! Go make an adventure list and be happy.

Best,

Cynthia Eden

cynthiaeden.com

More Books By Cynthia Eden

Protector & Defender Romance
- When He Protects
- When He Hunts
- When He Fights

Ice Breaker Cold Case Romance
- Frozen In Ice (Book 1)
- Falling For The Ice Queen (Book 2)
- Ice Cold Saint (Book 3)
- Touched By Ice (Book 4)
- Trapped In Ice (Book 5)
- Forged From Ice (Book 6)
- Buried Under Ice (Book 7)
- Ice Cold Kiss (Book 8)
- Locked In Ice (Book 9)
- Savage Ice (Book 10)
- Brutal Ice (Book 11)
- Cruel Ice (Book 12)
- Forbidden Ice (Book 13)
- Ice Cold Liar (Book 14)

Wilde Ways

- Protecting Piper (Book 1)
- Guarding Gwen (Book 2)
- Before Ben (Book 3)
- The Heart You Break (Book 4)
- Fighting For Her (Book 5)
- Ghost Of A Chance (Book 6)
- Crossing The Line (Book 7)
- Counting On Cole (Book 8)
- Chase After Me (Book 9)
- Say I Do (Book 10)
- Roman Will Fall (Book 11)
- The One Who Got Away (Book 12)
- Pretend You Want Me (Book 13)
- Cross My Heart (Book 14)
- The Bodyguard Next Door (Book 15)
- Ex Marks The Perfect Spot (Book 16)
- The Thief Who Loved Me (Book 17)

The Fallen Series

- Angel Of Darkness (Book 1)
- Angel Betrayed (Book 2)
- Angel In Chains (Book 3)
- Avenging Angel (Book 4)

Wilde Ways: Gone Rogue

- How To Protect A Princess (Book 1)
- How To Heal A Heartbreak (Book 2)
- How To Con A Crime Boss (Book 3)

Night Watch Paranormal Romance

- Hunt Me Down (Book 1)
- Slay My Name (Book 2)

- Face Your Demon (Book 3)

Trouble For Hire
- No Escape From War (Book 1)
- Don't Play With Odin (Book 2)
- Jinx, You're It (Book 3)
- Remember Ramsey (Book 4)

Death and Moonlight Mystery
- Step Into My Web (Book 1)
- Save Me From The Dark (Book 2)

Phoenix Fury
- Hot Enough To Burn (Book 1)
- Slow Burn (Book 2)
- Burn It Down (Book 3)

Dark Sins
- Don't Trust A Killer (Book 1)
- Don't Love A Liar (Book 2)

Lazarus Rising
- Never Let Go (Book One)
- Keep Me Close (Book Two)
- Stay With Me (Book Three)
- Run To Me (Book Four)
- Lie Close To Me (Book Five)
- Hold On Tight (Book Six)

Bad Things
- The Devil In Disguise (Book 1)
- On The Prowl (Book 2)
- Undead Or Alive (Book 3)

- Broken Angel (Book 4)
- Heart Of Stone (Book 5)
- Tempted By Fate (Book 6)
- Wicked And Wild (Book 7)
- Saint Or Sinner (Book 8)

Bite Series
- Forbidden Bite (Bite Book 1)
- Mating Bite (Bite Book 2)

Blood and Moonlight Series
- Bite The Dust (Book 1)
- Better Off Undead (Book 2)
- Bitter Blood (Book 3)

Mine Series
- Mine To Take (Book 1)
- Mine To Keep (Book 2)
- Mine To Hold (Book 3)
- Mine To Crave (Book 4)
- Mine To Have (Book 5)
- Mine To Protect (Book 6)

Dark Obsession Series
- Watch Me (Book 1)
- Want Me (Book 2)
- Need Me (Book 3)
- Beware Of Me (Book 4)

Purgatory Series
- The Wolf Within (Book 1)
- Marked By The Vampire (Book 2)
- Charming The Beast (Book 3)

- Deal with the Devil (Book 4)

Bound Series
- Bound By Blood (Book 1)
- Bound In Darkness (Book 2)
- Bound In Sin (Book 3)
- Bound By The Night (Book 4)
- Bound in Death (Book 5)

Stand-Alone Romantic Suspense
- Waiting For Christmas
- Monster Without Mercy
- Kiss Me This Christmas
- It's A Wonderful Werewolf
- Never Cry Werewolf
- Immortal Danger
- Deck The Halls
- Come Back To Me
- Put A Spell On Me
- Never Gonna Happen
- One Hot Holiday
- Slay All Day
- Midnight Bite
- Secret Admirer
- Christmas With A Spy
- Femme Fatale
- Until Death
- Sinful Secrets
- First Taste of Darkness
- A Vampire's Christmas Carol

About the Author

Cynthia Eden loves romance books, chocolate, and going on semi-lazy adventures. She is a *New York Times*, *USA Today*, *Digital Book World*, and *IndieReader* best-seller. She writes romantic suspense, paranormal romance, and fun contemporary novels. You can find out more about her work at www.cynthiaeden.com.

If you want to stay updated on her new releases and books deals, be sure to join her newsletter group: cynthiaeden. com/newsletter. When new readers sign up for her newsletter, they are automatically given a free Cynthia Eden ebook.